Dirty Little Secrets

Dirty Little Secrets

Joy King

ST. MARTIN'S GRIFFIN
NEW YORK

Published in the United States by St. Martin's Griffin, an imprint of St. Martin's Publishing Group

www.stmartins.com

The Library of Congress has cataloged the first St. Martin's Griffin
edition as follows:

King, Joy, 1978–
Dirty little secrets / Joy King.—1st ed.
p. cm.
ISBN-13: 978-0-312-35407-7
ISBN-10: 0-312-35407-X
1. African American women—Fiction.   2. Drugs and sex—New York
    (State)—New York—Fiction.   3. Man-woman relationships—Fiction.
1. Title.
PS3611.I582D57 2006
813'.6—dc22

2006040536

ISBN 978-1-250-80419-8 (trade paperback)

Our books may be purchased in bulk for promotional, educational, or business use. Please contact your local bookseller or the Macmillan Corporate and Premium Sales Department at 1-800-221-7945, extension 5442, or by email at MacmillanSpecialMarkets@macmillan.com.

Second St. Martin's Griffin Edition: 2021

10 9 8 7 6 5 4 3 2 1

Acknowledgments

Growing up I had so many dreams, but never did I dream of being an author. Sometimes in life, the path you are meant to follow chooses you. Meaning, because of my own trials and tribulations I felt an obligation to tell this story. Who knew that what started off as a voice speaking inside of me would find its way to the pages of a book? Now I can't imagine having any other dream but to be a successful writer.

First I want to thank my mother, Suzy Hoard, who not only gave me life but is also my best friend. Whenever I doubt myself, you are the one I turn to for guidance. My dad Ellery King, you always told me, "Beware of the fork in the road; sometimes the hunter gets captured by the game." It's those words of wisdom that make you so special to me. My dad James Hoard, your strength and determination are truly an inspiration. Robin King, you're the best sister ever. Ella, Edward, and Logan, you're the future of our family.

Monique Patterson, when God has a plan, the right people just seem to step into your life. I knew from the moment we first spoke that you were one of those people. We just clicked, and you saw all the potential in me as an author that I hadn't quite seen myself. You are such an amazing editor and so gifted at what you do. I'm honored to be a part of the whole St. Martin's Press team, and hope this is just the first of many books to come. Emily Drum, thank you for always getting back to me and being so professional. Marc Gerald, a toast to a long and prosperous relationship, hopefully one that is drama-free. George Urdea, thank you for a fabulous Web site!

To all my friends, you know who you are, I love you so much. But I have to shout out a few people: Theron Sisco, you were with me on this whole book thing from the start, much love, baby. Ron Outcalt, we haven't spoken in a minute, but our bond is everlasting. My brothers—Frank Horne, Reggie Laroche, Omar Hamilton, Charles Dixon, and Johnny; my sisters—Marsha Irving, Tasha Marbury, Adama Robinson, Trixie Matthews, Shemella Jones, Charmelle Coffield, Adiam Berhane, Lissa Resnitzky, and Medina. Special thanks to Terrence Brown, Keith Lemons, B. Lawson Thornton, Colin Thorne, Bobbie King, Wilma, and my Zip Code family.

Most important, to my readers: I hope this story captures your hearts and leaves you wanting more!

Dirty Little Secrets

1

A Star Is Born

They say to truly cleanse your soul, you first have to expose every forbidden sin. Most prefer to continue through life never revealing the dark roads they've traveled. But I've chosen to share my journey. Let me start from the beginning, and tell you about my Dirty Little Secrets.

I was born August 3, 1980, in Atlanta, Georgia. According to my mother, I had a head full of jet-black curly hair and was sweet and juicy. In her eyes, I was perfect. She tied a stunning pink bow in my hair, of course. I'm sure all parents think their newborn is the most beautiful baby in the world, and Mother was no different. When I was three, she said, "Darling, when you grow up you're going to be famous. That's why I named you Tyler Blake—because it's a movie star's name, and you were born ready for your cover shot."

Mother would sit on the bed brushing my hair and lovingly

tell me, "Tyler, you are everything I dreamed you would be—and more. You're my little princess, and one day a lucky man will make you his queen." Mother figured that if I didn't become famous, then surely some rich man would come and sweep me off my feet. Little did she know that my world would be turned upside down, searching for a man who would make me his queen.

I spent hours studying Mother as she brushed her long black wavy hair or applied makeup to her angelic face. Would I grow up to be as beautiful? I wondered. One morning Mother saw me admiring her in her vanity mirror; she smiled and said, "Observe and learn, Tyler, because when you blossom into a woman, you will meet a man who will promise you the stars, but you must also demand the moon. You're my little princess, and you can't accept any less." It seemed Mother instilled this notion in me from the day I was born.

My sister Ella and I created a make-believe world, which we called Barbie Land. I would make up the most glamorous stories and act them out with our Barbie dolls. They had big houses, cars, and designer clothes. I would dress them in fabulous beaded gowns, adorn them with sparkling jewelry, and comb their hair in seductive styles. Barbie lived a jet-set life, and Mother promised that one day, so would I.

That life, however, was somewhat hard for me to imagine when I scrutinized myself in the mirror. I never felt beautiful like my dolls. They were slender; I was chubby. They had long flowing hair, and although my hair was long, I wore it in a pigtail. But my dolls still inspired me. Along with the encouragement of Mother, they gave me hope that one day I would be transformed into a dazzling diva and live the glamorous life. Mother was determined to guarantee that for me, my sister, and herself. She even enrolled me in a children's theater group because she knew how much I loved acting out the stories I made up. Mother thought participating in plays would give me a platform on which to dress up and express my theatrical side. I remember how thrilled I was when I got the part of Cinderella. Mother let me wear my hair in Shirley Temple curls, and I wore a long pink dress. I even wore a tiara. When I performed onstage, it was as if I had left my body and become a different person. Mother said I looked like a real-life princess and that one day that life would be mine.

That life would be a far cry from the one I was living. It was obvious to Ella and me that our parents were married in name only. Mother was so cold and distant toward our daddy. She constantly complained about how hard she had to work to provide for the family and that he had no ambition, no goals. Daddy was content with our modest house on a tree-lined street, one family car, and nonexistent family vacations. Daddy's idea of a vacation was for all of us to go to the local park for a picnic of Mother's special barbecue chicken with potato salad and corn on the cob. He definitely had no desire to lounge on an exotic island, as Mother dreamed of doing. Like Mother, I too yearned for so much more.

As time passed, Mother's frustrations began to build. One night I woke up to the sounds of Mother and Daddy arguing. "I'm so tired of coming home and seeing you sitting on the couch doing nothing! Why don't you get a job?" Mother yelled.

"I have a job; business is slow right now," Daddy explained.

"Business is always slow. This isn't the life you promised me, Carter. You told me you were going to have your own business and make a lot of money. What happened to the big house, the cars, the furs? I would've been better off staying at Saks, working behind the makeup counter."

"Maria, I've done the best I can. Things just didn't work out the way I wanted them to. But I love you so much, and we have two beautiful daughters."

"Ella and Tyler are the only good things that came out of this marriage. Love don't pay no bills, Carter. But I will not stay trapped in this depressing life. I deserve more than this and, more importantly, so do my girls." That night I had a clearer understanding of why Mother was always so angry at Daddy. Mother felt Daddy had deceived her.

One evening, Mother came home late for the third night in a row. My daddy was waiting in his favorite chair, with a glass of Johnnie Walker in one hand and the remote control in the other. Ella and I knew the moment Mother walked through the door because the loud screams woke us. We jumped out of our twin beds and ran to the top of the stairs. Daddy rambled toward the front door and began yelling with a drunken slur, "I know you been with that man again! Don't lie to me, woman!"

Mother marched toward the kitchen, ignoring Daddy as if she didn't even see him. Her blatant disrespect pushed Daddy over the edge, and he lunged at Mother. "Maria, don't you walk away from me! I'm the man of this house, and you better treat me with respect!" Then Daddy grabbed Mother.

My heart sank when I heard Daddy speak those words. I knew Mother didn't respect him, and if anybody was the head of the household, it was her. Daddy was a self-employed plumber, making little money, but we lived in a middle-class suburban neighborhood with a house full of brand-new furniture and a big color television. Mother even managed to get us a brand-new car after Daddy's old hoopty kept breaking down. Ella and I never questioned where all the money came from, because Mother would always say, "No matter what, only the best for my two girls."

All of a sudden Daddy was on top of Mother, his hands around her neck, choking her. Ella and I remained frozen as Mother kicked her legs and tried to pry Daddy's fingers from her throat. "You think I don't know about that man you been seeing?" he said between clenched teeth. "You ain't nothin' but a whore. Sashaying out this house in your fancy new dresses and expensive perfume you bought with money you got from that man. I'm gonna choke the devil right out of you, do you hear me!"

I felt like I was watching a bad movie, and I desperately wanted to change the channel. But this was real life. My daddy was murdering my mother right before my eyes. I had never known Daddy to be violent, and his behavior was sending chills down my spine. As I sat there with my hands clutching the banister, I heard Ella whisper, "You stay here, Tyler. I'm going to save Mother." Five years older, Ella always felt the need to protect me. Normally she was shielding me from bullying kids in the neighborhood. Tonight it was from our daddy. She ran downstairs and picked up the glass vase Mother had bought in a local antique store. I screamed as it shattered and blood spilled from Daddy's head. He lay on the hardwood floor looking dazed and confused.

Mother gasped for air as Ella held her.

Later that night, as Mother packed up our clothes and whatever belongings could fit in the car, Daddy begged her to stay. "Maria, Maria, please don't leave me, baby. I'm sorry. I'll never put my hands on you again. I love you, Maria. You're my life." His cries fell on deaf ears.

When Mother made up her mind about something, she didn't look back. Daddy had been wrong for trying to kill Mother, but I still loved him and I hated to leave. Despite his sometimes drunken behavior, Daddy was the kindest man I ever met. He always believed in being fair, and my friends loved him because he thought all kids should be treated equally. If I had a new doll and didn't want to share it with my friends, he would sit me on his lap and say, "Tyler, sharing is the most rewarding gift you can give someone. If you don't learn to share, how will you ever appreciate all your blessings?" I never forgot those words, and I reflected on them every time I wanted to keep something all for myself.

As we drove off, Mother looked at Ella and me. "If a man hits you once," she said, "he will hit you for the rest of your life unless you decide to end his—or he decides to end yours. I want to live and I want your father to live, so we will never come back to this house again."

From the backseat I waved good-bye to Daddy and watched him as he chased after the car, still sobbing and begging for Mother to come back. That night we stayed at a hotel, and I cried myself to sleep. I couldn't believe that Daddy was gone and I would never see him again.

The next morning I heard Mother on the phone talking sweet to somebody. Before she hung up, she said, "I love you, too." For a brief hopeful moment I imagined that she was going to give Daddy another chance, but that illusion was quickly shattered. Mother turned to us, her face glowing and her eyes sparkling, and said, "Ella and Tyler, today you are going to meet your new daddy."

"But I already have a daddy, Mommy," I said, trying to hold back the tears swelling up in my eyes.

"No, baby, he isn't your daddy anymore. Your father tried to kill me last night. He is dead to us now."

"He didn't mean to hurt you, Mommy. He just wanted you to stay home with him like you used to."

Mother began stroking my hair. Then she picked me up and

sat me on her lap. "Tyler, I need for you to be a big girl for Mommy. I know you love your father, but your new daddy is going to take good care of us. Remember I told you that one day we would live in a big house with fancy cars and beautiful clothes?" I nodded. "Well, honey, all that is about to come true. Mommy has found her Prince Charming, and he has promised her the moon and the stars. All I ask is that you and Ella be the little dolls I raised you to be and treat your new daddy with the utmost respect. This is a new beginning for us, and we want the transition to be smooth. In order to make that possible, we must make your new daddy feel comfortable and secure with his position in your life. So after careful thought, Mommy thinks it would be best if you girls call the new man in our lives 'Daddy.' That would make me awfully happy. Will you do that for Mommy?" Ella and I looked at each other, and we reluctantly agreed to do as Mother asked. What choice did we have? She always got her way.

Mother produced a bag from some fancy department store and laid out two pink lace dresses with matching socks and shoes for Ella and me. She combed our hair into long ponytails and braided them going down our backs. With a couple of well-placed pink barrettes, we looked like the most perfect little girls.

After Mother got us dressed, she made us swear we would sit still and not get so much as a wrinkle in our dresses. I had never seen Mother so giddy and nervous at the same time. Forty-five minutes later, she stepped out of the bathroom looking like the winner of a beauty pageant. Mother was so beautiful, so pretty, and such a lady. She was always so pretty in pink. I don't mean that mother wore pink all the time, but she always exuded pink. She was soft, classy, and ladylike, but also strong and determined.

When I heard a knock at the door, my heart began pounding. I couldn't believe I was about to meet my new daddy. Ella and

I held hands tightly as Mother opened the door and a man grabbed her around her small waist and gave her an openmouthed kiss. I never saw Mother kiss my daddy like that. She would only let him kiss her on the cheek or give her a peck on the mouth. But she was allowing this man to kiss her like he was Billy Dee Williams or something. When the man finally released her from his embrace, mother had a schoolgirl grin on her face. With great joy she said, "Michael, these are your daughters, Ella and Tyler." She then turned back to us and said, "Come on, my little angels. Give your daddy a hug."

Ella and I walked toward the man and looked up at him. He was tall with a smooth milk-chocolate complexion. His short black hair had waves like the ocean. He smiled at us with perfect white teeth and knelt down to give us a hug. I was drawn to the strong but pleasant smell of his cologne. I held him a little tighter because his smell was hypnotizing me. I could feel the muscles in his arms moving beneath his expensive suit.

He looked at us and asked in a deep, reassuring voice, "What can I get for my little princesses? Would you like to go to the toy store and get some new dolls?"

"That would be perfect," Mother answered for us. My new daddy picked up our luggage, and we headed out the door. He was driving a big luxury car that had a leather interior, and it smelled like he just got it off the car lot. He put everything in the trunk, and Mother told us to get in the back. I wondered what she was going to do with her car, which was sitting in the hotel parking lot, but thought it better not to ask. We went straight from the hotel to FAO Schwarz, just as our new daddy had promised. When we walked in the store, all the saleswomen ran to assist him. Daddy oozed charm and sophistication.

The teenaged-looking saleswoman approached him and flirted

openly. "Good afternoon, sir. What can I help you with today?" she purred.

"I'm looking for the most beautiful dolls you have for my two little princesses."

"Isn't that nice? Your girls sure are pretty," she said, briefly glancing at us and then back to Daddy. Ella nudged my arm to let me know she was suspicious of the overly nice saleswoman.

"Yes, they are. They take after their gorgeous mother. Maria, come over here so this nice woman can see where my little princesses get their looks from."

Mother gladly strutted over to Daddy, and he put his arm around her and kissed her on the cheek. I could tell the saleswoman was not pleased with the way Daddy was fawning over Mother. The saleswoman gave a gracious but fake smile as she acknowledged Mother and reluctantly led us to a selection of beautiful dolls. Mother had a wide grin spread across her face. It didn't bother her in the least that the young woman was blatantly flirting with her man. She seemed almost flattered that the saleswoman wanted Daddy, but he was with her.

After shopping all day and eating at a fancy restaurant, we finally arrived at our new home in Cates Ridge. It was the biggest house I had ever seen. Mother was grinning from ear to ear as we walked up the driveway. Two luxury cars were parked outside. One was a small red sports car with a big bow on top. Daddy walked up to Mother and handed her a pair of car keys. "This is my welcome-home present to you," he said, and then he playfully patted her butt.

"Oh, Michael, I can't believe you did this."

"Maria, you are my queen. I'm going to give you the world." Mother beamed with joy. She'd finally found her Prince Charming, and he had swept her off her feet. As she sat in the driver's seat of her new car, I heard someone say, "Hey, Dad, what's going on out here?"

"Evan, remember I told you that today Maria and her daughters would be moving in? Say hello to my little princesses, Ella and Tyler, your new sisters."

"That's right," Evan said, as if just remembering. "Hi, Maria, it's nice to see you again." He waved at Mother, then turned to us and spoke in a soft eerie voice. "Hello, I'm Evan, your new big brother." He reached out to shake hands, and I immediately felt uncomfortable at his touch.

We all went into the house, and Mother took Ella and me to our new room. "Isn't our house beautiful?" Mother gushed, as though she could no longer contain her excitement. "You girls are welcome to have your own rooms, but I thought for now you would like to share." She was right; I needed to feel safe in my new surroundings, and although Ella was only five years older than I was, she seemed like a second mother. I needed to be near her in our new home. Plus the room was humongous. It was decorated in all-pink Hello Kitty, with two canopy beds, one on each side of the room. Mother even had posters of my favorite actresses on the wall, Brat Pack members, Demi Moore, Molly Ringwald, and supersexy Vanity. I loved her in *The Last Dragon*. We had our own big color television and loads of dolls and toys. It was as if this bedroom had been waiting for us all our lives.

After only a few months of living in our new home, Ella, Evan, and I were whisked off to Las Vegas for a quickie wedding between Mother and our new dad. That's when it truly hit me that my parents were divorced and there was no chance for reconciliation. Accepting that made it a lot easier to adjust to my new life.

Daddy showered us with presents and love, and Mother never seemed happier. The only thing I didn't like was my stepbrother, Evan, who was sixteen. He seemed sinister. Sometimes I would catch him staring at me, as if he were looking through me, not at me. And his eyes had a coldness to them. Evan gave off the negative energy of a dangerous young man. Even his relationship with Daddy seemed strained.

After we had been living in our new house about a year, I walked in the kitchen one afternoon and unexpectedly interrupted an argument. Daddy had his hand raised as if he was about to hit Evan. I had never seen Daddy so upset. When Daddy saw me, he quickly calmed down, but Evan gave me the creepiest grin as he turned and walked away. It was as if he purposely tried to upset Daddy to see how far he could push him. We were all relieved that Evan was leaving in a couple of days to stay with his mother for the summer. I always felt uneasy in his presence and couldn't wait to have him out of the house.

That night I woke up to use the bathroom. Mother had told me not to drink any more Kool-Aid before bed, but of course I didn't listen. When I walked out of the bathroom, Evan was standing in the hallway eating an oatmeal cookie Mother had baked earlier that day. He looked me over with his dark eyes and held out the cookie, offering me a piece. I shook my head and walked past him. I was completely taken off guard when he grabbed my arm and pulled me into his room. He had one hand across my mouth and used the other to kick the door. I couldn't comprehend what was going on, but I knew I was in trouble. Evan quietly whispered in my ear, "Tyler, I don't want to hurt you. When I take my hands from over your mouth, please don't scream or you'll be sorry. Do you understand?"

I nodded, but as soon as he released his hand I let out a short scream. He slapped me across the face and put his hand back over my mouth.

"I told you not to scream, you little bratty bitch!" He was breathing hard and my heart was racing. Evan lifted me up, one hand still across my mouth, and carried me over to his bed. My legs were kicking, but at six years old I was no match for this sixteen-year-old boy. After dropping me on his bed, he used his body to hold me still, one hand still over my mouth; with the other he began shoving down his blue boxer shorts. I finally realized what Evan planned to do to me. He was like an actor in the movies on television; Mother always warned me to stay away from men like that. I felt like I was going to throw up. Evan finally got his shorts down far enough, and I saw the hardness of his penis. I began to kick furiously. He yanked my cotton nightgown out of his way and reached for my floral panties. As he pressed my head down hard on the pillow, part of me wanted to give up the fight and give in to the inevitable, but I didn't want to be a victim. I didn't want to be like the little girls I heard about in school and church who had been raped or molested. But at the same time my mind and body were frozen, and I couldn't react. Fear held me and I felt sick and alone.

There was no sound in the room, except Evan's panting, the rustle of his frantic movements, and my sharp, frightened breathing. In the moonlight coming through the window I could see the depraved look in his eyes. A surge of energy came over me, and all of a sudden I started fighting as if my life depended on it. He was too strong and athletic, but feeling his cold hands invading my body made me fight harder. He got frustrated with my struggling and punched me in my jaw. My head rocked to the side from the impact, and from the corner of my eye I could see the door open slightly and a shadow run away. I wanted to scream for whoever it was to come back. Evan finally ripped off my panties and was about to violate me when the bedroom door burst open. I sobbed when I saw Mother, Daddy, and Ella standing in the doorway. Daddy threw on the light switch and stared in shock at Evan standing over me, one hand still on my mouth and his penis hanging out for all to see. Evan jumped up and stumbled backward, trying to stuff himself back into his pants.

A look of rage like I had never seen before filled Daddy's eyes. He looked like a demon. Suddenly he lunged at Evan, punching him with such force that Evan fell to the floor. He began stomping on him and yelling, "You sick sonofabitch! This is what you like to do? Fuck little girls?"

Mother ran forward. "Michael, calm down! You're going to kill him!"

"Any man who messes with a little girl deserves to die! And if it's a son of mine, I'm going to kill him myself because he's already dead to me." He continued to stomp Evan until he saw blood rolling down the side of his mouth and Evan could no longer beg for mercy.

Mother and Ella were now holding me close. Daddy had stopped kicking Evan and stood over him, fists clenched, breathing like a bull. "Boy, you are dead to me. As far as I'm concerned, I don't have a son. You were never born. You can stay here tonight, but first thing in the morning I'm going to put you on the plane for your mother's and I don't ever want to see your face again." As his father wandered away, Evan still lay on the floor, curled up in a fetal position.

When I woke in the morning, Evan was gone. Later that day

some movers came and cleaned out his entire room. Any picture or item that had to do with Evan was removed. Daddy had erased his memory as though he never existed. No one was to ever speak Evan's name, and Daddy tried even harder to spoil me, hoping I would forget the incident ever happened. But no matter how many gifts or trips to amusement parks I had, that dreadful night with Evan remained fixed in my mind.

2

Blossoming Flower

During the summer of 1994 I turned fourteen and began to transform from a caterpillar into a butterfly. I was now a curvaceous teenager with full breasts, a small waist, and a round butt. Lots of boys wanted to date me and I wanted to date, too, but not any of the clowns in my school. The boys gossiped more than the girls. They would brag about who was going all the way or who was just giving professionals. Their conversations always turned vulgar, and I was determined not to be a topic for any of them.

"Girl, we got our asses kicked tonight by Druid Hills. Our football team needs to step it up," my girlfriend Lisa said, full of frustration. Lisa had a big mouth, with a big butt and chest to go with it. Everybody told her she looked like Lauryn Hill, so she swore her shit didn't stink. Lisa got on most people's nerves with her sometimes obnoxious attitude, but I didn't pay her any mind. She was more of the in-your-face type, and I was more subtle, which made us click. The times she did get on my nerves, I would just put her on Pause for a minute.

"Who cares? I'm starving; let's go get something to eat," I said as we were leaving the football field.

"You always eating, and I don't know where all the weight goes wit yo little ass," Lisa said as she sucked her teeth.

"Whatever. Let's go," I said, agitated with Lisa. That was the one thing I hated about going to the football games with her. She always wanted to linger in the parking lot where all the fellas hung out, in search of her latest prey. Lisa called it shooting the breeze. I called it trying to get her pimp game on.

"Can I come with you?" a male voice asked. I turned around and was pleasantly surprised to see a well-built, butterscotch-complexioned hottie standing in front of me. Lisa immediately jumped beside me and stuck out her enormous chest, giving the guy one of her "sexy" looks.

"Aren't you Chad Mills, the star quarterback for Druid Hills?" Lisa asked, sounding like she was about to eat him up.

"Yeah, that's right. What's your friend's name?"

"Oh, that's just Tyler." Lisa waved her hand as if dismissing me. "I'm Lisa. It's a pleasure to meet you." She stepped forward, extending her hand. Chad did her one better by extending his hand directly toward me.

"Hi, Tyler. I'm Chad. It's nice to meet you," he said. He took my hand and held it, and I could feel myself blushing. Lisa made it worse by standing beside me with her lips poked out.

"I've never seen you before," Chad said. "Are you new to North Atlanta?"

"Yeah, this is actually my first year. I went to Sutton Middle School last year."

"Oh, so you're a freshman?"

"Yeah," I answered shyly.

"You have to be the prettiest freshman I've ever seen."

"You're sweet," I gushed, sounding like a love-struck teenager.

"I would love to call you. Can I get your number?"

"Sure," I said, smiling. Chad was just the type of guy I had been searching for. He was handsome, he was at least a junior so he had to be somewhat mature, and he made me feel at ease. Because Evan had assaulted me, when guys tried to date me, I always felt as if they had an ulterior motive. I was scared to be alone with them because I believed they would harm me in some way. With Chad, those thoughts did not cross my mind. Both his looks and his status as a football star would make all my friends envious of me. Plus he came across as a sweetheart. I definitely had stars in my eyes.

After our initial encounter, Chad and I were inseparable. He would come over and we'd make out for hours. My parents were oblivious of what we were doing because they thought Chad was the greatest. Chad's mother belonged to the same country club as my mother, and his father did business with Daddy, so they had no problem leaving us alone. Besides, my parents were trying to salvage what was left of their shaky marriage. For the last couple of years it had been deteriorating. It hit rock bottom when Ella left for college. Ella had been the glue holding our family together. She was the type of child who demanded we take family vacations and eat dinner together every night. Without her there to keep the family united, Daddy began to distance himself. Mother soon realized that Daddy, like so many other men, was having an affair, and so she began her own fling. Without constant praise and attention from Daddy, Mother became insecure and sought confirmation elsewhere that she was still beautiful.

One evening she was supposed to be at a country club meeting, preparing for a dinner honoring the female socialites of Atlanta. Worried when she never showed up, her friend Beatrice called the house looking for her. Daddy told her something had come up at the last minute and Mother couldn't make it.

When Mother came home, he asked her how her meeting went, and she said, "Great." Before Mother could even shut the door, Daddy was standing in the foyer ready to grill her. "Maria, don't fucking lie to me. Beatrice called here looking for you after you didn't show up."

"I know. I got there right after she got off the phone with you. I was held up trying to make some last-minute revisions, and I was late to the meeting." Mother always knew how to remain cool under pressure. She spoke so matter-of-factly that you couldn't help but want to believe her.

"Okay, then you'll have no problem getting Beatrice on the phone to confirm your story."

"I'm not a child, Michael, and I won't be calling Beatrice to ask her such a silly question." Once again, but now as a teenager, I stood at the top of the stairs watching a drama unfold.

"Maria, you better get Beatrice on the phone right now or—," Daddy said in a threatening voice.

"Or what, Michael? You're going to run out and go see your mistress? Tell her I said hello." Mother turned away.

It was like a flashback from the past when Daddy said, "Maria, don't you walk away from me!" Then he took off after her, and they were out of my sight. When I heard the loud thump of Mother hitting the marble floor in the foyer, I ran downstairs to save her, just as Ella had so many years ago.

"Daddy, stop!" I screamed, just as Daddy was about to land a second punch. He froze and stared at me with the same shameful look that Evan had had on his face when he got caught with his pants down.

"Tyler, go back upstairs. This is between your mother and me," Daddy said, standing over Mother and trying to hide the anger that had taken over him. Mother still lay on the floor, looking helpless and scared.

"Michael, please don't do this in front of Tyler. You promised that no matter how angry you got, you would never put your hands on me in front of the children." I stared in shock. Mother's face was riddled with shame and fear. What was she saying? Had Daddy hit her before and I just didn't know about it? Daddy took a deep breath, and Mother slowly began to stand up. I knew my parents had problems, but never did I believe the relationship had become abusive. Daddy walked downstairs to the entertainment room, and Mother grabbed my hand and asked me to follow her upstairs. We went in my bedroom and sat on the bed. Mother held my hand like she did when I was a little girl.

"Tyler, I'm sorry you had to witness the altercation between your father and me. I never expected him to hit me with you in the house."

"Has he hit you before?"

Mother glanced at me with sorrowful eyes, giving away the answer.

"But I thought you said if a man ever hits you, you must immediately leave him."

"Baby, look at everything your father has provided for us. We are accustomed to a lifestyle that most people only dream of. He has fulfilled our every fantasy." As Mother spoke, I was confused, torn, and disgusted.

With great sarcasm, I said, "So it's okay for a man to knock you around if he's rich and takes good care of you? But if he is poor, like my real father was, then it's not worth sticking around?"

"Tyler, you watch your mouth. Your father was worthless. He had no ambition and couldn't hold a decent job. If I stayed with him, we would be stuck in the land of the dead. Do you think you would be living in a million-dollar house and wearing designer jeans? Hell, no! Michael has provided us with a better life, and if he loses his temper once in a while, then so be it." Mother's face was red and her body was shaking.

I couldn't believe the words coming out of my mother's mouth. She had sold her soul for money and material gain. Not only was Daddy having an affair, but he was also beating her ass, and it was okay as long as the lifestyle continued. I wanted to lash out at her.

"So, the man you're fucking now . . . are you going to leave Daddy for him the way you left my father? Or are his pockets not deep enough?"

Mother stood up and slapped me. I grabbed my face and glared up at her.

"I know I haven't been the perfect mother, but everything I've done has been for the love of you and Ella. All I ever wanted was to provide a good life and not have you faced with the same struggles I had growing up. But no matter what I do or don't do, you will respect me. You respect the bullshit I endured in order to escape the dreadful existence that would have been your life if you didn't have a mother determined to find a better way. One day when you have your own kids and you want a better life for them, come have a conversation with me and let me know what you will and won't tolerate from a man." With that, Mother turned her back and walked away, but not before I saw the tears rolling down her cheeks. I had hurt her and I never wanted to do that. Mother was my hero, and I loved her more than life itself.

• • •

As the school year began to wind down, Chad and I had become closer than ever. He made me feel special. He would surprise me with flowers, romantic handmade cards, and little gifts. He seemed like the ideal boyfriend—good family, intelligent, a star athlete, and handsome. What more could a girl ask for? But I wasn't in love. I was physically attracted to him, but I wasn't passionate about him. Chad was safe because he was feeling more for me than I was feeling for him, so there was no way he could break my heart. After seeing the drama in both of my mother's marriages, I began thinking that love was way overrated. Still, I yearned for a man to make me feel loved.

Although I was only fifteen, that desire pushed me to take my relationship with Chad to the next level. My parents were out for dinner, and I asked Chad to come over and keep me company. We were watching 9½ Weeks, and I began teasing him about how sexy Mickey Rourke was. "Chad, look at how Mickey Rourke is fucking the shit out of Kim Basinger. I bet she has had at least three orgasms."

"What you know about an orgasm?" Chad asked. He thought I was a virgin—which I was.

"I've never had one, but my girlfriends tell me that once a man makes you reach your climax, you'll be in love with him for the rest of your life."

"Is that what they tell you? Well, why you don't find out for yourself?" Chad came closer to me on the couch and started kissing my neck. His lips always felt so warm on my skin, and my nipples became perky as his tongue made its way to my mouth.

He whispered in my ear, "Baby, do you want me to make love to you?" His breath smelled like Trident gum.

"Yeah, I want to feel you inside of me." Chad kissed my top

lip and then the bottom before slipping his tongue inside. As he kissed me, he unbuttoned my red silk shirt and unclipped my bra, exposing my voluptuous breasts. As his mouth swallowed my nipples, my pussy instantly became wet, and I unzipped his jeans longing to see and feel his dick. As he got up to take off his clothes, I stood in front of him in the new lace thong I had purchased from Victoria's Secret for this monumental occasion.

Chad looked at me with pure lust in his eyes. "I've been dying to be inside of you for so long. I promise you won't be disappointed." With that, I lay across the couch, waiting for him to finish undressing so we could make love.

I had never seen Chad stark naked, and I wasn't disappointed. All those sporting activities had left his body perfectly chiseled. He lay on top of me and began kissing all over my body. He literally licked me from head to toe. I was filled with lust and desire and could barely contain myself. The anticipation of what might happen next was driving me crazy. Looking at his erect penis, I knew all of him would fill me up. I kept saying, "Please put it in," and finally he did. Chad glided inside of me like silk. When he entered I felt pain, but it was the best sort of pain. Chad had been finger-popping me for so long with damn near three fingers that my pussy was not too tight to handle his well-endowed manhood.

I finally understood why when it felt right you could make love over and over because that was all I wanted to do after my first time with Chad. Wow, I thought, this whole sex thing is incredible. They say your first sexual experience will dictate how you feel about sex for the rest of your life, so I recommend that all women make their first time beautiful. But better yet, if possible wait until you're a lot older and more mature than I was.

• • •

For the next few months Chad and I made love every which way possible. But eventually I became bored. He had never mentally excited me, and I was becoming restless. Meanwhile, participating in drinking parties with my girlfriends was becoming increasingly more exciting. When my parents were out on the town, my girlfriends and I would raid their bar, mix all sorts of liquor together, and see who could drink the most and the fastest. Sometimes we would each have a bottle of champagne and see who could gulp down her bottle first. Talk about getting fucked up! Luckily my father had asked our housekeeper, Helena, to keep the bar well stocked, so my parents were oblivious of what was going on. One day Helena asked me about the depletion of the liquor, and I politely informed her that on more than one occasion I had seen her taking a swig. From that day on I never had a problem with her again.

I knew Chad and I had a dilemma when I preferred a bottle over some good loving. But I still tried to hang in there, thinking maybe I was just in a bad funk.

One weekend when Chad's parents went out of town, we were at his house lying in front of the fireplace after making love. It had been sensational, and I put my tongue into his right ear and nibbled on his earlobe trying to get him aroused for a second round. But "oh" boring Chad wanted to talk. He babbled on about going off to college the next year and how much he would miss me. As I lay on his chest, he lifted my chin up so we were looking in each other's eyes. "Tyler, if you promise not to be intimate with anyone else while I'm at college, when you graduate I want us to get married."

I thought to myself, I couldn't go two weeks without sex, let alone endless months.

"Chad, don't you think you're jumping the gun a little bit?

You don't know what will happen when you go off to college. You might meet some pretty little cheerleader and fall in love."

"Tyler, no one is prettier than you. You're my dream girl, and I want to spend the rest of my life with you." His words were cutting me deep. Yes, I wanted a man to love me and take care of me, but I also knew how destructive marriage could be. Plus I wasn't in love with Chad. The thought of him being the last man I would ever feel inside me was more than I could take.

"Baby, let's not talk about this now. School isn't even out yet, and we have the entire summer. Let's enjoy the time we have now and not worry about what the future holds."

What I considered a light conversation became more serious when Chad held my chin tightly and said, "Tyler, we belong together. My future is with you and only you." His eyes had a darkness to them that I had never seen before. It gave me an uneasy feeling.

"Okay, baby, whatever you say." I gave Chad a long kiss to defuse what now had become an intense vibe. This was one conversation I would delay for as long as I could.

After my evening with Chad I knew our relationship was on the road to nowhere. He was getting much too serious, and I wanted a lot more excitement—something different. I tried to go strong with my so-called first love, whom I had given my virginity to, but I think that whole "your first" is overrated. When I have flashbacks of my sexual experiences, "my first" is not the one that comes to mind. I cared deeply for Chad in my own way, but our relationship was a sinking ship.

I wanted a man who was the complete opposite of Chad: a man who would bring nonstop excitement to my life; someone edgier, who would stimulate my mind. I wanted a guy with a clean-cut appearance but a bad-boy mentality. I was also about to learn the hard way that you have to be careful what you wish for.

One night I went to a Clark Atlanta University talent show with Lisa. Lisa and I both looked a little older, especially with Lisa's size DD breasts. After the show, I was standing outside the bathroom waiting for her to come out. Just then I looked up and noticed this guy standing in front of me. "If I could rearrange the alphabet, I would put *U* and *I* together," he said. I laughed, and from then on I was intrigued. His name was Trey. He was another so-called pretty boy. He was wearing cream slacks with a cream cashmere sweater. Very clean-cut, just the way I envisioned my boyfriend would be. He was handsome, flashy, and confident, with a great sense of humor. We chatted and exchanged phone numbers even though he was twenty and I was only fifteen. He called me later on that night. Luckily I had my own line, so when the phone rang it didn't wake anyone.

"Hello," I said, trying to sound half-asleep although I was completely awake.

"What's up? This is Trey. Are you sleeping?"

"Almost, but I'll get up. What you doing?"

"Talking to you," he said with a slight snicker. "I'm surprised you're asleep. I just knew you'd be sitting by the phone waiting for me to call you." He sounded cocky. I began to fuck with his ego trying to see just how inflated it was.

"You know, Trey, you talk a lot of shit, but by the time I walk out of your life you're going to be so in love with me that I'll cause you to lose your mind." He laughed so loud, as if I had just told a Chris Tucker joke.

"Tyler, baby, no woman will ever cause me to lose my mind,

and the only person who ever walks away in my relationships is me," he barked with pure confidence.

"Oh, really?"

"Yes, really."

"Why is that?" I asked, like I really gave a fuck.

"Because every woman I'm with, I first blow out her back and then I blow her mind."

I had to admit that his confidence was turning me on. He sounded so sure of himself that I wanted to know if he could deliver the goods.

"Why don't you come over and try to blow out my back and blow my mind?" I suggested.

"You mean right now?"

"Yeah, right now." Thirty minutes later Trey pulled up in his black Ford Explorer. I had told him to park in the cul-de-sac, so from the top of the stairs through the vast glass windows, I saw him running toward the driveway. When I opened the Honduras mahogany doors, he stood in awe of the European-styled house. He gazed at the marble foyer and cathedral ceilings and couldn't manage to get a word out. I grabbed his hand and led him downstairs.

I turned on the night-light and put in my slow-jam CD. I was wearing a tiny pink teddy with no panties. We looked at one another, letting our eyes do all the talking. We came together with a lingering kiss. He led me toward the couch and laid me down, kissing me and fingering me at the same time. He then took that finger and licked it. He smiled and said, "You taste good."

He slid down my body and put his tongue deep inside me. He lifted my ass up as his tongue went deeper and deeper. He tongue-fucked me for what seemed like forever. When he finally lifted his head, I was ready to pass out. Obviously Trey could tell that he had already worn me out.

"Do you think I'm going to satisfy you and let you fall asleep? No, baby girl, it doesn't work like that. I've gotten this pussy nice and wet, and now it's time for me to get mine." Trey took off his clothes and dove in like he was taking a dip in a pool. He was pounding me hard and fucking me rough. He flipped me over and pulled my hair back as he talked dirty in my ears. Chad had never fucked me like this. But then again we had always made love. Trey and I definitely were fucking, and his intense energy and rough play were turning me on. He kept saying, "Yeah, you like this big dick inside of you."

"Yeah, baby, you feel good," I heard myself saying. By the time we had both collapsed in exhaustion, I was in complete awe of Trey. He had me open and he knew it. His confidence was definitely justified, and I decided I wanted him and I was going to have him.

After our night of passionate sex, I was totally caught up in Trey. I was running out of excuses for canceling dates with Chad, and I realized it was time to end our relationship. One warm spring night Chad and I were standing on the deck overlooking the pool. I looked in his eyes and said, "We need to talk." By the way he kept fidgeting I could tell he felt uneasy, but he tried to remain cool.

"You seem so serious, Tyler. What's going on?"

"Chad, you know that I care deeply for you and I always will, but I'm no longer happy in this relationship."

"What are you saying?" he asked, sounding taken aback.

"The relationship is over, Chad."

His eyes widened, and he looked as if I had just given him a death sentence.

"Tyler, what are you talking about? Did I do something wrong? We can fix this." Chad was blabbing on and on as if he couldn't help himself.

"Just stop, Chad. It isn't you; it's me. I don't love you anymore." The words rolled off my tongue, and I instantly regretted saying them. Chad sat on a patio chair and put his head down. I had only seen him look this defeated after his football team lost the state championship.

"Why, Tyler? I thought we were happy together."

"I haven't been happy for a while."

"Why didn't you say something before now?"

"I didn't know how to tell you."

"Answer this one question, and I want you to tell me the truth," he said somberly.

"What is it?" I asked, and my heart started to pound. I already knew what the question was, and I didn't know if I had the heart to answer honestly. But maybe Chad deserved that. I had led him on for so long, and I wanted him to be free to be happy with someone else.

As though it took every ounce of strength in his body, Chad finally said, "Tyler, are you seeing someone else?"

With great reluctance I nodded yes. Chad stood up, walked toward me, and I stepped back thinking he was about to become violent. But instead, Chad gently grabbed my face and kissed me good-bye. Just like that, I traded in my all-American football player in order to dance with the devil.

3

Eyes Wide Open

Trey was different from me in so many ways, but we were alike in so many others. Trey was from the streets and came from a broken home. He grew up with no guidance and went through life doing exactly what he wanted. He was in college, was highly intelligent, and had numerous admirable qualities, but on the inside he was fighting demons. He seemed haunted and brought the pain of those issues into our relationship.

After I broke up with Chad, I soon found out that Trey had a girlfriend who just happened to be Chad's ex-girlfriend, Chandler Thompson. A senior at my high school, she was a girl I had always admired. Chandler was beautiful and had a body to die for. Mocha chocolate with long black hair, she had a tiny waist with a bodacious butt. She was bootylicious way before Beyoncé or J. Lo. The fact that I was seeing her boyfriend astounded me;

but I wanted no part of any drama. As soon as I became aware of their relationship, I told Trey, "Until you straighten out your relationship with Chandler, we cannot see one another." Of course, he denied seeing her but I knew he was lying. I felt deceived that Trey was two-timing me but not surprised. He was young, handsome, and in college. I would've been surprised if Chandler was the only one.

I didn't quite believe that Trey was going to leave this gorgeous senior for a measly sophomore, but I certainly wasn't about to play second fiddle either. More important, I didn't want to develop a reputation for stealing other girls' boyfriends, a problem I had had to fight all through junior high.

One day between classes I stopped in the girls' bathroom. I was looking in the mirror trying to get something out of my eye when Chandler walked in, looking gorgeous as ever in a skintight red dress. She came right up to me, looking heated.

"Tyler, I need to speak to you about a nasty rumor that's been circulating around school."

"What rumor is that, Chandler?" I acted as though I didn't have a clue.

She sucked her teeth and looked me up and down as if she knew I was full of shit.

"The rumor about you and my man, Trey. You haven't heard anything about that?"

"Me and your man?" I pointed as though it was news to me. "Actually I'm single, Chandler, so whoever brought me into that rumor must have confused me with someone else."

"I don't think so because, see, I only know of one Tyler Blake, and that's yo ass." Chandler walked toward me with vengeance in her eyes. "Listen, you high-yellow heifer. I don't know what type of game you're trying to play, but you're playing it with the wrong bitch. Trey is my man, and if you know what is good for you, keep your young ass away from him."

My denial fell on deaf ears, and Chandler would hear none of it. After one last interrogation, she flashed her long red nails across my face as if she was going to scratch me. She left the bathroom with these departing words: "I got my eyes on you, bitch, so watch your back." On that note I decided to skip sixth period and take my ass home.

Later on that night while I was doing a pedicure, the phone rang. "Hello."

"Can I speak to Tyler?" The female voice sounded familiar.

"This is she," I responded, wishing I had never taken the call.

"This is Chandler."

"How did you get my number, and what do you want?"

"I called you, so I'm asking all the questions, and don't even think about hanging up," she blurted out, as if she was reading my mind. "Listen, Tyler, I'm not trying to cause you any problems, but I want to get to the bottom of this shit regarding Trey. I want to take a ride to his apartment and confront him about the rumors of him fucking with you."

"That's not necessary, Chandler. There is nothing going on between Trey and me."

"Well, I don't believe you."

"That sounds like a personal problem that I can't help you with. Now please leave me the fuck alone about this bullshit." I slammed the phone down, and after Chandler called back for the fifth time I took the phone off the hook. Before I went to bed I hung the phone up, and it rang less than a minute later. I let it ring three times while debating whether I wanted to take the chance of having Chandler on the other end. Something told me it wasn't her, so I picked up.

"Hello."

"Hi, Tyler, are you asleep?" the familiar voice asked.

"No, I'm still up, Chad. How are you?" When Chad and I first broke up, he would call me once a day to see if we could work things out. Then it became once a week. Finally the calls stopped altogether, so it was surprising to hear his voice.

"I'm doing good. I was calling to make sure you were doing okay."

"I'm fine; why wouldn't I be?"

"Well, I spoke to Chandler today, and she told me she heard you were seeing her boyfriend." My mouth dropped. When I broke up with Chad he knew I was seeing someone else, but I never told him who he was. For Chandler to go running to my ex was beyond pathetic.

"Why in the hell would Chandler call and tell you that?"

"Tyler, Chandler and I are still friends, and she wanted to know if you and I were still seeing each other."

"What did you tell her?"

"The truth—that it was over between us, although I wish it wasn't. Tyler, you don't need to be with a guy who already has a girlfriend. You deserve so much more than that. I still love you, and I know you must still care about me, too."

"Chad, I do care about you, I always will, but not in a romantic way. I know that's not what you want to hear, but it's the truth. I hope you understand."

"I do. But, Tyler, be careful. Whoever this guy is, he seems like bad news."

"I will. Thanks for your concern, Chad."

I couldn't believe that Chandler called Chad, getting him involved in my personal business. What was more mind-boggling was that someone as beautiful as Chandler Thompson was sweating a sophomore about her so-called man. Although I loved spending time with Trey, this was becoming way too complicated. The last thing I wanted was a whole bunch of girlfriend drama. I've never liked drama, and to this day I still don't. I run from unwanted drama.

After I could no longer duck Chandler in school, we had one last conversation. Well, it was more like she talked and I listened. After cornering me at my locker, she said bitterly, "I know you're fucking Trey, but now he's all yours. I refuse to share my man with some snotty Lolita who doesn't know how to keep her legs closed." With a devilish grin spread across her flawless face, she added, "By the way, I told Trey how old you really are. Tootles, bitch." As she turned her back to walk away, she tossed her long black hair in my face and sashayed down the hallway like she owned the place.

When I got home, Trey called and asked if he could come over to talk. I wasn't in the mood but agreed. The first question he asked as we sat on my bed was, "Why didn't you tell me how old you were?"

"Because you didn't ask."

"I assumed that since you were at a college function you were at least legal."

"I will be in a few months, but if you don't want to wait I totally understand." But I wanted to be with Trey now. Throughout this whole episode with Chandler we hadn't been intimate, and seeing him looking so sexy, I definitely wanted our relationship to continue.

"Well, what do you want to do?" he asked, sounding the same way I felt.

"It's up to you." When he reached over and began kissing me and rubbing his hand on my breast, I knew it meant the waiting wasn't necessary. Luckily my parents weren't home, because Trey and I immediately started catching up on lost time. From that day forward Trey and I were boyfriend and girlfriend.

In the beginning everything was new and exciting. I had never been with a guy like Trey before. He came into my life at a point when school, my friends, and my life in general were boring to me. He was like a head rush, and it was very addictive. We were glued at the hip. Most days I would hang out with him on the Clark Atlanta campus. Although I had only a learner's permit, my parents had gotten me a car, and I would drive myself to and from school. Whenever possible, I skipped classes to be with Trey. Hanging with him was more interesting than anything they were teaching me at school. To this day I still wonder how I was able to make decent grades and graduate. I even dropped out of the drama club. Although I still dreamed of being an actress someday, meeting four days a week for rehearsals interfered with my blossoming relationship with Trey.

On the rare occasion when Mother had time for me, we went to the Ritz-Carlton for Sunday brunch. Ever since I found out Daddy was physically abusive toward Mother, our relationship had been strained and we rarely talked about what was going on in each other's life. "So how's Chad doing?" Mother asked, unaware we had broken up a couple of months earlier.

"Chad and I aren't together anymore."

"Oh, you'll be back together. Did you have a little spat?"

"No, actually, I have a new boyfriend."

Mother looked at me suspiciously. "New boyfriend? I haven't met him. Does he go to your school?"

"Actually he attends Clark University," I said, all perky because I was proud to have a college boyfriend. Plus there was no need to lie and tell her he went to one of the local high schools. Mother knew the parents of just about all the students that she felt came from respectable families.

"He's in college." She paused. "Isn't that a little old for you?"

I lied and said he was only a freshman and had just turned eighteen.

"Would you like to see a picture of him?" Trey had given me a college calendar, for which he had posed for the month of April. I had it in my tote bag and was anxious to get Mother's reaction.

"Sure, honey," she said nonchalantly. I reached in my tote bag, pulled out the calendar, and flipped to Trey's picture. Mother's mouth dropped, and I knew she wasn't pleased. Trey was wearing a cream linen suit that complemented his light reddish skin, and he had a gun tucked inside his pants. I got a kick watching Mother's expression. I was proud to tell Mother this pretty boy was my new boyfriend. But she liked to have died.

"He is nothing but the devil, and you need to stay away from him," she said, fear in her voice. Of course, instead making me afraid, her reaction added to my excitement, and I wanted to be with Trey more than ever. After getting Mother riled up over my personal life, I decided to take the conversation in a different direction.

"Mother, can I ask you something?"

"Of course, dear. What is it?" she said, reading her paper.

"Where is my father?"

"Honey, I told you he had to go to San Francisco on business," Mother said, not taking her eyes off the paper.

"I'm talking about my real father, my biological one."

Mother put the paper down and looked at me. "Now why would you ask me where he is? Who cares? Haven't you had a wonderful life? Michael has been a fantastic father to you," she said, sounding upset.

"Yes, he has, but he still isn't my real father. Why hasn't my real daddy, Carter, ever come back for Ella and me? Doesn't he want to know how we are?"

"No! Carter doesn't care about you or Ella. I didn't want to tell you this, Tyler, but I reached out to your father, and he told me he had moved on and didn't want anything to do with you or your sister."

"*What?* But why? When I was little he was so sweet to me."

"You're not little anymore, and he doesn't want to be bothered. Honey, I'm sorry to be so cruel, but you have to get this fantasy about how wonderful your father is out of your head. He has always been irresponsible and never wanted to provide a good life for you and your sister. Michael is your father and always will be."

Mother's words crushed me. The only thing that had given me some solace was my belief that my real father had never come back for us because he didn't know where we were. To learn that he had turned his back on Ella and me was devastating. I couldn't help but feel that something must be wrong with me if my own father didn't want me.

Just as I grabbed my denim jacket and purse and got ready to head out to meet Lisa at the mall, the phone rang. "Hello," I said in a rushed voice.

"Hi, Tyler, are you busy?" I was surprised to hear Chad's voice. We hadn't spoken in over a month.

"No, how have you been?"

"Great. Just trying to get everything in order for college. I was actually calling to see if you would still go to the senior prom with me." He rushed the question as if he knew I was on my way out the door. "I know we're not together anymore, but I don't have anyone to go with."

"Oh, Chad, please, any girl would die to be your date for the prom."

"Yeah, maybe, but they wouldn't be you. Tyler, I'd really love it if you'd come, as friends of course."

"I would love to go." Although that wasn't exactly true.

"Wonderful. It's next Saturday, and I'll pick you up around seven." Chad quickly hung up, as if he thought I might change my mind. But I had no intention of doing that. I was looking forward to getting all dolled up and buying a new dress, but more than that I felt a sense of obligation to attend the event with Chad. I couldn't erase the sad look in his eyes the day I told him our relationship was over. I could've been more sensitive, and I hoped that attending the prom with him would ease my still-guilty conscience. I decided not to tell Trey, because he would be less than thrilled if he knew I was going on a date with my ex-boyfriend.

Mother was delighted to hear I was going to the prom with Chad. We went to Neiman Marcus to pick out a dress. As I tried on a beautiful white lace dress that hugged my curves in all the right places and dipped in the front, giving me an enticing cleavage, Mother beamed. "That's the one. You look beautiful, my little princess." Mother hadn't called me that in a long time, and it brought chills to know she still felt that way.

"Darling, I'm ecstatic you're getting back with Chad; he is a wonderful young man."

"Mother, Chad and I aren't back together. I only agreed to go to the prom with him; nothing more, nothing less."

"I just assumed you were over your fixation with that Trey character and were now thinking about your future."

"Mother, I'm only fifteen; I have plenty of time to think about my future."

"Time flies sooner than you think. If I'd planned ahead, I would've never wasted all those years with your father. Don't make the same mistake I did. Chad is a great catch. He is either going to be a professional football player or an attorney, so you know he will be a wonderful provider. He comes from an excellent family, and he's a very handsome young man. Tyler, you would be a fool not to stick it out with him. If you want to have meaningless dalliances with that Trey character, so be it, but by no means take him or the relationship seriously."

As Mother paid for my dress, I thought about what she'd said. Maybe I should stick it out with Chad. He was a wonderful guy and my first love. Trey was fun, but I wasn't sure if he was the type of guy I could be with on a long-term basis. Chad was boring, but he was also going off to college in a couple of months so I wouldn't have to deal with him on an everyday basis. I could always see Trey on the side.

When Mother and I got back from shopping, we noticed an unfamiliar car parked in front of one of the garages. Daddy was out of town and Ella was away at college, so we couldn't imagine who it could be. Mother pulled up beside the vehicle, but no one was inside. "Are you expecting a visitor, Tyler?"

"No. I don't know whose car that is."

"Maybe it's one of those door-to-door salespeople. Don't they have laws against such harassment?" Mother said, annoyed that she might have to talk to a stranger. We gathered our bags and made our way to the front door. The tall man in a suit was standing with his back turned to us. "I told you it was one of those salespeople," Mother said, exasperated. "Whatever you're selling, we're not buying, sir, so please excuse yourself."

"I'm not selling anything. I came to pay my family a visit." I dropped the bags that were in my hand when the man faced us. He was ten years older, but his eyes were still the same.

"What the hell are you doing here, Evan?" Mother screamed. "I want you off this property right now or I'll call the police!"

"That won't be necessary. Don't I have a right to see my father?" Evan directed his question toward me, and I put my head down, not wanting to see his face. I couldn't believe Evan was standing at our doorstep as if he hadn't tried to rob me of my innocence ten years earlier.

"Your father isn't here, and if he was, I doubt he would want to see your face. Remember, he is the one who disowned you," Mother said.

"How can I forget?" he said in an unremorseful tone. "I'm sure that must please you, Maria. Now you and your two little princesses can keep my father's money all to yourself." Even with Evan's model-perfect, chiseled face and smooth coffee-colored skin, there was no escaping the evilness that his eyes possessed. He had the same lean, muscular build of his father, but for all of his physical attributes, underneath lived a monster.

"Is that what this is about? You want money?" Mother said, visibly upset.

"I'm blood; if anyone deserves his money, it's me. Not some money-hungry woman and her two bratty daughters," Evan said smugly.

"You bastard," I said, furious. "The reason you don't have your father's money is because you tried to molest a little girl. You almost destroyed my life. I still have nightmares. I can't believe you have the audacity to show up here after what you did.

You belong in jail—or better yet, dead—for what you put me through."

"Tyler, relax. It's okay." Mother was trying to calm me down, but it wasn't working.

"No, it's not okay! I prayed I would never have to see your despicable face again, but here you are. Looking like the same evil snake you were ten years ago. You haven't changed. You're still the sick prick you've always been."

"Evan, get in your car and never come back here again. When Michael finds out you were here, he'll be furious, and you better hope he doesn't come looking for you to finish what I stopped." Mother was holding her cell phone, prepared to dial 911.

"I'm leaving, Maria, but you haven't heard the last of me. I don't know when, but your family will pay for what you took away from me."

"Don't you threaten my family, you sonofabitch! I should've let your father kill you."

"Should've, could've, would've, but I'm very much alive. Remember that." Evan walked past us toward his car. For a second I thought about picking up a tall vase and slamming it over his head, but decided against it. "Oh, by the way, Tyler, you've grown up to be such a beautiful young lady. But then you were certainly a beautiful little girl."

Mother and I watched Evan walk away, hoping he would never come back.

When Chad picked me up for the prom, he looked gorgeous. Both of us wore white, and we looked like the African American version of Ken and Barbie. It took us twenty minutes just to get out the door because Mother wouldn't stop taking pictures. When we arrived at the Peachtree Plaza for the prom, the ballroom was decorated beautifully, with orchids and roses everywhere. Monica's "Before You Walk Out of My Life" was playing, and Chad took my hand and led me to the dance floor. As he put his hands around my waist and we swayed to the music, he pulled me closer, as though he never wanted to let go. For a moment it seemed like old times.

The prom wound down, and Chad asked me to go upstairs to his suite for a drink. When we got upstairs, he pulled out a bottle of champagne, poured me a glass, and tuned the radio to 107.9. We chatted about the college he'd decided to attend and how happy he was to get a full scholarship. I got caught up in the moment and had a slight buzz from the champagne, so when Chad kissed me, I kissed him back. But when he unzipped the back of my dress, I gently pushed him away. "This isn't right."

"What are you talking about? Nothing could be more right. Tyler, we belong together," he said as he continued to kiss my neck.

Pushing him away, I huffed, "That may be true, but not now, not like this. I need time, Chad."

"Time for what?" he said, anger creeping across his face.

"To think things over."

"What fucking things, Tyler?" he asked as he grabbed my arm.

"Chad, you're hurting me; let go of my arm." I tried to break free, but he was too strong. The look in Chad's eyes was scaring me. It was a look I could never erase from my mind—depraved and full of rage. It was the same look I had seen in Evan's eyes ten years ago. I shook my head in disbelief; it wasn't possible for Chad to be that sort of monster.

"Chad, please let me go; you're hurting my arm," I repeated. But Chad's eyes were empty. It was as if he had zoned out. I decided to make my getaway. Looking around, I didn't see anything within reach that I could pick up and hit Chad with; so I swung my left arm with all my strength and hit Chad in his neck, knocking him off balance. He fell back, releasing me, and I made a dash toward the door.

As I reached for the doorknob, I heard, "Tyler, where the fuck do you think you're going?" My neck snapped back as Chad grabbed me by my hair, and I fell to the floor.

Within seconds Chad was on top of me, ripping off the beautiful dress Mother had bought me. "No! Chad, please stop! You don't want to do this, please!" I begged to no avail. It was like he was possessed and there was no bringing him back. I screamed at the top of my lungs, but my cries were drowned out by the music playing on the radio. Even so, Chad put his hand over my mouth.

"No one can hear you, Tyler. I have you all to myself. You used to let me make love to you, but I guess now you want me to take it." I lay in the middle of the hotel suite pinned to the floor. As I felt Chad spread my legs apart and rip off my panties, I couldn't believe this was happening to me again. But this time there was no Daddy coming to the rescue. My eyes filled with tears as Chad jammed his dick inside of me and pounded me over and over again, releasing all the hatred he had inside. After what seemed like a lifetime, Chad finally let out a loud moan. His heavy body felt like a car rolling over my foot. But my energy was so drained that I didn't have the strength to try to move him off. I could see the sweat trickling down the side of Chad's neck, and after five more minutes of intense breathing he finally rolled off me and stood up. As he zipped up his pants, he gave me the glance-over and shrieked, "Why did you make me do this, Tyler? It didn't have to be this way."

I couldn't believe my ears. Chad was blaming me for the rape he had just committed. "You sick bastard! You just raped me, and you have the nerve to stand there and blame me!"

Chad walked toward me and knelt down on the floor I was still lying on. "Don't you ever say that again. I didn't rape you. This was a lovers' quarrel that got out of hand."

"Is that the lie you're running with? Because a ripped dress, torn panties, and bruises on my arms and thighs all symbolize rape to me, you sonofabitch." My attitude had now shifted from fear and pain to relentless anger. I stood up, looking at my destroyed dress and bruised body. "Chad, you will not get away with this. I'm going to tell my parents, and they will no doubt report you to the police."

"Yeah, you do that, Tyler, and I'll let everyone know what a whore you are."

"*Whore?*" I shouted. "*You raped me!*"

"So you say, but I could tell the police you like it rough. What do you think people will say when they find out you have a boyfriend but went to the prom with your ex? You need to think long and hard before you start throwing around accusations."

"These aren't accusations; they are facts, and the fact is that you raped me, do you hear me?" My voice cracked as I got louder and louder.

"Well, you go right ahead, but by the time you make it to court, everyone will know that sweet little Tyler is nothing but a freak. Fucking a grown-ass man and fucking me too; no one will feel sorry for you. They will think you are nothing but a hot-ass bitch who has no self-control. Your boyfriend will be brought up on statutory rape charges, and your family will be embarrassed and disgraced."

A wave of despair flooded through my body. The emotional roller coaster I was on now took another turn. I went from fear to anger and now shame. I put my head down, replaying the words Chad had just spoken to me. Everyone would think I was a whore. My parents would find out how old Trey really was, and he would know I lied about hanging out with Lisa that night. He'd find out I was actually with Chad. I felt helpless.

At his insistence, Chad drove me home. Luckily my parents were asleep. I went in the bathroom and turned on the light switch. The reflection in the mirror of the once beautiful face with the perfectly applied makeup had two raccoon eyes from the tears smearing my eyeliner and mascara. I took off all my clothes, put them in a plastic bag, and planned to toss them in the trash. I pulled back the floral shower curtain and turned the knob to Hot. I stepped inside and let the burning water drench my hair and entire body. I was hoping all the evil that had just violated my body would be washed away. That was the best I could hope for. After going over my options, I decided to keep this horrific night to myself. I convinced myself that I got what I deserved for even going to the prom with Chad. The shame I felt was too much to share with anyone, let alone my parents or the police. This was a chapter of my life I would put behind me. Or so I thought.

In the months after the rape, I fell into a deep depression. I did a good job hiding it from my family and friends, but every night I would cry myself to sleep. With Ella away at college, Mother focusing on her social life, and Daddy traveling more and more on his so-called business trips, the only person I had was Trey. Besides going to school, I spent all my time with him. We had been together for over a year, but our relationship had begun taking on a different dimension.

One day Trey arrived to take me to a barbecue at his friend Patrick's house. I colored my normally black hair a lighter brown and wore a snug-fitting halter dress. As soon as I stepped in the car, the insults started. "Why did you dye your hair that color? It looks nasty because it washes out your complexion. And that dress makes you look fat," he said, even though I was no more than a hundred and fifteen pounds. The other side of Trey was showing its ugly face, and it was far from the fun-loving guy I fell in love with. Trey was screwed up emotionally and I was already unstable, so he started to screw me up even more.

"I like my hair color, and I think this dress fits me good," I replied confidently, trying to mask how bad Trey had hurt my feelings.

"I didn't ask you what you think. You don't know anything anyway. I'm a man. I know what looks good and what doesn't. Trust me, you look like shit."

For the entire barbecue I sat in a corner feeling too insecure to walk around or mingle with anybody. After that day Trey's cruelty became an all-out daily assault that slowly chipped away my self-esteem and left me lacking confidence.

Trey was excited about his new apartment and finally having no roommate. Between going to school during the day and promoting parties at night, he was making decent money and was able to afford a one-bedroom unit in a brand-new luxury apartment complex. In Trey's bedroom I was unpacking a box full of tapes, CDs, and videocassettes when I came across a tape that had "Joy Time" written in bold black ink. It was dated a month earlier. Curious, I slid it in the VCR. An image flashed across the screen—it was Trey, sitting on the couch in his old apartment, speaking into the camera. Then he walked over to the camera, took it from someone's hand, and turned the camera on her. It was a pretty ebony-complexioned woman in her early twenties. I heard Trey's voice in the background, saying, "Come on, Nikki, do a striptease show for me." Music was playing in the background, and then another young woman stepped into the camera's view.

"That's right, ladies. Move that ass to the music. Take it all off." The women were now completely naked and grinding to reggae music. "Play with each other's tits while Daddy watches." The women were rubbing each other down and sucked each other's nipples like they were babies nursing. The whole scene was bizarre. I had never seen two women making out before. Right when I was about to push Eject, Trey propped the camcorder in a prime position. He was now butt naked, frolicking with the ladies.

"Come here, Stephanie," Trey said, grabbing her gigantic ass. She was giggling as she made her way toward him. "I want you to deep throat it for me like you did last night," Trey demanded. This was all too much. The girl got on her hands and knees and swallowed Trey's manhood.

The other girl, Nikki, chimed, "Ya not gonna leave me out the mix." Then she grabbed Trey's hand, and he lay on the floor while Stephanie continued to suck him dry. Nikki sat on Trey's face, and he ate her pussy as if it were a prime piece of steak. I couldn't bring myself to turn off the tape; I was entranced. I sat on Trey's bed in disgust, not believing the threesome taking place in front of my eyes with my boyfriend playing the starring role. I put my hands on my forehead, shaking my head in disbelief, when Trey walked in.

His eyes popped out as he saw the sex tape he had made only a month earlier. He ran to the VCR and struggled clumsily to rip the tape out. But the damage had already been done. "Tyler, it's not what you think; this tape is from a couple of years ago."

"Trey, I saw the date. You made it last month." Honestly, I didn't even care. I knew Trey was cheating on me, but I was at such a low point in my life that it didn't matter. Plus since Chad raped me, I didn't even enjoy sex anymore. I preferred to be left alone. I gave into Trey sexually only because I felt obligated.

"Nah, baby, that's the right date but the wrong year," he countered.

"Save it, Trey. No need to explain; the tape speaks for itself. It's actually a good thing. I've been having reservations about our relationship, and this tape makes it clear that it's time for us to go our separate ways."

"What the fuck did you say?" Trey's demeanor changed in less than eight seconds. He went from denying and apologetic to hostile and aggressive. "I know you not trying to end this over some bullshit tape with some chicken-heads."

"Yeah, some chicken-heads—one who had your dick in her mouth and the other who had her pussy spread across your face. That's funny," I chuckled. "Trey, it's all good. Shit happens, but this is the last time it will happen with me." I stepped off the bed preparing to leave, but as soon as my feet touched the carpet, Trey punched me in the left eye. I fell back on the bed.

"Bitch, you think you gonna leave me? Hell, no! I told you, don't nobody leave me." Trey stood over me, yelling like a three-year-old having a temper tantrum. Spit was flaring from his mouth as he continued to rant and rave. He lifted his leg and put his Nike shoe to my throat. "You ain't never gonna leave me. You hear me?" He pressed his shoe deeper into my throat, and I began to lose my breath. Trey knelt down and grabbed my hair and dragged me to the mirror in his bathroom. My eye was now swollen and red from the punch he had planted on my face.

"Take a long look at yourself. If you ever leave me, I'll have this pretty little face so disfigured, your own mama won't recognize you."

Trey's words stung. Was this my life? What had I done to deserve my miserable existence? That night Trey fucked me while forcing me to watch his porno tape over and over. He said it was to teach me not to go through his shit.

For the next few months I grew more and more afraid of Trey. After enduring busted lips, black eyes, and constant beat downs, I was afraid of what he might do next. I had become so alienated from my family and friends that it seemed like nobody cared. Part of me felt that something about me must be so terrible that I deserved Trey's constant abuse. I spent most nights at Trey's apartment, and because my parents were busy living their own separate lives, they never made time to see how I was doing. I could've left for a month, and no one would've noticed.

Besides Trey, I spent time with only one other person, and that was Patrick. I first met Patrick at his barbecue, but that was only briefly. He was so occupied with entertaining his guests that we didn't have an opportunity to talk. Then one day when I was waiting for Trey after a class, Patrick saw me.

"Hi, Tyler, are you waiting for Trey?"

"Yeah." I smiled shyly. I knew Trey wouldn't appreciate me talking to Patrick, although they were friends.

"Is everything okay? You have a sad look on your face," he said.

"I do? I'm fine, just a little tired," I said, not wanting to reveal that the look on my face was an indication of how miserable I was with Trey.

"Okay, but if you ever need to talk, let me know."

"I'll do that," I said as Patrick turned and walked away. For a brief moment I wondered why Trey couldn't be sensitive like Patrick.

One night during a heated argument with Trey, he punched me in the nose. Blood was everywhere. I ran out of the apartment and drove off. While driving back and forth on Peachtree Street, I called Patrick from my cell. He told me to come over. When I got there, he examined my nose, and luckily it wasn't broken. He gave me some cold towels to stop the bleeding and had me tilt my head back. The questioning immediately kicked in.

"Why does a girl like you, who has so much going for herself, stay with a man like Trey?" Patrick asked as he pressed the towel around my nose.

"It's a long complicated story," I sighed.

"I'm in no rush," Patrick said with a warm smile. He had a way of making me feel at ease. I could talk to him for hours without even realizing the time was passing us by.

"When I first met Trey, he was fun and exciting. Different from the other guys I dated. He was the quintessential bad boy, and I was attracted to that. Never did I think he would turn out to be so demonic."

"So why stay?"

"The first time Trey hit me, in so many words, he threatened to end my life if I ever tried to leave him. No one had ever placed that sort of fear in my heart. Part of me also feels unworthy of any type of real love."

Patrick turned my face to his and lovingly placed his hand on my shoulder. "How can you say that? You come from a good family, and the world is yours for the taking."

"You mean I come from a rich family, because nothing about it is good. Living in a big house and having nice cars doesn't make a good family, Patrick. No one even notices when I'm not around. My father is too busy having an affair, and my mother is so wrapped up with her socialite friends and her casual flings that they couldn't care less whether I'm coming or going. My life is empty."

"I'm sorry, Tyler. I had no idea your family life was causing you so much pain, but then again, it should have been easy to figure out. If your parents were paying any attention to you, they would see how volatile your relationship with Trey is. But, Tyler, I'm here to tell you that you deserve more. You're a beautiful, smart, and loving young woman with so much to give. You deserve more than Trey. I can't force you to leave him, but if you're only staying out of fear, I will make sure that he never puts his hands on you again."

I moved closer to Patrick and gave him a long lingering kiss. No one had ever made me feel so safe and secure. "Patrick, I want to give myself to you. Please make love to me."

"Tyler, you have more to give than just your body. I want all of you: your mind, your body, and your soul. But that will take time. Right now you need to focus on ending things with Trey and focusing on healing yourself." Patrick was right. I had so many inner demons I needed to fight, and the first one was Trey. I also knew that this situation had to be dealt with delicately. Trey would flip if I started a relationship with Patrick, but part of me didn't care. I so desperately wanted to escape the torture I was enduring with Trey and be with a loving, gentle person like Patrick that I was willing to take the risk.

"Instead of making love, can we lie in the bed and you just hold me until I fall asleep?" I asked.

"I'll do more than that; I'll hold you until you wake up." Patrick reached for my hand and led me to his bedroom. He gave me a T-shirt to put on, and we slid under the covers. Patrick held me all night as I fell into the deepest sleep I had had in many months.

When I woke up early the next morning, Patrick was still asleep. I moved his arm from around me and quietly got out the bed. I threw on my clothes, wrote Patrick a note telling him I would call him later, and headed out the door. When I got in the car, I had twenty missed calls and ten new voice messages, all from Trey.

As I drove up the driveway, I felt a great sense of relief to be home. When I opened the front door, my parents were sitting on the stairs in their pajamas as though they had been up all night.

"Tyler, where have you been and what happened to your nose?" Mother asked, the look of death on her face. My parents hadn't questioned my whereabouts in so long that I was thrown off.

"I spent the night at . . . Lisa's house, and I accidentally banged my nose on her bathroom door."

"Don't lie to your mother," Daddy said, as if he was disappointed with where the conversation was going.

"I called Lisa last night, and she tried to cover for you, but once I explained the severity of the situation, she admitted she hadn't spoken to you." What severe situation was Mother speaking of? I wondered.

"Did something happen to Ella?"

"No, Ella is fine. The emergency is you." Mother's lip began to quiver as it did when she was either stressed or extremely nervous.

"Me? What about me?"

"Last night, Trey kept calling here looking for you. He said you weren't answering your phone and thought maybe we knew where you were. After the third call he became irate and started cursing and screaming, saying I was lying about knowing your whereabouts. I didn't know it, but he was calling from outside the house. Before I could tell your father about the conversation there was a knock at the door, and when Daddy opened it, Trey put a gun to his head. He told your father to tell you that if you don't come back to him, you're as good as dead. What the hell is going on, Tyler?"

All the built-up pain and fear emerged from inside me, and I burst out crying. Father ran toward me and wrapped his arms around me. Mother stood there, looking confused. "I'm so sorry," I wailed. "Trey beat me up last night, and I stayed with my friend Patrick because I was afraid and didn't want to come home."

"Beat you up? Is that what happened to your nose?" Mother asked.

"Yes."

"Was that the first time he hit you?"

"No, Daddy, he has hit me many, many times." My body fell into his chest as I purged one of my painful secrets.

"My little princess," Daddy kept saying over and over as he rubbed my back.

"I knew that man was evil. How dare he do this to a daughter of mine? We called the police after Trey left, and they came over and filled out an incident report. I want you to press charges for the busted nose he gave you."

"Mother, I just want to forget any of this ever happened and forget Trey ever existed."

"Are you crazy? You have a maniac after you, and you want to act like you're not in danger?" Mother hissed.

"You have a lot of nerve," I said, pushing myself away from Daddy. "Mother, you allow Daddy to knock you around on the rare occasions that he's home. And Daddy, you're out having an affair as if your family is nonexistent. The two of you are part of the reason I stayed with Trey—I thought he was the only one who gave a damn about me. Maybe he abused me, but at least he gave me attention and acknowledged my existence. Both of you are so caught up in your own lives that you don't care what's going on with me."

Daddy stared at me, stunned. "Tyler, that's not true," he said lovingly. Your mother and I love you very much, and I'll admit we have been selfish, and I'm so sorry. Despite all our faults, you still have to be realistic about the situation. This isn't just going to go away. We need to take the necessary steps to protect you, and that means going to the police." He was right. Trey was crazy, and there was no telling what he might do. Maybe if he knew the police were involved, it would scare him enough to leave me alone.

My parents drove me to the police station, where I filed a criminal complaint, and the police issued a temporary restraining order against Trey. I finally felt that Trey was completely out of my life.

Initially Trey continued to call with threats, and he even came to my house and school looking for me. But after he was arrested for violating the restraining order, he seemed to get the message and he backed off. Patrick was there for me the whole time. Although we hadn't been intimate, we were closer than any two people could be. He was truly my rock, and I felt blessed to have him in my corner. The tragic events in my life had briefly united my parents, and they seemed to rekindle their love. But after things cooled down, Daddy was back to the mistress and Mother was back to her social life.

"Let's go check out that new Denzel Washington movie tonight," Patrick said.

"That sounds good. I'll be at your crib in an hour." After hanging up, I jumped in the shower. I put on the new baby blue minidress I'd picked up at a boutique in Lenox Square mall. It was a warm summer night, and I put the top down on my new BMW 325. It was a present for my seventeenth birthday, which had just passed. I blasted "Hypnotized" by the late great Biggie Smalls as I made my way to Patrick's house. While bopping to the music, I realized that a black Jeep had been behind me for the last ten minutes. My heart started jumping, and instantly I thought of Trey. While I dialed Patrick's number to relay my fear, the Jeep made a right turn at the light. I laughed at myself for being so paranoid. When I reached Patrick's crib I blew the horn, and he came running outside. He jumped in the passenger seat and gave me a kiss on the lips, and we headed off to the movies.

"That movie was crazy. Did you see how Denzel blasted that dude?" Patrick asked, all hyped.

"Forget that. Did you see how Denzel put it down with that chick? He has got to be the sexiest man in the world—next to you, of course." I laughed before giving Patrick a kiss.

"Isn't this special, my friend and my girl all hugged up together?" As Patrick and I stood in front of the car, for the first time in over three months Trey was standing in front of me. My hands began shaking, and Patrick pulled me closer.

"Trey, I think it's best that you leave. Now!" Patrick stood in front of me without the least bit of fear.

"Or what, Patrick? Huh, what you gone do?" he continued, a smug look on his face. "You might think you got yourself a prime piece of pussy, but that's my bitch you're fucking. She will always be my bitch."

"Whatever, man, you keep holding on to those memories because that's all you have left." With those words, Trey snapped and swung his fist, barely missing Patrick's jaw. I stepped back as Patrick and Trey went to blows.

"Trey, please leave!" I screamed, hoping he'd realize he was fighting a losing battle. But they were in a full-blown fight. People were gathering around, wondering what the hell was going on. After Patrick landed two straight jabs, one in Trey's stomach and the other under his chin, the fight seemed over. Trey was bent over in pain, looking defeated.

"Take that, you bitch-ass motherfucker. You like pounding on women, but you can't pound on no man. Don't you ever bother Tyler again, or I swear I'll kill you." Patrick grabbed my hand to walk away, and Trey reached in the back of his pants and pulled out a gun.

All I heard was people screaming, "He has a gun! He has a gun!" Everyone was ducking behind cars and running for cover. Patrick squeezed my hand tightly as if to tell me not to be afraid. But I was beyond afraid. Trey pointed the gun toward us.

I didn't want to die, and I felt the need to plead for my life. "Trey, don't do this. Killing Patrick and me won't change anything. I know you're better than this." The tears were rolling down my face as I prayed my words would make a difference. Trey stepped closer to us with the gun pointed steady in our direction. I was hoping that Patrick wouldn't try to be a hero and get ahold of the gun.

"All I ever wanted to do was love you, Tyler. You're my life. Never in my wildest dreams did I believe I would have a girl like you. You can't blame me for doing whatever I had to do to keep you. But you've moved on, and I can't let you be happy without me." My chest was thumping and I was becoming dizzy because I knew Trey was about to put a bullet in Patrick's head and in mine. I heard police sirens in the distance, but they were too far away to make a difference. All it would take was a second for Trey to end our lives. He yanked the gun forward with intensity, as if he was about to pull the trigger. I knelt forward, still holding Patrick's arm, knowing we were about to die together.

"Tyler, I'll love you forever. Remember this moment because my face will haunt you for the rest of your life." Everything after that seemed to happen in slow motion. Patrick tried to use his body to cover me, but I moved forward and looked directly at Trey, as if I wanted to look my death in the face. Trey's arm was raised, and the next thing I heard was what sounded like a large explosion. Everyone gasped in horror as Trey's brains splashed across the concrete.

I screamed, *"Noooooooooooo!"* as Trey's body fell to the ground. I hated the way Trey had treated me, but never did I want him to die. But there he was, lying before me dead. As the police arrived and ran toward Trey's dead body, I realized it could've been mine.

4

Letting Go

"I want to give a shout out to the class of 1998's North Atlanta High School graduates, Lisa Duncan and Tyler Blake," the DJ yelled over the mike. "It's All About the Benjamins" was blaring from the speakers, and Lisa and I were grinding to the music at Club 112. I didn't know how Lisa got Chris to announce that over the mike, especially since you're supposed to be twenty-one to get in the club. But who cared? I was so psyched about being free from high school that I wanted to party all night long. With eyes closed, I was running my fingers through my hair, dancing in my own world, when I felt a pair of strong arms wrapped around my waist. The arms felt so good that I didn't even move them. I was in a zone and I slowly grinded in their embrace. My eyes were still closed when the soft lips kissed my neck and their sensual scent intoxicated me. Whoever was holding me felt so right.

The kiss on my earlobe got me aroused, and the whisper in my ear ended the mystery.

"You just letting any old nigga run up on you?"

"Nah, only one that I miss, like you, Patrick." I turned around and faced him.

"How did you know it was me?" he said, sounding surprised and happy that I wasn't letting just anybody grind on me.

"I didn't at first, but then your voice gave you away."

"Oh, so you didn't know who I was and you still allowed me to feel up on you like that?"

"Yeah, shit, you had me in a zone. I was already vibing with the music, and when you touched me it felt so right. Anyway, how can you question me when I haven't seen you in over six months?"

After Trey killed himself, I had totally lost my mind. I couldn't sleep or eat, and all I saw was his face. Patrick tried to console me, but I was inconsolable. Being close to him kept reminding me of that fateful night. Eventually he dropped out of school and disappeared, and we lost all contact. My parents had me see a therapist for a while, and eventually I somewhat pulled it together mentally. But when I tried to find Patrick, I hit a dead end. It was as if Patrick just vanished off the face of the earth. I knew I was the one who pushed him away, and I had no right to think that once my mind was stable he would still be right there waiting for me. But Patrick and I had been through so much together that it caused me to take his feelings for granted. Not once did I consider that he might've needed my support. But now here he was, standing in front of me. I stared at him for a good minute. With his tall, dark strong build, Patrick's presence was always felt, but even more so now with his new bling-bling look. He was wearing a flashy Rolex watch and had two huge diamond studs in his ears. He was always a stylish dresser, but now he was immaculate.

"Damn, Patrick, you looking good. I guess wherever you've been they've been treating you right."

"Not as good as if I had you."

"Funny, you seem to be doing just fine without me—not a card, a phone call, nothing," I said, feeling genuinely disappointed. Patrick used to be my rock. I was attracted to how fly he was looking, but more than that, Patrick had the warmest smile I had ever seen.

"Tyler, you know you're the one who pushed me away. I couldn't get you on the phone, and when I went to your house your father said you didn't want to see me. I was devastated. There was nothing left for me here, so I bounced."

"I did come looking for you once I got my mind right, but you were nowhere to be found. Where have you been?"

"I live in Chicago now."

"What you do in Chicago?"

"A little bit of this, a little bit of that." I glanced over Patrick again, checking out his gear. He looked like nothing but money. Young black man, doing this and that, looking like a million bucks, sounded like a pharmaceutical dealer to me. But no matter what his profession, Patrick still had the same gentle nature that attracted me to him in the first place.

"So what brings you back to Atlanta?"

"I had some business to take care of, but now that I ran into you hopefully it will also be pleasure." Patrick smiled and I smiled back. I was happy to see him again, and I didn't want him to leave. Patrick was supposed to be in and out of Atlanta quickly, but after our encounter he got a suite at the Four Seasons Hotel and I stayed with him. My best friend was finally back, and I started feeling complete again.

The following weekend both of my parents were out of town, so I invited Patrick over for dinner and a movie. In the middle of dessert, out of a clear blue sky, Patrick said, "Tyler, do you ever think about that night?"

"What night is that?" I asked, knowing he was talking about Trey's death but trying to avoid the conversation.

"Tyler, you know what night I'm talking about," he said, determined not to let it go.

"Patrick, it's so hard. It seemed like it took forever for me to get over it, which I still haven't. Things are going so good for us. Do we have to ruin everything by discussing Trey?"

"Tyler, we can't move forward until we can address the past. That incident is what tore us apart in the first place."

"I know, but it's just so hard. I can't get the image out of my mind of Trey blowing his brains out."

"Do you blame me for what happened? Tell me the truth."

"Of course not, Patrick; if anything, I blame myself. I know it must have been devastating for Trey to know his ex-girlfriend and his close friend were involved. I can't help but wonder if maybe I should've been more sensitive to his feelings."

"Tyler, that wasn't your fault. Trey had issues that ran deeper than anyone realized; you can't blame yourself," Patrick said as he held my hand.

"I know; that's what my therapist said, but it's hard not to feel some sort of guilt," I said, playing with the ice cream that was now melted.

"Honestly, for a while I felt some responsibility for what happened to Trey. Then one day I had to admit the truth to myself.

When Trey had that gun, it could've just as easily been us lying there dead. Trey was a ticking time bomb, ready to explode. Instead of blaming ourselves and letting that dark cloud continue to linger above us, we need to count our blessings and thank God that we're alive and able to go on with our lives."

"Baby, I knew that was true, but I needed to hear it from you."

I gave Patrick a hug, relieved that we had finally discussed that night and our unresolved feelings. After getting over that emotional hurdle, Patrick's and my relationship began to prosper.

"So, baby girl, what you wanna do today?" Patrick and I had gone to every fancy restaurant, seen every movie, and shopped nonstop. I didn't know what was left, besides making love. The funny thing was that as close as Patrick and I were, we had never made love. It didn't seem to bother him, but he was a man and I'm sure he had needs.

"How about we go to the park and have a picnic?"

"A picnic? You're kidding, right?"

"No, what's wrong with a picnic?"

"I have a better idea. Why don't you go to the dresser, open the top drawer, and look inside the box?" I gave Patrick a quizzical look but followed his directions. When I opened the drawer, I found a Tiffany and Company box along with an envelope. I opened the box first.

"Patrick, you got this for me? I can't believe it. It's the most beautiful bracelet I've ever seen." The tennis bracelet had over forty huge diamonds that were clear and flawless. It was stunning. I looked back at him, still shaking my head in disbelief.

"Why don't you open the envelope?" Patrick prodded. I had

momentarily forgotten about it because I was so caught up in the iced-out bracelet. I opened the envelope and saw a first-class ticket to Chicago dated for next Friday.

"Will you come, please?" Patrick was now standing next to me, and he held my hand as he asked me the question.

"How can I say no after you just gave me this unbelievable gift?"

"I don't want you to come because of the bracelet; I want you to come for me." The sincerity in his voice moved me.

"Of course I'll come, and not for the bracelet but for you."

After Patrick left, I missed him immediately. We so enjoyed each other's company, and I was looking forward to visiting him in Chicago.

Because of all the time I spent with Patrick during his visit, I barely had a moment to hang out with Lisa. We decided to meet for lunch since I knew I would be going out of town in a few days. "What's up, stranger?" Lisa said when she sat down at our table in the Cheesecake Factory.

"Girl, what is good? I like your braids; when did you get them done?" I asked, checking out her micros.

"Tawana did them a week ago."

"Damn, she has gotten good. Your shit look tight."

"Thank you," Lisa said, posing to give me side views. "But enough about my hair, girl; I thought you had run off and gotten married to Patrick. I haven't seen you since you ran into him at the club. That was so crazy."

"Wasn't it? I thought Patrick had disappeared from my life forever, and then to see him again while we were celebrating our graduation was almost too good to be true. He just left the other day and I already miss him. I can't wait to go to Chicago so we can be together again." As I continued to go on about Patrick, I noticed that Lisa couldn't take her eyes off my wrist.

"Tyler, where did you get that bracelet from?" she said, holding my arm and examining the diamonds. "Is it real?"

"It's very real. Patrick gave it to me before he left. Isn't it beautiful?" I said smiling.

"Beautiful is putting it lightly. You always get everything, Tyler; it isn't fair," Lisa said, slumping back in her seat. "Why is your life so perfect?"

"Lisa, my life is far from perfect. Let's not forget I witnessed my ex-boyfriend killing himself." Lisa rolled her eyes as if it that incident wasn't a big deal.

"Besides that, you have it all. You live in a big house, drive a convertible BMW, have the best clothes, and now you have a boyfriend who is loaded. Why couldn't that be my life?" I didn't know how to take what Lisa was saying. Yes, her house was modest compared to mine, and she drove a used car, not a brand-new one like mine, but we were so close, I never gave it much thought. But it was obvious that Lisa did, and I felt bad.

"Lisa, you have a great life. You're smart, pretty, and your parents adore you." I always admired the dedication Lisa's parents had for her. Her mother was a schoolteacher and always encouraged Lisa to do her best, and her father was an accountant. No, her parents didn't have a lot of money, and sometimes Lisa would complain about what a strict budget her family was on, but I knew from watching my parents' marriage that it took more than money to make you happy.

"That's easy for the girl that has it all to say."

"Lisa, stop it. One day we'll both be rich, and it will be our own money. Wait and see. Until then, we'll have fun spending everyone else's money, starting with Patrick's. After lunch, which is my treat, of course, let's go to Lenox Mall. You can pick out whatever outfit you want. Within reason, of course," I added. I hoped that a trip to the mall would ease her discontentment. For the first time in a very long time I was happy, and I wanted to share that with Lisa.

The following weekend when I visited Patrick in Chicago I decided we would take it all the way. He booked a premier suite at the Ritz-Carlton. When I realized it had convenient indoor access to the exclusive Michigan Avenue shops, I was ecstatic. I spent my day at the Carlton Club spa and then did a little shopping. That evening I met Patrick at the Greenhouse for drinks. I wore a fitted white Dolce & Gabbana pantsuit, with my hair up and a few cascading curls framing my face. After a few drinks, admiring the view of the city and listening to the beautiful "My Funny Valentine" coming from the piano, I was ready to go to our suite and make passionate love.

By the time we reached the thirtieth floor, we were basically undressed. Luckily Patrick had managed to take out the room key, and when he opened the door we began a long lingering kiss that lasted until we reached the king-size bed. He fingered my nipples, and then his warm mouth kissed my breast. I moaned with ecstasy while caressing his manhood. He started going down on me, and I screamed with pure pleasure. Then he stopped and marveled at my beauty before we made love. We made love for a long time before becoming exhausted and falling asleep in each other's arms. Patrick's strong muscular body next to mine made me feel so loved. The next morning when I opened my eyes, Patrick had already ordered breakfast. I ate a couple of strawberries before going into the marble bathroom to take a shower. As soon as I walked in, I saw that Patrick had already prepared a bath for me. He also had a mimosa on the table next to the bathtub. He remembered it was my favorite drink in the morning. After I lounged in the Jacuzzi for a while, I joined Patrick in bed and we made love once again.

Looking out at the Chicago skyline and the lakefront view, I was relieved that Patrick and I were compatible sexually because now we had a chance at a serious relationship. At the same time, he knew so much about my past, I was afraid it would cause problems in the future. You should never, ever date a guy who was your best friend and knows all of your secrets. Patrick never believed in us. I guess he shouldn't have, because although I loved him, I wasn't *in* love with Patrick and he knew it. He was older and ready to settle down and have a family. Although I was young and having fun, I never wanted to be locked down and have a baby with someone in the pharmaceutical business. What type of life is that? I had bigger goals and ambitions in life. Patrick was someone who was intriguing to me at the moment. I loved driving around in his brand new red 500 SL in front of my friends. He was the first guy to give me a thousand here and two thousand there just to go shopping, and that was big to me. I felt like I was balling. Here I was, still a teenager, and this guy was treating me like a princess. All my friends were envious of me, and I loved it.

"Oh, fuck, if I throw up one more time, I'm going to die," I screamed out loud on my way to the bathroom. Being sick had already caused me to skip my classes at Spelman, and with exams coming up I couldn't afford to miss anymore. I had been extremely nauseated for a week, and a red flag was waving steady. I purchased a pregnancy test, and of course I was pregnant.

"I can't believe this shit," I kept saying, walking back and forth in my room. I simply wasn't about to have Patrick's baby. I flipped through the yellow pages and made an appointment to have an abortion. I knew Patrick would be devastated because he was twenty-six and had no children. He wanted a baby more than anything in this world, but it wasn't going to be with me. As much as I loved Patrick, I knew having a baby with him would never work. For one, although he never discussed it with me, I knew Patrick was involved in illegal activities. How else could he explain his endless money without having any sort of known job? With Patrick there were too many risks that he could end up in jail or, God forbid, dead. That wasn't the life I wanted for our child.

The next day was my appointment, and I didn't have anyone to go with me. I decided to bite the bullet and call Lisa. If I had my way, no one would know about the abortion, but I had to have someone to drive me home after the procedure.

"Hello," I heard Lisa say under the sound of loud-ass music.

"Girl, turn that shit down."

"What is it?" Lisa asked, sounding aggravated at my request.

"I need you to come with me to the doctor's office tomorrow."

"Doctor's office? For what?"

"I'm having an abortion, and I need someone to drive me home afterward," I said matter-of-factly.

"Abortion! Girl, your mama is going to kill you." Lisa could be so damn dramatic. That's why I didn't want to even tell her silly ass, but my options were limited.

"If all goes well, there is no need for her to find out about it, dumb ass."

"Don't be getting smart wit me; I'm doing yo yellow ass a favor."

"Whatever, Lisa. I'll pick you up at nine o'clock in the morning."

"Hold up. Why can't Patrick go with you?"

I wanted to reach through the phone and smack Lisa because she knew damn well I couldn't ask Patrick. I complained to her on several occasions about the constant hint-dropping Patrick did about me having his child. She knew that if Patrick ever found out I killed his baby, he would never forgive me.

"Lisa, you know if Patrick knew I was pregnant, he would lock me up for the whole nine months. You are my only option, so please stop with the third degree and just be there for me."

"All right, girl; I'll see you in the morning."

A couple of days after my abortion I went to Chicago to see Patrick. We were lying in the bed asleep when a sharp pain woke me up. "Oh, goodness," I sighed.

"What's wrong, baby?" Patrick asked, still half-asleep. The pain was becoming more intense, and my arms were wrapped around my stomach trying to minimize the impact.

"Oh, shit, I'm bleeding," I screamed as I looked down and saw the blood on my thighs. "Baby, please take me to the emergency room." When we got to the hospital, a nurse escorted me to an examining room, and I waited for the doctor to come in. I asked Patrick to sit in the waiting room because I didn't want him to hear the conversation I was about to have with the doctor. Patrick reluctantly agreed.

Before the doctor examined me, he asked me a series of questions: Was I pregnant? Had I had an abortion recently?

"I had an abortion a few days ago." The doctor examined me while continuing his line of questioning. Then he paused and looked at me.

"Ms. Blake, unfortunately you had a botched abortion."

"What does that mean?" I asked nervously. Ignoring my question, the doctor proceeded.

"Was your procedure done in the Chicago area?"

"No, I'm from Atlanta." I was now shaking, and I wanted the doctor to explain what the hell a botched abortion was.

"Whoever performed the abortion did not completely remove the fetus."

"Excuse me?" I said, horrified.

"Your abortion is what we would consider incomplete. The doctor who performed this procedure was incompetent."

"I actually don't know who the doctor was. I didn't go to my family physician because I was afraid my parents would find out. So I flipped through the yellow pages and picked someone who could perform the surgery quickly and cheaply." The doctor was shaking his head in what looked like a combination of disappointment and disgust.

"Ms. Blake, an abortion is a very serious procedure and shouldn't be taken lightly. Women have died during this sort of operation. When making a decision like this, you have to do what is safest, not what is cheapest or quickest." I felt ashamed as the doctor lectured me.

"You need surgery immediately to make sure the entire fetus is removed or you could develop a life-threatening infection." Tears were pouring out of my eyes. I didn't know how I was going to explain this to Patrick.

"Will I be able to get pregnant again and have a baby?"

"Yes, if we perform the surgery right away there should be no permanent damage." I breathed a sigh of relief, thinking that all hope wasn't lost.

"Doctor, can I see my boyfriend before you take me to the operating room?"

"Sure, but only briefly. I'll have the nurse call him in." I nervously rubbed my hands, wondering what I was going to say to Patrick. When he walked through the door, Patrick looked so afraid for me.

"Tyler, what is going on? The nurse said they're about to take you in for emergency surgery."

"Baby, I had a miscarriage. I didn't even know I was pregnant. They don't think the entire fetus came out, and they need to perform surgery so I don't get an infection." The lie just started flowing, so I rolled with it. It sounded a lot better than the truth. Patrick's eyes swelled with tears as he wrapped his arms around me.

"Tyler, I'm so sorry. Everything will be okay. I'll be here waiting for you." Guilt had taken over my body. Patrick was so caring and understanding, unaware of all my lies. But it was for the best. Patrick would be devastated if he knew the truth. The nurse came in and told me they were ready for me. Patrick kissed me on the forehead, and with a tear rolling down his cheek, he waved goodbye.

When I woke up the next morning, Patrick was at my bedside, sitting in a chair in a deep sleep. The doctor came in and told me the surgery went fine and I could check out of the hospital. He gave me a prescription for an antibiotic, and I gave him my thanks. I was anxious to get the hell outta there.

After picking up the prescription and stopping to get a bite to eat, Patrick and I headed home. There had been complete silence between us, and I knew Patrick was in deep pain. He finally reached over and took my hand. "Tyler, I'm so sorry this happened. I know how much we both wanted a baby, but don't blame yourself. It's not your fault. We can always try again after your body heals."

"I know," I said quietly.

When we got home, I immediately went upstairs and took a long hot shower. While I washed away my sins in the hot water, I heard my cell phone ringing. But after a couple of rings it stopped, and I thought whoever called must have hung up. When Patrick's home phone started ringing, my gut told me there was about to be trouble. I stepped out of the shower and quietly picked up the phone in the bathroom. I listened intensely as I caught the conversation from the very beginning.

"Hello," Patrick said as he answered the phone.

"Hi, is that you, Patrick?"

"Yeah, who else would it be?"

"Nobody. Why didn't Tyler answer her cell phone?"

"She's in the shower. I saw your name show up on my caller ID so I picked up."

"Oh, so you wanted to speak to me?" Lisa said, being flirtatious.

"Actually I thought maybe you were calling to check up on her."

"Why, is she okay?"

"Actually she's a little upset. Last night she had a miscarriage. She didn't even know she was pregnant."

"You mean an abortion?" Lisa said, trying to sound like she misunderstood him, but knowing exactly what she was doing.

"Nah, I said miscarriage. Tyler wouldn't have no abortion."

"Oh, I thought you were talking about the abortion I took her to have a few days ago."

"Excuse me? What the fuck are you talking about?"

"I'm sorry, Patrick. I must have misunderstood you. I took Tyler to have an abortion a few days ago, and when you said she was upset I thought maybe it was because she felt guilty." I wanted to reach through the phone and give Lisa the ass-whipping of her life.

"I guess I'm the one who misunderstood," Patrick said, knowing full well that the concerned speech Lisa just gave was bullshit. But regardless, if what Lisa said was true, then I had a lot of explaining to do.

"I'll tell Tyler you called, Lisa." My whole body began shaking. I let the shower keep running as I waited in the bathroom for a few minutes, trying to regain my composure and decide how I would play this. When I finally came out, Patrick was standing in front of the window looking at the view of the city. Patrick threw down the phone.

"Baby, let's stay in the bed all day and watch movies. How does that sound?" Patrick ignored my question. I walked toward him, knowing he could explode at any moment. As I came closer he turned around and looked at me. His eyes were red, and his expression was ice cold.

"Lisa called while you were in the shower. She first tried your cell, and when you didn't answer she called my home line."

"Oh, what did she want?"

"Nothing really. I thought maybe you called her earlier about the miscarriage and she was checking up on you."

"Oh." I was biting my bottom lip so hard, I thought it was going to start bleeding. My head was spinning, remembering every word Lisa said to Patrick. I couldn't believe my best friend would sell me out. I always knew Lisa was envious of me, but in trying to destroy my relationship with Patrick, she had crossed a line.

I would have to deal with Lisa later, but right now I had to figure out a way to explain my actions to Patrick. I already knew what Lisa told him, and it showed all over my face.

Patrick continued to stare me down. "When I told Lisa you were upset, she assumed I was talking about the abortion you had a few days ago. She thought you were feeling guilty. What do—?"

I cut Patrick off before he could continue. "It's not what you think. I didn't mean to deceive you, Patrick, but I wasn't ready to have a baby."

"So you went and had a fucking abortion behind my back, then gave me this song and dance about a miscarriage? You lying bitch! Why the fuck did you really have to have surgery?" I was overwhelmed and couldn't speak. "Answer me, Tyler! What the fuck was the surgery for?" Patrick was now screaming at the top of his lungs. I finally managed to speak up.

"The doctor who did the abortion didn't remove the entire fetus. If I didn't have the operation, I could've developed a life-threatening infection." Patrick's eyes were full of hate and disgust. "Sweetheart, the surgery went fine, and we can have another baby. I promise."

Patrick put his hand around my throat and held me like I was an enemy. "You killed my seed. Do you think I want to have a baby with you? You are an evil, sick woman. I can't believe I ever fell in love with you. Now I know why Trey killed himself—because you are nothing but poison." Patrick tossed me down on the bed like I meant nothing to him. He turned around and looked at me. "When I get back, I want you out of my house. Don't ever contact me again." Patrick went to his drawer and tossed an envelope at me. "Use this to do whatever you need to do to get the hell out of my life." After Patrick stormed out and I heard the door slam downstairs, I looked inside the envelope. It was full of thousand-dollar bills. I burst into tears and fell on the bed and buried my head in the pillows. Patrick hated me, and now I felt like I had no one.

I called a taxi, then waited for it in the living room. I didn't want to think about Patrick's words, so instead I focused on the chest of drawers in the foyer. The body had a rich cordovan finish, while the legs and trim were executed with silver-leaf detail. Patrick's exquisite taste amazed me, and once again I realized why we were best friends. Soon I heard the taxi honking its horn; I walked to the door and looked around the beautiful duplex one last time before I said good-bye.

To this day I wish I had never crossed that line with Patrick. I decided never to get involved with a man who started out as my best friend. Knowing the type of person I am, my friendships would outlast a romantic relationship any day. I learned a valuable lesson with Patrick, and if I had the opportunity to go back, I would change so many things.

5

Just Got Off the Bus

"Mother, I'll be ready to leave for the airport in about thirty minutes."

"Okay, honey. I have to run to the store right quick; I'll be back in fifteen minutes."

"Okay, don't be late. I don't want to miss my flight." After my relationship with Patrick ended, I started thinking about what I was going to do with my life and what type of career I wanted. I wanted to get out of town, do something bigger and better, and leave all my demons behind. I decided to transfer from Spelman to New York University. Ella was now attending grad school at the Fashion Institute of Technology in Manhattan, so the location was perfect. She said I could stay with her until I found my own place. I was looking forward to beginning my new life.

The phone rang as I was packing up my last bag.

"Hi, I wanted to say bye before you left." I recognized Lisa's voice, and my first instinct was to hang up. We hadn't spoken since the day I cursed her out for revealing my secret to Patrick. But I was leaving, starting a new life, and there was no need to hold a grudge.

"Thanks, Lisa," I said blandly.

"What time does your flight leave?"

"In a couple of hours. I'm leaving soon though—you know how hectic the airport can be."

"Yeah, I know. Tyler, I want to tell you something before you leave."

"What?" I said indifferently.

"I never said sorry for telling Patrick about the abortion. I know I swore that I told him by accident, but you were right; it was intentional."

"But why?" Now I was curious about her confession.

"Tyler, you were always the prettiest, and all the guys liked you. Of course, I never understood why you dumped Chad for that deranged Trey . . . but anyway then you had Patrick, and you had no time for anybody else. You were always showing off the ice he gave you or the shopping sprees he took you on, and I was sick of you flossing in his Benz all the time."

"So you were jealous," I said abruptly.

"Yeah, I was jealous. I knew Patrick would dump you if he found out the truth, and I wanted to make sure he did. I know that is malicious, Tyler, and now I feel terrible. I feel like you're leaving because of what I did, and I don't want you to leave." Part of me wished Lisa had kept her confession to herself because it wasn't going to bring Patrick back to me; but then maybe I needed to hear it to finally close the door on my life in Georgia.

"Lisa, I don't know what to say. We've been friends forever and you are like a sister to me, but I have to leave. There are too many painful memories for me here, and I'm in search of happiness. I can't get that in Georgia. But Lisa, I accept your apology, and I will always love you."

"I love you too, Tyler, and please don't forget about me. Pick up the phone and call sometime."

"I will." I hung up the phone feeling a sense of closure. I looked around my room and stood admiring the Barbie collection I began when I was five years old. It made me revisit all the dreams I had growing up as a little girl. Leaving was the first step to accomplishing the life I had visualized. Even with all the drama I engaged in, I always wanted to be somebody. Staying focused was my biggest obstacle. I continuously went back and forth being with some man in some relationship that kept me off course, but now for the first time I had a preliminary sketch. All the details weren't mapped out, but I was letting go of the past and opening a new door. I was full of anticipation of what could be waiting for me. Maybe my world hadn't been perfect, but I decided that I would go to New York City, start fresh, and leave all my secrets behind.

When I arrived in New York, I tried to leave the past behind me. Inside I felt like I had "just got off the bus," but I knew I had to put on my game face. There were endless opportunities there for me, and though I had made a ton of mistakes thus far in my journey, the mistakes were still mine to make. I take full responsibility for all of them. Always remember one thing. If you take responsibility and blame yourself, you have the power to change things. But if you put responsibility on someone else, then you are giving them the power to decide your fate.

On January 8, 1999, I reached New York. Once I got off that plane, I had stars in my eyes and money to burn—or so I thought. Ella let me stay in her dorm-style apartment with her two roommates until I found a place of my own. I wasn't able to get campus housing, which I didn't want anyway. I figured I would get an apartment of my own. I later found out that apartment hunting in New York City wasn't quite that easy. Instead of getting a part-time job, I opted to whoop it up with Ella all over town. We splurged on shopping sprees, wined and dined at fancy restaurants, reveled in Broadway shows; we just balled. There was almost twenty thousand dollars in the envelope Patrick gave me, but we all know that if you have no money coming in and you are running around spending, then twenty thousand dollars is no money. Hey, I was young. The best thing I did was spend the last bit I had on securing a cozy room in an apartment building on Seventy-seventh and Broadway. Within a month, I had gone through all my money.

I was attending NYU and pursuing my dream of becoming an actress. I figured my big break was right around the corner. Ella and I were sitting in her room watching TV, and she asked me about my future plans.

"So, Tyler, now that you're here, what exactly do you want to do? I mean, while you're attending school, because of course that comes first."

"Well, I figured I would concentrate on the books and juggle acting auditions. Maybe do the Broadway circuit and then get into film; I mean, how hard can it be? Look at all the no-talent faces in the movie and music business today."

"Yeah, that's true, but there are also a lot of beautiful women with a lot of talent on the same mission as you." It hadn't dawned on me that there were a million other girls running around thinking the exact same thing. I knew there would always be girls who were prettier and more talented, but Mother had instilled in me that I was special and I felt like I was born to be a star. I just had to focus and pursue my dream to the fullest extent. But I hadn't figured out how I should go about making it happen, and so I was grabbing in the dark.

One day on my way to an audition I came across a flyer about a hot new label, Get Money Records. I remembered when I was in Georgia and was in awe of a guy named T-Roc, who I saw in a music video. He was sexy, and Lisa laughed at me when I told her one day I'd be in his bed. Now here I was in his city, looking at a flyer about his new label. I truly believe that if you visualize something, want something, and put that energy out there, that whatever your heart desires will come true. What you're yearning for may not come to you in the exact way you envisioned but it will be obtained. This was no different. That is why you must be careful about what you want and try to reserve your energy for something positive and productive. It took me many years to finally understand that.

After a delicious lunch with Ella at the Pink Tea Cup, I felt energized. Not only did she pay for the fried chicken and pancakes I devoured, but she also gave me a week's worth of subway tokens, which I desperately needed. I was strolling down the street counting my blessings on the way to an audition, and to my surprise, the street happened to be the same block where T-Roc's office was located. One of his many workers was standing outside.

"What's up cutie? What's your name?" the ultra iced-out guy said.

"Tyler," I sneered, continuing to prance by.

"My name's Jason; I work at Get Money Records." My antennae instantly went up because I knew that was the label T-Roc owned, and I stopped in my tracks.

"I just moved to New York, so I don't know anything about record labels," I lied, not wanting him to think I was impressed.

"Well, that's okay; you hang with me and maybe you can learn how to run one," he said with an I'm-so-sure-of-myself laugh. "I have an idea. There's a private party tonight where you can get your first taste of the music industry. How 'bout it?"

"Sure," I said calmly. I gave Jason my phone number, and he said he would call around seven. As I strolled down Twenty-third Street and Seventh Avenue, all sorts of possibilities were flashing in my mind. Would I actually see—or better yet meet—T-Roc even though I'd been in NYC for only two months? Could I be that lucky? By the time I reached home, Jason had left a message. I called him back, and he said he would pick me up in an hour.

I was elated about the possibility of meeting my crush, but at the same time I was extremely nervous. I didn't know what to wear, so I played it safe and went with a simple pair of tight black pants and a cream top. Then I dabbed on my favorite Mac lip gloss, "Oh Baby," and headed out the door.

Jason pulled up in a white Range Rover with dark tinted windows and chromed-out rims. Before I even got comfortable in the car, he said, "We have to make a stop on our way to the party." I didn't ask any questions about where the party was or what it was for. Instead I chose to stay quiet and go with the flow. It's always been my philosophy that when you are around people you don't know, it's better to remain silent and observe.

To my delight we met up with T-Roc and his friends to head to the private affair. Just like that, I was on the red carpet with paparazzi taking T-Roc's picture. He was a huge star and basked in all the attention. He was the hip-hop king of New York. Everyone wanted a piece of him, and I was caught up. I couldn't conceive that this man I had seen in heavy rotation on BET and MTV and doing interviews for *Entertainment Tonight* was actually just a few feet away from me and we were going into the same party. Little old me, Tyler Blake from Georgia, was in the mix and about to rub shoulders with the movers and shakers of the hip-hop industry.

The event coordinators escorted T-Roc's large entourage into the VIP section, and the next thing I knew they were popping bottles and I was drinking Cristal. Yes, I had had champagne a million and one times before, but it was never like this. Eyeballing the room, I felt out of my element. All the women seemed glamorous and different from the ones I was used to back home. With my simple black pants, cream shirt, and curly bob, I didn't fit in with these chic ladies. But in the scheme of things it didn't matter, because I was in touching distance of the man I'd always wanted to meet.

That night I partied, had a couple glasses of champagne, and began living out one of my dreams. Those days back in Georgia, partying with my girlfriends and thinking we were whooping it up, was no comparison to how the rich and famous partied. Arriving home at the crack of dawn, I kept replaying every moment of that night and feeling butterflies in my stomach. It had been the most fun ever, and I wanted to savor every moment. Although T-Roc hadn't even noticed me, I was overjoyed by the whole experience. There were many other celebrities there too, and all of them looked much shorter and thinner in person, which was a little shocking but exciting all the same.

The next day to my surprise Jason called. "What's up, Georgia

Peach?" I wasn't expecting to hear from him so soon, and I was elated he called.

"Nothing much; I had a blast last night."

"Cool. Does that mean you're up to doing it again tonight?"

"Of course," I said, knowing good and well I needed to study for an English exam.

"What you doing right now? How would you like to come by the label and see for yourself how Get Money Records is bringing in the millions?"

"That would be great 'cause I've never been inside a record label before." This was all new to me. Plus I'd take any opportunity to meet T-Roc. Working with what I had, I selected a pair of low-rise jeans and a cropped turtleneck revealing my toned stomach.

Jason picked me up and we headed over to the label. No matter how much I wanted to scream with enthusiasm, acting laid-back was—and still is—one of my strengths. When I walked through Get Money's doors, the atmosphere seemed hectic and fast-paced. The energy was strong, and everyone that was working at the label was about the hustle and bustle. There was something alluring about the chaotic atmosphere, and I understood why so many people—including me—wanted to be part of that world. Jason told me to have a seat and said he would be right back to show me around.

As I sat there watching people running back and forth like they were developing a cure for some life-threatening disease, I heard someone say, "I'm T-Roc; what's your name?"

T-Roc reached out to shake my hand, and I tried to remain calm so he wouldn't see the stars in my eyes. But inside, my heart was pounding so hard that I thought the building would start shaking. Gazing into T-Roc's persuasive eyes, I knew I was in deep infatuation. I had had enough experience to know it certainly wasn't love, but it was the best type of infatuation I had ever encountered.

"Hi, I'm Tyler." I remained cool, thinking he would then walk away, but instead he began flirting with me.

"Tyler. That's a pretty name for a very pretty girl." This was better than any Barbie story I had ever made up.

"Are you coming out with us again tonight?" I realized he had noticed me the night before, which made me feel like a gold medalist.

I innocently said, "If you would like me to."

Later that night, I was at it again, partying with the hip and stylish, taking note that I simply had to invest in a New York–chic wardrobe. In Georgia I was in style and used to being the center of attention. Here I stood out like a sore thumb. But it wasn't the time to dwell on that, because I was simply having too much fun. They were playing "Hate Me Now" by Nas, and T-Roc grabbed me by my waist and escorted me to the dance floor. He was grinding against me from behind with his face against the side of my cheek, and the essence of his cologne had me caught in his rapture. Up until that moment, I wasn't sure T-Roc was attracted to me.

Although I felt cute, my confidence was a little low. Here I was, in a new city, at these industry parties, surrounded by women who looked like they had just stepped out of *InStyle*. Everywhere I turned there were beautiful women, but T-Roc was dancing with me. I felt special because I was dancing with the man that every other girl wanted. Why wouldn't they? Not only was T-Roc on top of his game businesswise, but he was also a very clean-cut, sharp-looking guy. Nobody possessed his style, and his star presence was undeniable.

"How about you come home with me after the party?" T-Roc whispered in my ear before turning me around so we were face-to-face. It took all my strength to resist his offer, but I knew what would happen and I wasn't quite ready yet.

"I want to but I can't."

"Why can't you?" he asked. His arms were still around me.

"I really have to study. I have an English test coming up, and if I don't pass it, I might fail the class." T-Roc gave me a bizarre look, like "Bitch, you can't be serious," but I was. No, I wasn't going to fail the class over this test, but I had to say something to get out of going home with him.

"I tell you what, pretty girl; you take your test, and I'll catch you the next time around." As T-Roc let go of my waist and left me standing on the dance floor, I felt my prom king had left his queen.

I lay in bed dreaming about how it would be for T-Roc to make love to me. It had been months since I had been intimate with someone, and wouldn't it be the icing on the cake if my next man was T-Roc?

A couple of days passed, and I didn't hear from Jason. I was a tad disappointed, but at the same time I needed to concentrate on school. Once again I wasn't focusing. More and more I was thinking that school wasn't for me. But until I found something more productive, I figured I needed to stick it out. Tired of calling my parents for money every other week, I decided I needed a job. There was a restaurant right down the street from me looking for a part-time waitress, and I jumped on the opportunity. I put down a bunch of bogus prior waitressing experience, but they obviously didn't check to see if it was true. To my delight I got the job. Once I was hired, a young woman named Chrissie was assigned to train me. She was a cute petite white woman who put me in mind of a younger version of Sarah Jessica Parker. To my surprise, Chrissie also attended NYU. We instantly clicked, and I finally had my first girlfriend in New York.

During one of my rare moments of studying, Jason phoned to say that he was on his way to pick me up. That was fine by me; I was more than happy to close my English book and take an extended break. I hoped my mogul had told Jason that he wanted to see me because the last time I saw T-Roc he seemed a little put off that I declined his invitation to his crib. I'm sure he hadn't gotten that type of brush-off often.

Jason and I went to the label, where I sat for a while without T-Roc saying two words to me. He was busy running a label, and I started to wonder what I was doing there. It was amazing to see him at work because he was a very hands-on type of guy and an extreme perfectionist. When something didn't go exactly the way he wanted, he had no qualms about having a tantrum right in front of everybody. After two hours of no one saying a word to me, Jason emerged. "Are you hungry?"

"A little bit." Actually I was starving, but that was too much information.

"Cool, we're going to pick up some food and stop by my friend's house to chill for a while." *Cool* was Jason's favorite word, I thought to myself.

My mind was made up. If I was presented with another invitation by T-Roc, I would not decline. I had a strong inkling that he was the friend Jason was talking about. We stopped at a soul food restaurant called the Shark Bar, Jason picked up the food he had ordered, and a short time later we pulled up to a brownstone in the city. I took a quick look around the quaint neighborhood while Jason rang the doorbell. I was bubbling over on the inside when T-Roc answered the door. He greeted me with a sly smile and said, "Hello, Tyler. How did you do on your English test?" His question threw me off balance, but I quickly regained my composure.

"It went great;" I said shyly, and gave a smile. On the outside, the building looked historic and old-fashioned. On the inside it was all high-tech and ultramodern. Here I was, sitting and eating barbecued salmon, yams, and rice with my crush. It was too good to be true. The three of us were laughing, joking, and enjoying the delicious food. After a couple of hours Jason said he had to run an errand. That was fine with me, because I could finally have some alone time with T-Roc.

"Tyler, what school do you attend? Not high school, I hope." I tried to get a read on T-Roc's face because I couldn't tell if he was serious or playing.

"NYU."

"What's your major?"

"Journalism."

"Oh, you look very young; how old are you?"

"Eighteen. I'll be nineteen later this year," I said eagerly, not wanting to seem so young.

"Don't rush it, pretty girl. There will come a time when you'll be wishing you could push your age back, not forward." As T-Roc talked, my mind began drifting off, thinking about the hundreds of cute girls he had conquered and the many more who would follow me, But you know what? I didn't give a shit. I couldn't have cared less. When I wanted something, that is what I wanted—no ands, ifs, or buts about it! At this moment in my life, I wanted to know what it felt like to make love to T-Roc. I didn't care if it turned out to be a one-night stand, because personally I thought that would be more romantic. This guy was a known ladies' man, and I wasn't naive enough to believe I could change him or that I would be "the one." Every girl he slept with was probably trying to lock him down, so I figured I'd do one better and treat him as a casual sexual encounter. This was about me fulfilling yet another one of my fantasies, no more and no less.

We began kissing, and I started feeling myself getting aroused. "Tyler, how about we go upstairs where we can get comfortable?" T-Roc took my hand and led me upstairs to his bedroom where a huge plush bed awaited us.

Leaning back on his bed, he said, "I want to watch you undress." My mind began racing, and the shy, insecure, and self-conscious side of me took a seat as the other side—the bitchy, fiery, and confident side—showed its face. I gave him a look that said, Oh please, I'm not taking off my clothes for you. All these episodes in my life are like movies to me, and I've created scripts that have to be exciting and fun. I knew sleeping with him was going to happen, but I couldn't let him think that he would just snap his fingers and my clothes would fall off. I had to make him believe that he had somewhat coerced me.

"No, baby, I don't think so. This isn't Scores, and I'm no stripper."

"Pretty girl, I just want to see you naked. Please." I did have on a soft pink Natori bra and panty set that I wanted him to view. If I wasn't comfortable with anything else, I pretty much always liked my figure and enjoyed showing it off in cute undergarments. I didn't want to seem too eager to please, though, and this was my script, so I needed to start setting the pace. In my mind I was telling T-Roc to back it up, buddy, I'm running this show. I sauntered over to the bed and began kissing him again. His lips were so soft and his skin so smooth. He was being very gentle with me and taking his time letting me explore his body. He led my hand down to his hardness so I could feel how aroused he was. His hands were slowly moving up my skirt, and he began gently squeezing the flesh of my thighs and buttocks. He got anxious and started to unbutton his pants and tried to push my head down to give him a professional.

Now I might do a lot of things, but I was not about to give him head. That performance is strictly executed for my man, and he definitely wasn't that. Some women prefer to give a professional over sex, but I think that it is way too personal and should only be shared with a select few.

"Nah, that's not happening, T-Roc. I don't know you like that to be giving you head." After a little back and forth, he finally accepted that it wasn't going to happen, and we moved on to taking off our clothes and making love. T-Roc made love with the same passion and intensity he had in his professional life. He was a good lover, and the experience was pleasurable.

Once he reached his climax I could close this chapter. It was like wanting something and getting it, and then being done with it; because most of the time it's never what you think it's all cracked up to be. This sexual encounter with my crush was no different. I got up and began putting on my clothes because I was ready to go. I never like to sit around and engage in small talk after having sex with someone unless it's my man.

"Where you trying to run off to?" T-Roc asked with irritation in his voice.

"I'm sure Jason is coming back soon, and I want to be ready when he gets here."

"You want to be ready for what? To leave?" He seemed surprised and offended by my suggestion that it was time to go.

"Well, aren't we finished here? You got yours and I somewhat got mine; what's left for us to do? Talk? I don't really care for all that."

"Aren't you a feisty little bitch? Who the fuck do you think you're talking to?"

"Unless I was misinformed, your name is T-Roc, and I know exactly who I'm talking to."

T-Roc walked toward me and firmly grabbed my hair, pulling my neck slightly back. "You pop a lot of shit for an eighteen-year-old brat from nowhere. You need to decide whether you want to remain a nobody with your schoolbooks and English tests, or if you want to be somebody and keep me as a friend."

"Oh," I said, with my head still tilted back, "that choice is easy." T-Roc smiled and relaxed on the grip to my hair, assuming the crucial decision was a thumbs-up in his favor.

"I'd rather be my own nobody than your somebody."

T-Roc had the look men get when they're about to bitch slap you. Just then, Jason walked in. T-Roc released me, as if he didn't have a choice due to Jason's arrival. Relieved, I couldn't get out of T-Roc's house fast enough.

After my short-lived but memorable encounter with T-Roc, I decided to focus on school and my pursuit of stardom. I also worked additional hours at my part-time job when I could. It was basically for clothes. I decided after my brief introduction to the glamorous life that I had to invest in some new designer outfits. I also went on a couple of auditions, but I wasn't being consistent with the grind work necessary to get any sort of break.

Early one morning my agent called about an audition for a music video for a hot up-and-coming R&B group. He assured me it wasn't one of those typical music videos with every girl running around naked, so I said, "Okay, why not give it a try?" I got the lead, playing the waitress girlfriend of one of the group's members. The next day we started shooting, and it was inspiring sitting in the chair having professional people do my hair and makeup, and styling me. This could be the beginning of better gigs to come, I thought.

Both the owner, who was also a rap star named Tah Tah, and Mark, the CEO and co-owner, were at the shoot. Tah Tah, coming off his fourth multiplatinum CD, seemed to be a real gentleman, and Mark was charming in his own way. But he definitely had an overinflated ego. The shoot wrapped for the day, but they summoned me to be back early the next morning, and so I yearned to go home and crawl into bed. The moment I stepped outside on the pavement, however, Mark was standing in front of his white Benz with an "I've been waiting for you" demeanor.

"Hi, can I talk to you for a minute?" Mark gestured for me to come over.

"What's your name again?" Mark asked as I made my way to his car.

"Tyler Blake," I said. I didn't want to be bothered with the egotistical record honcho, but he was the CEO and was overseeing the music video.

"What do you do besides music videos?"

"Actually I don't do videos. I'm an actress, but my agent thought this would be easy work, and it pays decent money. I also attend NYU; my major is journalism." I didn't like Mark's attitude, and I decided to make it clear I wasn't some dumb, desperate industry ho whose greatest ambition was sucking his dick for a part in a video. When I slept with T-Roc I did it because I was attracted to him and wanted to. To have sex with Mark would be more like a job then an adventure.

"That's cool, but have you ever thought about getting into the music business?"

"The music business?" I paused. "In what capacity?"

"A rapper."

I burst out laughing. "I can't rhyme."

"Never say can't. Female rappers are big shit right now. Look at Lil' Kim, Foxy Brown, and Eve. We're trying to find a badass chick right now to be the first lady of our label. You fit the look perfectly. With your face and that body you'll be the hottest chick out there."

"I don't think you heard me. I can't rap."

"Baby, I got this. You have an excellent tone to your voice, and you speak well. I can have Tah Tah or one of our other rappers write your rhymes. All you would have to do is make a sellable delivery. You think all those female rappers out there is writing their own shit? Hell, no! You know how many niggas got Jay-Z on their payroll as their ghostwriter?"

I was listening to Mark, wondering if he was serious. Or was this some type of over-the-top ploy to get me in bed? But then again there were at least ten pretty girls on the video set who would have willingly dropped their panties for him, so all this gassing wasn't necessary if he wanted some pussy. But me as a rapper? That was a stretch. I finally said, "I don't know, Mark. I never really envisioned myself as a female MC."

"Think about it tonight, and we'll talk further in the morning." I agreed to do that and headed home. On my way I stopped by a newsstand and picked up *Source*, *Vibe*, and *XXL*. I sat on my bed flipping through the magazines to see who the hottest female rapper was and what music producers were lacing their tracks. When I saw Lil' Kim being ghetto fabulous with the Christian Dior and the bling bling, I thought being a female rap superstar might not be all that bad.

• • •

"Did you think about what we discussed last night?" Mark asked as soon as I arrived on the video set.

"Actually I did. I'm curious to hear what your game plan is."

"We're wrapping up early today, so how 'bout coming with me to the office so we can iron out a few things?"

"Sounds like a plan to me." I shot my last scene around two o'clock in the afternoon and was dressed and ready to leave with Mark within twenty minutes. When we got to his office, there were platinum plaques everywhere and the setup was immaculate. I sat down on a plush red couch as he went through some papers while handling a business call. Obviously LaFamilia Records was on top of its game, and Mark knew it.

"My head A and R is going to join us so we can throw some ideas around." The next minute a tall skinny guy walked in.

"What's up, Mark?"

"What's going on, Cassidy? This is Tyler, the female rapper I was telling you about." Cassidy checked me out and nodded his head in approval.

"Yeah, she's hot. We can do big things with her. What's the name looking like?"

"I wanted you to help me come up with a couple of ideas— something hot and sexy like the artist herself." The two of them kept going back and forth like I wasn't even in the room. Not once did Cassidy ask to hear me rhyme—or even if I could. Their only concern was image and packaging.

"Yo, I got it!" Cassidy practically belted, as if he just had a brilliant idea. "Her name should be Citrus. You know, like the fruit."

"A fruit," I retorted, put off by the name. They two men scanned me in unison, as though they had forgotten I was in the room; then without hesitation they disregarded my statement.

"That's hot," Mark said, nodding his head in agreement. "Citrus, Citrus, Citrus. Sweet, juicy, and sexy; that's it, Cassidy."

"I hate it," I said, a serrated edge to my voice.

"Tyler, baby, let us handle the business side; we're pros at this. All you have to do is stay looking beautiful and keep that body tight. You do what I ask, and everything will be copastetic."

"Copastetic? Is that even a word?" I said, examining him with confusion.

"Yeah, it's my word."

"What the hell does it mean?" I asked.

"I don't know what the dictionary definition is, but in the Markionary it means everything will go smoothly. So remember that," he warned after winking his eye.

After my unsettling meeting with Mark and Cassidy, I called Ella.

"Hi, Ella; it's me, Tyler."

"I know my own sister's voice," Ella snapped with a slight attitude. We'd both been so busy that I hadn't talked to her in a while. I was only giving her a friendly reminder.

"Sorry, but check this out: while I was doing a music video I met the owner of LaFamilia Records, and he wants to make me into a rap superstar."

"What? Did I hear you correctly? A rapper? You can't be serious, Tyler."

"Actually I'm very serious."

"What happened to your acting career?"

"I can still pursue that after I get my first platinum CD."

"You sound crazy; did you tell Mother about your new career?"

"We keep playing phone tag."

"I guess that means you don't know about the separation or the fact that Daddy has basically gone broke."

"What are you talking about?" I asked, surprised. Daddy made an excellent living as an investment banker. How could he be broke?

"Mother said he claims he made some bad investments and is broke. She believes that because she wants a divorce he is trying to keep all the money to himself. No money, no alimony."

Before I left for New York, I hardly ever saw Daddy. He stayed away so long on business trips that I secretly wondered if he'd set up house with his mistress. When I moved, it seemed all communication between us ceased to exist. Then the few times I did get Mother on the phone, the conversation lasted all of five minutes. Once she knew I was physically fine and had no emergencies she'd tell me she was busy and would call me back later. Of course that call would never come. During our brief talks, not once did Mother mention she wanted a divorce, so I was surprised by what Ella was telling me.

After I got off the phone with Ella, I called Mother, but there was no answer. I left a message asking her to call me ASAP. I began to get worried, but then I remembered this was Mother. She probably already had a new husband lined up.

Early the next morning the phone rang, shaking me from a deep sleep, "Hello," I uttered, not quite awake.

"Yo, Citrus, wake up!" the voice screamed. I realized it was Mark. His comment made me alert because I simply detested the name he had given me.

"What's up, Mark? Can I call you back in a couple of hours? I'm still asleep." I glanced over at my clock. It was eight thirty in the morning. It was Wednesday, and I always slept late on Wednesday because I had no classes.

"Can't do that; you've got work to do. Meet me at my office in an hour. Don't be late." I heard the phone click, and I put the pillow over my face, not believing Mark was summoning me to his office so early in the morning. I was under the impression that music cats slept all day and worked all night.

I managed to get out of bed, take a quick hot shower, and head out the door. I stopped by Starbucks and got a caramel frappuccino to wake me up. By the time I reached Mark's office, I was wide awake and bright-eyed.

"Very good," Mark said as he eyed his watch, realizing I was on time. "We have a lot to do today. Cassidy is taking you over to the studio so you can listen to Tah Tah lay down some vocals. I want you to pay attention to his delivery and his breathing. Those two elements are key: your flow has to be tight, and you have to control your breathing."

"Okay, I think I can manage that."

"I've also brought a stylist and a fitness trainer on board. I want you to be perfect at all times. Once we announce you're the first lady of LaFamilia, you're going to be under a microscope. They'll be inspecting everything from what hairstyle you're rocking to what color polish you use for your pedicure. You have to be on point because when you make your grand entrance you're bodying all these other bitches."

"Mark, you're not a little bit skeptical about all of this? I have no experience as a female rapper. What if I suck?"

"That's a possibility, but you have the hardest quality there is to find."

"What's that?"

"That X factor. It's what I call true star quality. When you first walked on the set for the music video, I knew it immediately. It's the same quality I saw in Tah Tah. It is rare. Many people have talent and good looks, and they even have successful careers. But very few entertainers have the aura to be a superstar. If you follow my lead, I promise you will be huge. Whether it is TV, movies, or whatever, it's all yours."

I nodded my head, imagining life as a superstar. I definitely wanted it, but I was still trying to swallow the whole Citrus rap-stress thing.

Cassidy walked in, interrupting my thoughts. "What's good this morning, Citrus?"

"Cassidy, can you please call me Tyler?"

"No," he said firmly. "You have to be in Citrus mode at all times. That's your life until you go to sleep at night. But first thing in the morning when you wake up, it's back to Citrus, so get used to it." Cassidy turned to Mark and handed him a folder full of pictures.

"These are a few fashion ideas the stylist came up with." Mark was examining each picture, tossing some to the side and putting others in a neat pile.

"These work right here."

"Yeah, those are the same ones I like too," Cassidy chimed in. "Who were you thinking about as far as producers go?"

"Maybe Money-B; he just blessed Tah Tah with a blazing track."

"Okay, that's cool. Who else?"

"What about Trackmasters, Timbaland, and maybe Dr. Dre? You know all the hot producers," I interrupted, wanting some say-so.

"Damn, baby, you talking about big names, which means big budgets."

"You said we're doing superstar status. Well, then I need superstar producers, right?"

"No doubt." There was a slight pause. "By the way, do you have an attorney?"

"No."

"Don't worry about it; I'll hook you up with one I'm familiar with. He's excellent."

Cassidy and I left Mark's office and headed over to Right Track Studio. I'd never been in a music studio, and it was cool to watch Tah Tah in the vocal booth, spitting his rhymes. His lyrics were sick, and his delivery was crazy. Everybody compared his sarcasm to Jay-Z, his poetic lyrics to Nas, and his lyrical gift to the late great Biggie. He was like damn all across the board. When Tah Tah stepped out of the booth, he headed straight toward me and introduced himself.

"So you're the first lady of LaFamilia," he said with a smile. "I'm Tah Tah and welcome to the family." He gave me a hug like we'd known each other forever. A couple of weeks ago I was taking English exams and waiting tables; now here I was in the studio hugging one of the biggest rappers in the business.

For the next few weeks I practically lived in the studio. I was either studying Tah Tah or practicing my flow and delivery. I was constantly trying to mimic Tah Tah and make my voice a little deeper. He'd get frustrated and scream at me and say, "Rap in your natural tone; stop trying to imitate me, and tighten your own shit up."

That was easier said than done. Developing my own style was not as simple as I thought it would be. I wasn't an authentic rapper; I was a packaged product that Mark was creating. If I wasn't in the studio, then I was meeting with the stylist selecting clothes that would be ideal for Citrus, or I was in the gym trying to get my body perfectly tight. But I wasn't enjoying any of it and was having second thoughts about the whole concept. My cell phone rang, disrupting my reverie, and I noticed Mark's name. I picked up, dreading to hear the itinerary for the rest of my day.

"Hi, Mark," I said, trying to sound cheerful although I was becoming increasingly miserable.

"Listen, baby, I know you've been working hard and might be feeling stressed." That's an understatement, I said to myself.

"I'm taking you to dinner tonight, so you can relax and we can discuss the plans I have laid out for your future. I'll pick you up at eight." Dinner sounded nice, but I would've preferred an all-day spa pass. Sitting with Mark discussing my future as a rap star wasn't exactly appealing to me. Maybe tonight I would explain that to Mark. I hadn't signed anything, and the lawyers were still working out the terms of my contract for the label. It all seemed suspect to me. When Mark introduced me to the attorney he hooked me up with, he was rushing me to sign the papers without explaining shit to me. I opted instead to go with an attorney Ella was dating, and he told me the deal was garbage and I would be signing away my life and my firstborn. I heard Mark's specialty was fucked-up contracts, and I told him to forget it. He tried to pacify me, so my attorney and the label's attorney had been in negotiations ever since.

Mark picked me up right on time, which pleased me because it meant I could make our dinner short and be back home in a couple of hours.

"You look beautiful tonight, Tyler." I was happy to hear him call me by my given name and not that ridiculous Citrus, although I was somewhat dressed like a citrus. I was wearing an orange chiffon baby doll dress that the stylist picked up from Versace. She'd decided that my wardrobe needed to reflect the whole Citrus idea, and I was going to look like a fruit all year round. The whole concept was ludicrous.

"Thanks, Mark. Have you decided where we're going for dinner?"

"I had my chef prepare an intimate dinner at my place. There we can have privacy and talk about your future with LaFamilia." That sounded good to me. Maybe I wouldn't be home in a couple of hours like I planned, but at least I wouldn't have to be in a restaurant around a bunch of people. Plus I wanted some privacy when I broke the news to Mark that I no longer wanted to pursue the female rapper profession.

We pulled up to Mark's elaborate house in New Jersey. I had never been there before, but I'd heard how beautiful it was. When we walked inside, I saw that it was undeniably stunning, but I had lived in and been around houses like this since I was a little girl. It was going to take more than this to impress me. We walked to the dining room, where the table was perfectly prepared. Mark poured me a glass of champagne as the chef fixed our plates. After finishing up the delicious gourmet meal, Mark and I stayed at the table making small talk. After an hour, Mark excused the chef and his two helpers, telling them he would see them tomorrow. I was also ready to leave, but I hadn't yet discussed my plans to end my brand-new profession. Mark came back to the table after seeing the chef and his helpers to the door and making sure it was locked.

"Tyler, we finally have the house to ourselves," Mark said in a mac daddy voice. I gave him a bewildering stare because I wasn't yet sure if his tone was purposeful. When he swaggered over to my chair and caressed his fingers through the loose curls in my hair, I instantly became uncomfortable.

"What are you doing, Mark?" I asked. I shifted my head to let him know his behavior was inappropriate.

"What do you think I'm doing, Tyler?"

"I don't know, but you're making me very uncomfortable, so please stop."

"That's what I love about you, Tyler; you have entitlement issues. You truly believe that you have a right to do and say whatever you want. I'm going to enjoy teaching you otherwise. Once I break you down, our working relationship will be so much easier."

"Excuse me!"

"I didn't stutter. It's time to introduce you to the real world and get you out of that fantasy princess shit you live in."

"Mark, you sound real crazy, so I'm ready to go—now."

"See what I mean? You're under the impression that you can leave just because Tyler wants to. It doesn't work like that. You leave when I tell you to. But before you go anywhere, I want you to come over here like a good little girl and kiss Daddy's dick."

I watched Mark in disgust. This was all the fat fuck wanted from the start. Did he really think I was going to suck his dick? He was sorely mistaken. I would bite the shit off before I would suck it.

"Mark, maybe the champagne has you a little tipsy, or you've just lost your fucking mind, but regardless, none of that is jumpin' off."

"If you want to become the next big thing, you better make it jump off. Understand, Tyler, I make you—you don't make me, because I'm already made. I've got my millions, and I will make millions more. I can go out tomorrow and find another Tyler Blake and turn her into Citrus. Nobody will know the difference. So if I was you, I would crawl on my hands and knees and suck this dick until I beg you to stop or your career as a superstar is over. Do you understand me, you ungrateful cunt?"

I laughed uncontrollably and couldn't stop. I could tell Mark thought I was on something and wasn't sure whether to shake the shit out of me, or ask for whatever I was on so he could laugh too. But once he realized I was laughing at him, his attitude shifted back to what it was. I continued to laugh before turning serious.

"You think I care about being your quote superstar? Baby, I'm already a star; the world just doesn't know it yet. But look at you. You're nobody's star. You're just a fat fuck with an overinflated ego. Nobody would give a shit about you if you hadn't bamboozled your way into this business with your drug money and ridden the coattails of a real talent like Tah Tah. Nigga, I don't need you or LaFamilia Records. As a matter of fact, I was going to tell you I wanted out of this farce of a career. I'm no rapper, never was. I let you get me caught up in some bullshit dream that I never wanted to be part of. When I do become a star and make my millions, it won't be by sucking the dick of a clown-ass wannabe Berry Gordy cat like you."

I picked up my purse and pulled out my cell phone to call a cab. I knew the look Mark had on his face meant trouble, but it wasn't happening tonight. There was a champagne bottle sitting right in front of me on the table, and if Mark stepped any closer, I was busting it over his head. Somebody was going to die tonight if that motherfucker put his hands on me. The thought of being raped again was too much for me to handle. At this point I would rather take my chances catching a case than letting another man violate my body.

"Mark, whatever you're thinking, rethink it fast. If you put your hands on me, you better kill me; because if I make it out of this house alive, not only will I file criminal charges against you,

I will make it my mission to destroy whatever respectable reputation you think you have in the music business."

The intense look on Mark's face told me he knew I wasn't bluffing. "Have it your way, Tyler, but we will cross paths again, and next time I might not be so willing to let you go. I'm sure you'll have no problem finding your way home."

With that, Mark went upstairs and left me alone. I called a car service and finished drinking the last glass of champagne while waiting for my ride. Once again I was back to square one trying to figure out my life. I wondered how much longer I would have to battle for my rightful place. Until the answers were revealed to me, I would keep fighting for the little girl in me that needed to be protected.

After my awful experience with Mark, I couldn't seem to find my place. I started to get back on the acting scene, but the constant rejection was slowly making me lose hope. I didn't expect to see my name in bright lights overnight, but I'd hoped to have made more progress. I needed to take a step back and gather my thoughts. The course I was on was leading me nowhere, and I couldn't seem to get on track. I decided I needed to regroup and regain my strength. After leaving numerous messages, I finally spoke to Mother. Daddy was no longer living at the house, and she was going on a month-long cruise with her girlfriends. I used that opportunity to go to Georgia and escape the hectic life of New York City. I did a lot of soul-searching and decided that no matter what, I would make it in NYC, and I wouldn't go back to Georgia to live for anything in the world. I was a survivor and determined to be a success. The day I had to go back to Georgia would mean that I failed, and that wasn't in the cards. After a week of regrouping I headed back home to face my challenges in New York.

As soon as I walked through the door, my friend Chrissie called. Not only did we work together, but she was also my nightclub sidekick.

"What's up, Chrissie?" I was happy to hear her bubbly and cheerful voice on the phone.

"Nothing much. I wanted to go to Lot 61 tonight; do you feel up to it?"

"I just got back from Georgia—I literally just walked through the door. But I've been kinda in a funk, and going out to party might brighten my spirits."

"Yeah, Tyler, this is exactly what you need. You know we always have a blast when we go out."

"Okay. I'm going to jump in the shower and get dressed. Meet me here about eleven."

"Cool, I'll see you then." Besides releasing my stress on the dance floor, I desperately needed a drink. After my awful experience with Mark, I was once again developing a yearning for alcohol. I hadn't had this urge since high school, when I participated in drinking parties with my friends. The only reason I wasn't drinking on a daily basis was because of my tight budget. To me, liquor was a luxury not a necessity, although lately I was beginning to see it the other way.

After taking a ten-minute shower, I looked through my closet trying to decide what to wear. From the clothes I bought myself after being intimidated by the stylish New York women, to the clothes the stylist bought for my new life as superstar Citrus, I had a ton of outfits to choose from. I opted for the sexy tight leopard pants I bought at a boutique on Columbus Avenue, with a black fitted shirt and black snakeskin boots. I dabbed on my favorite Mac lip gloss and went downstairs to meet Chrissie. I loved my neighborhood because it was surrounded by so many cool spots, from clothing boutiques and restaurants to theaters and clubs. Everything was just a step away. When Chrissie saw me, she ran up and gave me a hug and a kiss, "You look hot tonight, Tyler. I love those pants."

"Thanks, you look pretty damn sexy yourself." Which she did. Chrissie not only looked like Sarah Jessica Parker, but she had the style of Carrie Bradshaw and the body. We hailed a cab and were on our way. We'd been to Lot 61 a couple of times before, and we'd always had a fantastic time because the DJ played great music and we both loved to dance. But tonight I was going to have fun of another kind. After shaking our asses to the sounds of Jay-Z, Chrissie and I went to the bar. When I was about to pay for our drinks, I heard a gentleman tell the bartender they were on him. I turned around to see who made the offer because the last thing I wanted was some dork sniffing around me all night because he paid for a couple of drinks. I would rather pay for them myself.

"Hi, I'm Ian," the tall gorgeous caramel-complexioned vision said. I stood there with my mouth wide open until Chrissie nudged my arm. I was almost drooling over the flawless creature.

"Hi, I'm Tyler, and this is my friend Chrissie."

"Nice to meet you." Ian and Chrissie shook hands. He then turned back to me with a smile that was worth at least a million bucks.

"So, Tyler, do you live in New York, or are you just visiting?"

"I actually go to school here; Chrissie and I go to NYU."

"Oh, that's cool. I'm just visiting, but I would love to spend some time with you. Do you mind sitting with me at my booth?"

I glanced over at Chrissie, and she gave me the "I'm okay" wink, and I followed Ian to his table.

What attracted me to Ian besides his athletic build, beautiful smile, and gorgeous color was that when he introduced himself, he seemed kind of shy and innocent. We sat down and began to talk, and we instantly clicked. I hate how when people meet you they always ask what you do, so I never ask that question. I wait for the person to volunteer the information. Ian didn't mention his profession, but with his beautiful face and tall lean body I thought maybe he was an up-and-coming supermodel like Tyson Beckford. I didn't care though. All I knew was that he made me feel at ease, and I felt a connection with him, so when he asked me to go to his hotel, I didn't hesitate.

Ian's limo pulled up to the W Hotel, and I was excited about what would happen when we got to his room. I expected that as soon as he opened the door we would begin passionately kissing and taking off each other's clothes, but we didn't. All Ian wanted to do was talk. Eventually we fell asleep in the bed, and he just held me all night. I went to sleep full of disappointment. I hadn't had any good loving in so long, and I was about to burst. I was on tension overload and needed to release myself. I had to settle with dreaming about an earth-shattering, mind-blowing sexual experience.

The phone rang early the next morning, waking us up. After Ian hung up, he said, "I have to leave and go to Philly for a basketball game, but I would love for you to come with me." When Ian mentioned his profession, I was impressed. It all made sense. I didn't recognize him because except for Michael Jordan I wasn't up on basketball players.

"Ian, thank you for the invitation, but I can't go. I was just in Georgia for a week, and I haven't even unpacked my bags. Plus

I'm scheduled to work, and more importantly, I'm determined to hit the books and concentrate on school. I hope you understand."

"I guess, but I have to admit I'm disappointed. I was looking forward to spending some quality time with you."

"I want to spend time with you too, but right now the timing is terrible." Although I was extremely attracted to Ian, for the first time I was trying to have some priorities and stick with them. By the vexed look on his face it was obvious Ian didn't take the rejection well, but he still asked for my number. I wrote my cell number on a piece of paper from a hotel notepad so I wouldn't miss his call.

During a break at work I flipped through the newspaper to the sports section. That's how I discovered Ian Addison was a franchise player and the league had very high aspirations for him. I kept fidgeting all day waiting for his call, but nothing came and I soon realized I hadn't received a call all day. To my dismay, that very same day my cell phone service was cut off, so I concluded maybe Ian and I weren't meant to be. Still, I began to follow basketball, hoping to find out what was going on with Ian on and off the court.

A month later Chrissie and I were sitting in the student union. I was reviewing my notes for an upcoming test, and Chrissie was reading the *New York Post*. "Oh, my goodness, Tyler! Ian is in town!"

"How do you know?" I asked, full of hope that maybe I would see him again.

"It's right here in the sports section. The Pistons are playing the Knicks tomorrow night. That means Ian is probably here right now."

"Do you think he'll be at the club tonight?"

"There's only one way to find out." I decided to go back to the same club where Ian and I first met, and if he really, really liked me, he would be there looking for me . . . like I was looking for him. That night turned out to be hectic because my waitress shift lasted longer than expected, and at the last minute Chrissie canceled and couldn't go to the club with me. Running late, I ran home, unbuttoning my shirt and pants while on the elevator. Once I reached my apartment, I jumped out of my clothes and grabbed my low-rider Seven Jeans and pink tank top. I slicked my hair back in a ponytail, dabbed on some lip gloss, and ran out to catch a cab. I figured Ian would be long gone by the time I got there, if he had come at all. All the same, I was anxious, so I screamed to the taxi driver to speed it up. As I was walking into the club, I saw groups of drunken guys staggering out but none of them were Ian.

Then my eyes lit up, and I swallowed hard when I noticed a tall muscular brown-skinned guy, wearing a huge platinum-and-diamond chain, about to leave. It was Ian. Luckily he noticed me too, and grabbed my arm. The first thing that came out of his mouth was, "You gave me the wrong number."

"No, I didn't. My phone was—"

Ian cut me off midsentence and continued to vent. "I've been in this club for two hours waiting for you to come. I was about to leave and go to my hotel because I didn't think you were going to show up."

I thought that was so romantic. Wow, this guy really likes me! I thought. He likes me! "I'm sorry, I would've been here hours ago, but I had to work later than expected. I'm so glad you waited."

Ian grabbed my hand and said, "Let's get out of here." Once

again, I was feeling special because some guy was wanting me. That night, we left the club and went back to his hotel, and of course we made love. But no, I did not see fireworks. I was not madly in love and I wasn't overcome with passion, but there was something about Ian that made me feel safe and that was enough for now. The next day he had a game, and when he asked me to attend I was delighted.

It was my first time going to Madison Square Garden to watch the New York Knicks. Ian left two tickets, so I took Chrissie. Chrissie was from California, so she had never been to a Knicks game either. "This is so exciting! Tyler, I can't believe we have floor seats."

I couldn't believe it either. Usually floor seats were reserved for the home team. I knew that because Patrick had had a friend who played on the Atlanta Hawks, and he was only able to get him prime seats when the team was playing at home.

"Isn't that Will Smith sitting across from us?" Chrissie said enthusiastically.

"Yeah, it is; but Chrissie, please calm down before you embarrass both of us."

"I'm sorry, Tyler, but I'm from Temecula, California, and I never saw any celebrities back home."

"Chrissie, you're so sweet; I love your honesty." Chrissie *was* sweet and honest. I felt that I could trust her as much as I was capable of trusting anyone. She didn't seem to be jealous of me the way Lisa was. I got the feeling she was genuinely happy about my new relationship with Ian.

"Chrissie, how do you think the life of a star NBA player's girlfriend—or wife—is?"

"I would think totally cool. Like unlimited shopping sprees, the best restaurants, everything just first class all the way."

All those things were cool, but Chrissie's mind-set was so limited. I wanted bigger things in life than that. I had already worn designer clothes and eaten at fancy restaurants; now I wanted to live like a star. After the game I met Ian in the section for family and friends, and we said our good-byes. He promised he would call soon and I could go to Detroit to visit. I made sure he had my home number this time, and I hoped he would keep his promise. He did.

I talked to Ian every day for a week while he was on the road. When he was finally headed home, he said, "Tyler, do you think you can get away for a couple of days? I really want to see you."

"Sure," I said, excited about seeing Ian again.

"Cool, I'll have my travel agent book you a flight. Is tomorrow good?"

"Yeah, that's fine; just make it an afternoon flight."

"Okay, I'll call you later on with all the details. Tyler, I miss you."

The next day I was on an American Airlines flight to Detroit. It was thrilling. Here I was flying high in the sky, first class all the way. All I wondered was, could Ian really want to be with me, because I was totally digging him.

Ian pulled up at the airport in a silver big-body Benz and greeted me with a sweet hug and kiss. "Baby you look even prettier than I remember."

"Shut up, Ian; don't try to pump my head up," I giggled.

"No, baby, it's the truth. Maybe I just miss you so much."

"Not as much as I miss you."

"Why do you say that?" Ian asked as he cruised down the highway.

"Because if you missed me as much as I missed you, it would mean you are smitten, and I'm sure you're not smitten."

I smiled as I said those words, and Ian smiled back. With a look of love in his eyes he said, "I think I'm just that."

Something about Ian was so childlike, and it only added to his charm. When we arrived at his house, I was surprised by how modest it was. I was expecting some huge mansion on an estate. He explained that this was his temporary house while his permanent house was being built. Of course, he had the standard flunky that all basketball players have, the guy who lives with them and builds his whole life around kissing their asses. But TJ, Ian's flunky, was cool. After we got settled, we went out to dinner at an Italian restaurant, and we spent the majority of time stealing kisses and Ian playing with my hair. We were like two love-struck teenagers.

The next evening I attended Ian's basketball game and sat in the section where the girlfriends, wives, or whatever you want to call them were sitting. It was cold so some of the women had on long fur coats. And they were all done up. I wore a pair of sleek black Richard Tyler pants, a red fitted sweater, and a simple black leather jacket. I definitely wasn't looking like bimbo Barbie. I was more subtle and sophisticated. A Nia Long look-alike and her girlfriend were staring me up and down with a "Die, bitch" look. I heard one of them whisper, "She's sitting in Ian's seats. Is she supposed to be his new girlfriend? She looks like she belongs in the library." They laughed loudly.

"As opposed to a brothel," I said, turning around to get a look at both women. An older white man sitting beside them bust out laughing, but when the women gaped at him with hate in their eyes, he quickly turned back to the game.

"You must have misunderstood us, because we weren't talking about you."

"Oh, then I apologize. I assumed because I don't look like I just stepped out of a Pimp 'n Ho video that you all were making catty remarks about my attire."

"Excuse me, are you trying to say we look like hos?" the Nia Long look-alike snapped.

I sat back and put my finger to my mouth and glanced up as though contemplating her question. "Yeah, basically," I said. I turned back around in my seat, waiting to hear a response from the two haters, but they sat there mum for the rest of the game. I figured my comment must have shut them up.

After the game, I went in the back to wait for Ian. It was the first time I saw how women throw themselves at athletes. They were like vultures! There were grown-ass women standing out in the area where fans and kids were waiting to get autographs. These women had their best clothes on, their hair and makeup was done to perfection, and they wore long fur coats as they waited for the players, hoping they would catch their attention. I don't condone Kobe Bryant for cheating on his wife, but I can definitely understand how it happened. It must be difficult for a guy to pass on some pussy when it is just thrown in his face every day. It made me wonder why Ian wanted me. I wasn't all glamorous and dolled up like these women. But it didn't matter, because he had chosen me. I had something pink and innocent about me; whatever it was, he was with me, not with one of the girls standing on the sideline with their Sunday best on trying to throw him their number. I was relieved when we finally left the building because I was sickened by all the fake glamour surrounding me. It was enough to make me choke.

"Did you enjoy the game?" Ian asked, like a kid wanting approval.

"I enjoyed watching you."

"Perfect answer."

"It's the truth," I said, giving Ian a peck on the cheek. He made me feel like a young girl experiencing puppy love for the first time.

On our way home we picked up something to eat and took it back to his house. We went downstairs and sat on his tan sectional to chill out. We were drinking, and he was smoking weed. At that time I had a little alcohol problem—I was a drunk. I never knew when enough was enough. I was a drunk, and Ian was a pothead and a drunk too. Now a drunk and a pothead don't mesh at all. TJ was there, and we were all bugging out and laughing. Ian mentioned that I had moved to New York to pursue an acting career. But I was still surprised when out the blue he said, "Tyler, baby, stand up there and sing a song for me."

"Baby, you so silly," I said, playfully slapping my hand on his shoulder.

"I ain't silly; I'm dead-ass serious," Ian babbled, sounding like a drunken sailor.

"Baby, I'm not really a singer, and I definitely don't feel like performing right now," I said, laughing slightly. I told Ian no for a few reasons: one, I was drunk; two, I was in no mood to put on a show; and three, let's just say that sometimes I can be shy.

"You better get up there and perform." Ian was shoving me off the couch. He put me on the spot, but I still thought he was playing until, to my horror, he began a huge argument.

With a drunken slur he yammered, "You better get up there and do something, or you gonna make me smack that ass up." I was on the edge of the couch glaring at him. Ian went on to preach about how his cousin was some big-time music guy, and if you're not able to perform at the drop of a dime, you can't be an entertainer.

My eyes were glassy, and Ian's were bloodshot. His body seemed to be pulsating as he began ridiculing me, putting me down, yelling at me. All over my refusal to sing. Suddenly Ian lifted me up and threw me against the wall.

"Ouch," I screamed, as my back hit the wall. "Why the fuck did you just do that, dumb shit? Because what, you're bigger and stronger than me, and I'm in your house?" Ian had the audacity to throw me around like he was on the court passing the ball—all over a stupid song!

I weighed a hundred and fifteen pounds wet, and Ian was robust, so it seemed as though I was literally flying when he threw me. I could hear my back crack when I hit the wall. I was now popping shit, especially because of my drunken state; I was furious!

"You should have done what the fuck I asked you to, instead of making some simple-ass shit all complicated," Ian hissed.

"You know what? I'm so out of here. I'm not about to deal with you and this bullshit. I don't give a damn how many endorsement deals you have—you're fucking crazy!" Ian's eyes seemed cold and distant as he stared me down like I was the disturbed one. I ran upstairs and started packing so I could get the hell out of there. It was one o'clock in the morning, but I didn't care. After getting my belongings together, I went back downstairs and told Ian I was ready to go.

"I ain't taking you nowhere. You sound stupid right now," he scolded.

"I want to leave now. I'd rather sleep in the airport than stay in the same house as you. Now let's go!"

Ian reluctantly drove me to the airport. "You a dumb-ass chick leaving my house in the middle of the night. Where the fuck is you going? You going to sit in the damn airport by your-self?"

"Exactly. That's a lot more appealing than being anywhere near a cocky sonofabitch like you."

"Yeah, we'll see if you still feel that way when you start freezing in that cold-ass airport."

By this time Ian had totally fucked up my high, and I was considering clawing his eyes out before I got out of the car. He continued to call me names, and I tossed names right back. When he pulled up to the airport terminal, I jumped out of the car, slammed the door, and didn't look back. I went inside to find out the earliest flight back to NYC. The next flight wasn't until 6:30 a.m. and it was now maybe 2:30 a.m. I found myself a comfortable chair and called Ella.

"Hello," she answered in a groggy voice.

"Ella, I'm sorry to be calling you so late, but I needed some-one to talk to."

"Aren't you out of town? Why are you calling me?" she asked, irritated.

"Ella, please just listen to me for a minute," I said, pleading.

She took a deep breath, and I heard her situating herself in what I assumed was her bed. "Go ahead; I'm up."

"Well, Ian and I got in this huge argument, and he sorta hit me."

"Someone doesn't sorta hit you, Tyler; either they hit you or they don't."

"If throwing you across the room fits in the category of hitting, then that's what he did."

"He threw you across the room?" she said, sounding shocked.

"Where are you now? At the police department filing criminal charges?" she said in an annoying, here-we-go-again tone.

"No, I'm at the airport."

"This time of night? Well, at least you left."

"I did, but I'm not sure I made the right decision. Maybe he didn't mean it."

"Maybe he didn't mean it?" she repeated, her voice rising. "Tyler, when are you going to learn? Didn't you figure out from your relationship with Trey that once the abuse starts it never stops unless the man can admit he has a problem and gets some serious help? I'm glad you left, and you need to stay as far away from Ian Addison as possible. I'm serious, Tyler."

"You're right, Ella. Having Ian out of my life is the best thing for me." I hung up the phone, closed my eyes, and instantly fell into a deep sleep. An hour later, I felt a hand shaking me awake. I opened my eyes to find Ian standing in front of me.

"Tyler, baby, I'm so sorry. I was so fucked up and acted like a real ass. Will you please forgive me?" Of course, my initial reaction was to think, This is so romantic. Instantly I forgot about the brutality that had brought me to the airport in the first place. I kept saying to myself, He came back for me, he missed me, and so he must care. But I wasn't quite sure if that was the truth or if I was once again clinging to a relationship that had bad news written all over it.

"Of course I forgive you; I should've just sung a damn song," I said, a slight smile on my face. When Ian held out his hand I grabbed it lovingly, and he picked up my suitcase with the other hand as we walked back to his car.

That night we made passionate love, and our kisses were so intense. As I straddled Ian, he kissed my neck and brushed his hands across my breasts before putting my nipples in his moist mouth. I couldn't feel him deep enough inside of me. My fingernails pressed deep into his warm back, and we both moaned with desire. As we gazed into each other's eyes, for the first time Ian said, "I love you, Tyler. Would you please have my baby?"

"Yes. I would love to have your baby, Ian," I moaned.

(Now, when a guy tells you he loves you and wants to have babies with you, it means that he likes to have sex with you for free! All the same I thought, Wow, he loves me. He didn't have to come back for me. He could've sent me packing back to New York City and never spoken to me again. Ian Addison was a superstar athlete. He had the choice of any woman he wanted, but he came back for me.)

The next day Ian cooked me a big breakfast, and took me on one of those shopping sprees Chrissie dreamed about. We talked, laughed, and got to know each other better. I loved how sexy Ian looked when I asked him a question: right before he responded he would lick his lips and smile. I was becoming more smitten with him every day. When we got back home, I dashed upstairs and rumbled through my bags so I could admire all the new outfits and shoes Ian bought me. For the first time in so long I felt like a princess again. Maybe I had finally found my Prince Charming in Ian.

The following day I was back on the plane to New York. When Ian kissed me good-bye, I longed for the day I would be with him again, and he reassured me it would be soon. "I'll be in New York in a couple of weeks, so be a good girl until I come. Call me when you get home." Ian gave me a loving kiss before we parted.

While waiting for takeoff, I admitted to myself that I was more than smitten with Ian, I had fallen in love. No, I hadn't forgotten that he threw me against a wall, but at the same time I had been through a lot worse. Plus I was blaming his behavior on the weed. Never mind that he was high a lot. I'd never dated a professional athlete, and he was exposing me to a whole other life, and I relished in it.

Once I got back to New York, reality set in. It was time to hit the books. I wasn't bored, but although I was going to school I was definitely not into it. Some of the classes were fun, but the other subjects could never hold my attention. I was going to a few auditions, but nothing was panning out. I would get extra work here and there, but I had to sit around sets for hours and hours just to earn enough money to buy something to eat. It couldn't pay my bills!

I found auditions exhausting because I needed money and I wasn't making any, New York is expensive and something had to give. Although Ian had plenty of paper, it was much too soon to ask for a handout. I didn't want to come off as some hard-up gold digger, even though he'd told me if I needed anything to just ask. I figured if the relationship continued on the path we were on, soon he'd start handing over whatever money I needed.

I was meeting Chrissie at the restaurant Cafeteria for lunch, and we were seeing each other for the first time since I got back from my visit with Ian. Chrissie was exuding her normal *Sex and the City* getup, mixing shorts with a bustier and her standard four-inch heels. Besides Carrie Bradshaw, Chrissie was the only person I knew of who could get away with wearing such eyebrow-raising outfits and actually look good doing it. We sat down at a corner table, sipping our usual glass of wine, and Chrissie dove right in with the questions.

"So how was your visit with Ian?"

"Let's just say I'm totally crazy about him. We did have a minor altercation at first, but we managed to work things out."

"What type of altercation?" I gave Chrissie the play-by-play while she sat with her mouth wide open.

"Oh, my gosh, I can't believe that! What an egomaniac. All his money has made him a pompous ass. Josh would never behave like that." Josh, Chrissie's broke boyfriend, always had his hand out, begging her for a dollar.

"Don't get me wrong; Ian's behavior was irrational, but he's still a great catch. At the end of the day you can fall in love with a rich man just as easy as a poor man, because underneath both men are still the same. They are going to want to control your life and tell you what to do. Men are dominating by nature, so why be bothered with some broke-ass man running around trying to drive you crazy, when you can have a rich one who can at least give you a better life?"

"Tyler, you're so jaded. Josh doesn't try to control me."

"Yeah, because you do whatever he wants you to do. Just wait until the word 'no' comes out of your mouth, and then you'll see just how compliant Josh really is."

Chrissie, like so many other women, had this game all confused. In her limited mind an unambitious wuss like Josh was somehow a better man than Ian because he never asked for anything but money and time. Most women are so desperate for companionship that they will give their last dollar and the time they need to put toward themselves to a man whose only interest is how he can benefit from them. I refused to let that be my existence. I understood that my relationship with Ian wasn't exactly normal, but it seemed a lot more fulfilling than Chrissie's. Ian had his flaws and was far from perfect, but since my arrival to the big city, he was the closest form of perfection for me.

6

Holding On to My Secret Fantasies

A lie is so much easier to believe than the truth. Someone can tell you they want you to be honest, but then everyone hates honesty. It's highly overrated. You want that person to stop before they say something you may regret hearing—and before you accuse them of deliberately misleading you. All my life I created a fantasy because I didn't want to face reality. But sometimes reality slaps you in the face, and you can no longer run from the inevitable.

I kept eyeing my watch as the hairstylist at the Dominican spot blew my hair straight. Two weeks had seemed to fly by, and in a couple of hours Ian would be picking me up at my apartment. We were going to some party, and I had no idea what to wear. Ian hadn't given me any details; he'd just told me to look sexy. I was debating whether to wear my red Narciso Rodriguez dress or my silk animal-print Jenny Packham. Both were extremely seductive, and Ian would like either one since he had picked them both out.

When I got home, I heard my phone ringing from the hallway, but I managed to answer it right before the answering machine picked up.

"Hello," I said, out of breath.

"Where the fuck have you been? I've left you three messages."

"I went to get my hair done. Why didn't you call me on my cell?"

"Because you don't ever answer that shit. You should've called and told me where you were. I don't have time to try and track you down."

"I'm sorry."

"Yeah, you should be," Ian said. Then he instantly jumped to another subject. "So what are you wearing tonight?"

Ian was becoming a tyrant. We would speak every day, and he would want a detailed report of my activities. If he called at a certain time and I wasn't home, he would scold me like I was a five-year-old. When Ian's behavior became unbearable, I sometimes wondered if my mother's views were rubbing off on me. I did love Ian, but would I be putting up with his intolerable attitude if he wasn't rich and famous? Or would I gladly show him the front door? I had to believe that it was love, because I hated the fact that Mother stayed with Daddy because she wanted a certain lifestyle.

"Either the red Narciso Rodriguez or the silk animal print."

"No, wear that nude-color Gucci dress. I love the way it hugs your ass."

"Okay, whatever you say."

"Hurry up, because I'll be downstairs in twenty minutes."

"Twenty." I heard the phone go dead before my thought was completed. With no time to waste, I did a quick fresh-me-up, applied my makeup the exact way Ian liked, put on my shoes, grabbed my purse, and zoomed downstairs. His limo was downstairs, right on time. The driver opened the door for me, and Ian, who was on his cell phone, did not seem to notice as I got inside. I reached over to give him a kiss, and he put his hand up, gesturing me to wait. When Ian finally finished his conversation, I was anxious for him to acknowledge me.

"Come sit over here." Ian patted the spot right next to him. "You look so fucking sexy! I'm ready to do you right here in this limo, but I want you to stay looking perfect; maybe we'll make love on our way back to the hotel."

"I forgot to bring my overnight bag."

"Don't worry about it; you can pick some things up from the store in the morning. I have a surprise for you."

My eyes brightened. "Really? What is it?" Ian handed me a Jacob the Jeweler box with the most beautiful diamond necklace I had ever seen. I couldn't take my eyes off the sparkler.

"This is for me?" I said, full of shock.

"No doubt. Turn around. I want you to wear this tonight with your dress. Now you look perfect," Ian said as he examined me from head to toe. We pulled up to a penthouse on Madison Avenue, and there were limos lined up down the block.

"Whose party is this, Ian?"

"My cousin's; he's celebrating his birthday." My mind was spinning, wondering who the hell his cousin was. When we entered the town house, the layout was magnificent.

"This is your cousin's place?" I was in awe because it was breathtaking.

"Yeah, he's doing big things. Come with me; I want to

introduce you to him." I followed Ian up some wraparound stairs that led to a huge open space where about fifty people were lounging on big, cream-colored plush couches. Everyone from Russell Simmons, Mary J. Blige, and Martha Stewart was socializing and taking glasses of champagne from the waiters sauntering around the room.

Ian finally came to a cloud of people and stepped through, and I heard him saying, "What's up, cuz? Happy birthday." There were a couple of models blocking my view so I still couldn't see Ian's cousin. People began dispersing as Ian pulled me in and the guests realized the superstar basketball player and the guest of honor wanted a private moment. As my view cleared and I glimpsed up before completely focusing, I heard Ian say, "Man, this is my girl-friend, Tyler. And Tyler, this is my cousin, T-Roc."

My heart dropped as T-Roc extended his hand. "Tyler, that's a pretty name for a very pretty girl." The same words he used the very first time he introduced himself to me.

"Thank you," I said dryly.

"You're a lucky man, Ian. How long have you been together?" Ian glanced at me, but I wasn't saying a word.

"A couple of months, but it seems longer. I think she's the one." Ian beamed. T-Roc was undressing me right before his cousin's eyes, but Ian was oblivious.

"Ian, I need to go to the restroom."

"Do you want me to show you where it is?"

"No, I can find it." I darted off before letting either one of them speak another word to me. This was too much. I found the bathroom, shut the door, and sat on top of the toilet, over-whelmed by the turn of events. Should I tell Ian that I slept with his cousin or will T-Roc tell him? Maybe I should just keep it to myself? Maybe T-Roc will? But the way he ogled me, like we shared some sordid secret . . . I gulped down the two glasses of champagne I had picked up on my way to the bathroom. Then I inspected myself in the mirror. I applied fresh lip gloss, fixed my hair, and adjusted my dress, prepared to go back to Ian like nothing was wrong. But when I opened the door, T-Roc pushed me back inside and locked the door.

"What are you doing?" I protested. T-Roc put his finger to my lips.

"Shh, there is no need to get upset," T-Roc managed to say in a cool, calm voice. "First me, now my cousin; you're turning this into a real family affair, Tyler."

"I didn't know he was your cousin, and if I had . . ." My words faded.

"What? You wouldn't have fucked with him? I seriously doubt that. The two of you seem very much in love, but then from our past encounter I can tell what type of woman you are, and you're not capable of love."

"You don't even know me; you have no idea how I feel about Ian."

"A great part of my success is attributed to my gift of interpreting people from limited time spent with them. My diagnosis of you is that you're an ice princess."

"I don't give a damn what you think of me."

"Maybe, but I'm sure Ian may feel differently."

"What do you want from me, T-Roc?"

"I want us to pick up where we left off." T-Roc stared into my eyes and when his lips touched mine, my body became weak and I gave in to him. I couldn't deny my attraction for T-Roc; he had this powerful aura that almost put me in a hypnotic trance. His hands glided up my dress, and he slid my panties to the side as his finger easily slithered inside me. I moaned as he kissed my neck and then my breast. In what seemed like one quick motion he lifted me up on the sink, raised my dress, and scooted my body forward so he could taste all of me. Right when I was about to reach my climax, T-Roc stopped. Handing me his business card, he said, "You better call me tomorrow no later than two o'clock, or I'll be having a heart-to-heart with my cousin about his new girlfriend."

"I can't. I'll be with Ian tomorrow."

"Well, you better get creative." T-Roc exited the bathroom, leaving me to wonder how I got myself in this predicament.

I woke up spooned against Ian, dreading the rest of my day before it had even started. I tossed and turned all night due to T-Roc's face flashing through my mind. It was too late to come clean with Ian about my past encounter with T-Roc, especially after our bathroom episode. But at the same time I wasn't going to let T-Roc dangle our relationship over my head. I had to settle this situation with T-Roc once and for all, which meant I needed to get home and get my mind right before my two-o'clock phone call. Right when I was about to slide out of bed, Ian's erect penis was rubbing against my butt, meaning it was time for his morning fix. As I slowly moved out of the bed, Ian grabbed me, pulling me toward him. "Where you think you're going?"

"Baby, I have a million things to do this morning. I have to get home."

"What? You better get your pretty ass back in this bed." I fell back in Ian's arms, giving him an impetuous kiss before jumping out of the bed.

"Ian, you know I have finals this week; please don't give me a hard time." Finals were actually the following week, but he didn't need to know that.

"Damn, I have a photo shoot for my Reebok ad, and I wanted you to come with me."

"How about I call you after my final and I'll meet you there. Is that cool?"

"Yeah, that works, but you better come."

"I will; I promise."

On the way home I sat in a cab replaying exactly what I planned to say to T-Roc. There was no way I was going to let him ruin my relationship with Ian. He was the best thing to happen to me in so long, and T-Roc wasn't going to suck me into whatever sick game he was trying to play. By the time the cab pulled up in front of my building, I had my T-Roc speech all worked out.

I paced back and forth in my living room as the clock ticked closer to two. I knew T-Roc said to call him by two, but I figured if I called him closer to the cutoff time, then maybe he wouldn't know how shook he had me. I took a deep breath before picking up the cordless phone and dialed his number. The phone rang once, then twice. "Hello," a distinct voice said.

"Hi, can I speak to T-Roc?" I asked, although I knew it was him on the phone.

"Speaking. Who's this?"

"Tyler."

"Right at two. I'm sure you purposely pushed the time."

"No, I just walked in the house."

"Whatever you say, Tyler." His confidence aggravated the hell out of me. I wanted this conversation over with so I could forget I ever had a crush on a man named T-Roc.

"Listen, I'm gonna make this quick because I have somewhere I need to be. Last night was a big mistake. I had a few glasses of champagne, which made my thinking skills zero. As far as what took place a few months ago, it is in the past and that is where it should stay." There was a long silence before T-Roc spoke.

"Tyler, you're right, and I apologize for putting you in an uncomfortable predicament," T-Roc said with what seemed like genuine sincerity.

"Does that mean you won't be telling Ian about our connection?"

"Is that what you think we have? A connection?"

"You know what I mean," I said, becoming flustered.

"If you're asking me if I'll keep our past relationship a secret from Ian, the answer is yes."

"Thank you; I have to go now." I hung up the phone before T-Roc could lure me in. It blew my mind how cooperative he was. How obliging he was confused me, and it had me on edge. The ring of my cell phone jarred me from my thoughts. It was Ian, and I scurried to pick up. Before I got a word out, Ian belted, "Where the fuck are you? Why aren't you here yet?"

I stuttered trying to explain myself. "I'm so sorry; I'm coming right now." It was almost three, and I had told Ian I would meet him no later than two thirty. He hated waiting, especially for me.

The traffic was terrible getting to the East Side, and by the time I arrived, Ian was standing in front of his limo talking to an older white guy in a business suit. I waited until they finished before walking up to him. "Hi, baby. Sorry I'm so late." Ian strong-armed me in the car and slammed the door.

"Where the fuck was you at?" Before he let me answer, he smacked me in the face. My hands went up in defense mode because he looked like he was about to strike again.

"Ian, don't." I sighed, feeling perplexed because the driver was surveying us from the front seat. Ian was too preoccupied scolding me to notice, or he just didn't care.

"How you gon have me waitin' for you? When I tell you to be somewhere, that's where you be, do you understand?" I didn't answer right away, and Ian shouted again. "I said, Do you understand?"

In a soft, lost tone I said, "Yes."

Ian leaned back and put his head down as though I had ruined his day. For the rest of the car ride and even when we shopped in Jeffrey, he didn't say two words to me. The silence was driving me nuts, and I'd become so desperate for his approval that I blurted out, "I'll never disappoint you again. Whatever you want, that's what I'll do."

"You promise," Ian commanded.

"I promise." With my pledge of assurance Ian tongued me down with a wet kiss and led my head to his hardness. I pleasured him for the duration of our ride, believing that I had earned his love again.

The next morning Ian left, and I missed him immediately. Luckily school was almost over and I could spend the summer with him. Until then, studying was my number one priority. While listening to my answering-machine messages, I was surprised to hear my agent saying there was an emergency and please call him back. We hadn't spoken since I went through my rapper phase, and I was curious about the urgency. I replayed the message one more time before dialing his number. "Hi, Chris; it's me, Tyler."

"Tyler, Tyler, Tyler, sweetie, I've been trying to track you down." Chris's usual grumpy voice was upbeat and friendly.

"Yeah, I got your message. What's so urgent?" I asked with suspicion in my voice.

"I got a call today from a guy who's the VP of the new female clothing line, Be Me. Some photographer hired to shoot the ad campaign saw you on that video you did for LaFamilia Records and thought you'd be perfect. He presented the idea to the owner, and she loved it."

"So are you saying I got an ad campaign for a clothing line?" I didn't believe it was true.

"Exactly. The shoot starts first thing tomorrow morning. The ad will consist of you and two other women, but you'll be the lead. Isn't this fantastic? I'm negotiating for top dollar."

"But, Chris, I'm no model. I'm an actress."

"Actress, smactress. Who gives a fuck? It's money. They want you. They're paying you, so let's do it. I'll call you in an hour with the details. Congratulations, Tyler." I had to put this whole situation on odd, or maybe I was just lucky. But then I always thought luck was for people who served the devil and that blessings came from God. So was this a blessing?

Early in the morning a car service was waiting to take me to a studio in SoHo. When I arrived the atmosphere was chaotic, and Marvin Gaye's greatest hits were blaring from the speakers. There were a couple of other models—the two Chris spoke of— some executive types, and Sasha McIntire, the owner of Be Me clothes. She was some ex-supermodel-turned-designer. She had had great success with a lingerie line and was now branching off into women's clothing, shoes, and accessories. Sasha pranced toward me as though on the catwalk. "Hi, you must be Tyler. It's a pleasure to meet you," she said in a fake Hollywood tone. The epitome of overindulgence at its finest, she had enough bling to put Fred Leighton out of business.

"Thank you. I appreciate the opportunity to be included in your ad campaign."

"Don't be silly. You're gorgeous, and that body of yours will look perfect in my designs."

"Thanks."

"Follow me over here so I can choose your first outfit for the shoot." Sasha picked out some tiny pale-pink satin shorts—which no one but Chrissie would have the balls to wear in public—with a matching white and pale-pink tube top. Thank goodness I had nothing for breakfast, because a dry piece of toast would have added ten pounds in this getup. While I was pulling my outfit, Sasha formally introduced me to Brianna and Sierra. Brianna was a tall Brazilian-looking chick, and Sierra was a mix of Asian and black. Both women were tall and gorgeous, and I still wondered how I fit in this mix.

During the shoot, the photographer placed me in the center and put the other girls behind me, like Kelly and Michelle in Destiny's Child. I felt like I was Beyoncé and they were the step-sisters. During a break, Sierra and I were in the middle of idle chatter when I noticed Sasha and Brianna kissing in the corner.

"Isn't Sasha engaged to some big-time movie honcho?" Sierra was now viewing the spectacle that warranted my comment.

"Oh, she's bisexual, but so is her fiancé. They're swingers, so they'll have the perfect marriage." Sierra responded like this was normal, acceptable behavior.

"Oh, okay, whatever works for them."

We worked from 8:30 a.m. to 8:30 p.m. until the last picture snapped and it was a wrap. It was hard, but it was the easiest work I'd ever done for the amount of money they were paying me. Plus the exposure would be priceless. Maybe Sasha's husband would see the pictures and think I was perfect for a role. I put my street clothes back on, said good-bye to Brianna and Sierra and the rest of the crew, and darted downstairs. That whole scene wasn't for me. They had basically turned the studio into a club. Everyone was drinking champagne and snorting coke. I had no problem with the bubbly, but I stopped short of fucking with the white girl. I exited the building feeling a warm spring breeze, and a silver Bentley Azure was parked in the spot I assumed the Town Car would be in. The driver stepped out and opened the back door, and there was T-Roc. "Tyler, get in the car." I scanned the area seeing where I could run for cover, but the street was isolated and deserted. With hesitation I got in the car, and the door slammed behind me.

"How was your shoot today?" T-Roc asked.

"Who told you about that?"

"You're not that naive, are you, Tyler?"

"Ian?" I asked, looking puzzled. Last night I called Ian excited about the gig; of course he didn't share in my enthusiasm, but why would he tell T-Roc? But how else would he know? The answer dawned on me when T-Roc said, "I wanted to give you something that would make you happy."

"No, you want me to owe you."

"I already have that. This was just a gift to you."

"How in the hell did you maneuver that? Did you beg Sasha for a favor?"

"I don't beg for anything. I'm a silent partner. I own fifty percent of the company. But you're a beautiful girl, Tyler, and once I showed Sasha your picture, she had no problem hiring you for the job. See, it's all about who you know."

"Why? Why did you do this?" I was confused by T-Roc's actions. I looked at him inquisitively, searching for the answers.

"Because I can, and I want you. The best way to win a woman over is to give her what she wants the most. You want to be a star, and I can make that happen for you."

"T-Roc, I'm in love with Ian, your cousin," I said sarcastically, because he seemed to have forgotten.

T-Roc chuckled slightly. "Tyler, you're not in love with anyone, and I doubt you ever have been. But what I can give you is a whole lot better than love anyway, and it will last."

"Forget it; I don't want any part of it."

"Have it your way," T-Roc said nonchalantly.

"I guess that means you're scrapping me from the Be Me ads."

"Tyler, like I said before, you're perfect for that ad. I only gave you an opportunity that most people never get because they don't have the necessary relationships. But you do; we're family. Well, here we are." I peered out the window, and we were in front of my apartment building. I had moved since first meeting Jason and I wondered how T-Roc had my new address; but then again T-Roc probably knew everything.

"Thanks for the ride and the modeling job," I said, feeling a twinge of gratitude. T-Roc just nodded his head not speaking a word. That night before I went to bed I spoke to Ian for about an hour, but T-Roc was the one on my mind. His actions were confusing to me, and I couldn't seem to figure him out. He honestly couldn't believe I would leave Ian and run into his arms because he got me a modeling job? It was so obvious his motives were insincere. Still, what he did worked because he was the one I fell asleep thinking about.

After my final exams, I took a break to spend some time with Ian. His dream house was completed, and he was living in a fabulous mansion on acres of land with its very own lake. His home was truly spectacular, and Ian knew it. He especially loved the custom-made Steinway grand piano that stood in front of his living-room window, which had a view of the lake. He said playing soothed his mind. Unfortunately it didn't soothe him enough, and the visit turned out to be another volatile encounter.

Ian was pissed that I'd gotten the modeling job and still wanted to pursue a career in the entertainment industry. On several occasions we discussed me transferring to a college in the Detroit area so we could be together year-round. But I had bigger ambitions than being some basketball player's girlfriend or wife. Having a successful career would give me the sense of purpose and direction I longed for. Being with Ian was a one-sided relationship that was becoming increasingly annoying.

One evening we had dinner with one of Ian's teammates and his girlfriend at the Whitney. In the middle of relishing my chocolate-glazed bombe, the conversation turned bothersome. Ian boasted, "No matter how bad a man fucks up, the woman is suppose to stand by his side and hold her position. The man is the leader. The sooner women understand that, the more content they'll be."

"You sound like a complete male chauvinist," I said.

"Get over yourself, Tyler. You know who controls this relationship." Ian gave his rookie teammate a pound. The wet-behind-the-ear rookie obviously idolized Ian and would agree with anything he said. I stared at the rookie's girlfriend to get a read on what she thought, but the sexy Spanish girl sat there with a blank expression.

"So my opinion doesn't matter?"

"Basically." Ian laughed, still showing off in front of his rookie flunky. Was this my life, trailing behind an arrogant, overpaid, egotistical maniac?

After dinner we said our good-byes to the empty couple and headed to the car. Once inside, Ian exploded. "Don't you ever question what I say in front of nobody!"

"Ian, you were being a complete asshole in there."

"You better watch your mouth, or you'll be footin' it back home."

"How can you talk to me like that, like I'm nothing?"

"Don't get all sentimental with me; you know what time it is. Everything you got on I paid for. That rock on your finger, I just bought that. The new apartment you're living in, I pay the rent. You were a struggling student when I met you; now you don't want for nothing. So if that means you better keep your mouth shut when I say something you don't like, then that's what you do."

"You bastard! Fuck you and your damn money!" I screamed. Ian cursed me out, calling me bitch, whore, and slut—all the names that men throw at women when they can't put together a coherent sentence. Instead of saying something that makes sense, they call you everything but your given name. Ian was driving all crazy, swerving into the other cars' lanes. I thought we were going to crash.

With fear I squealed, "Ian, slow down!" Ian had all this built-up frustration due to his presumption that I wasn't putting him first in my life. He wasn't interested in me pursuing a career. He wanted a twenty-four-hour sex slave at his beck and call, and damn the bitch who wasn't down for the cause. Luckily we made it back to the house in one piece, but the argument continued. This time, there was no Ian coming to the airport to save me, there was no Ian being my knight in shining armor. I was annoyed and disgusted with his attitude. Never one to hold my tongue, it was my pleasure to tell Ian what an idiot he was.

That night there was no making up and making love. Ian was sprawled out on one side of the king-size bed, and I slept on the other. In the morning, he left without saying good-bye. I stayed home and surmised where our relationship was going. Circumstances were different this time. At the end of the day, what could we really do? We were two different people. I wanted to be successful in my own right. I wanted to have my own money, my own possessions. Ian wanted a doormat. Our personalities were on complete opposite sides of the spectrum.

I lounged by the pool waiting for Ian to come home, dreading our talk. He finally made an appearance five hours later.

"Where have you been?" I asked, part missing him and part hating him for leaving me for so long without even a call.

"Out," Ian snapped.

"Out doing what?" I thought maybe he had been with another woman.

"Doing me," Ian said, throwing me shade. The conversation was going nowhere.

"That's cool; your stank attitude is speaking volumes. You obviously feel that whatever is out there is better than what you have right here, so you win."

"What you mean, I win?" he asked.

"It means that the relationship is over. Finished."

"Finished?"

"Yeah, finished. You do know what finished means? Over. To bring something to an end, which in this case is our relationship."

"What are you going to do without me, Tyler? I'm the best you'll ever get."

"Well, then you must have a low opinion of me, if you're the best that I can get." I cruised past Ian with contempt. How dare he insult my intelligence as if he were the be-all and the end-all. Ian remained at the pool smoking his weed and drinking some Hennessy. He was in his own zone and didn't seem to either realize or care when I packed my bags and left. It was good-bye to Detroit and hello to New York.

Chrissie and I were lying out in Central Park in our pink bikinis, soaking up the sun. It was a beautiful Tuesday afternoon and we both needed the relaxation. I was dozing off to sleep when Chrissie decided to strike up a heart-to-heart chat.

"How are you dealing with the whole Ian situation? I know you must miss him." Chrissie knew that I didn't want to discuss Ian, but *insistent* was Chrissie's middle name.

"I'm doing okay. I talked to him yesterday, but his attitude hasn't changed much. He is totally stubborn. But he did say he was willing to try to change some of his barbaric ways. It's not much, but a start." When I first got back to New York, Ian had left numerous messages berating me for leaving. It wasn't until he'd gone upstairs and noticed all my stuff was gone that he realized I had left. He was furious. But finally calmed down and gave me a half-ass apology.

"I agree. With Ian being such a tyrant, that's a huge step for him. Plus I know how much you love him," Chrissie said.

"Yeah, I do love him. What can I say? Maybe it's wishful thinking, but I'm still hoping that Ian can get control of his temper and we can be happy together. He's coming to New York sometime this week for a couple of days. We're going to try to work things out."

"Great, but Tyler, don't let him pressure you into conforming to his barbaric ways."

"Okaaaaay," I gestured. Chrissie was right: I had to remain strong because Ian could be so persuasive.

But my outlook on our relationship was different now. No longer was I on cloud nine and caught up in the excitement of being with a star athlete. I was maturing and trying to grow up. Even though the ad campaign was courtesy of T-Roc, making my own money was liberating and a natural high. I wasn't getting that same high attending basketball games, eating at fancy restaurants, or shopping. At the end of the day, how many designer bags did I really need? It was becoming a bit repetitive. Plus Ian wasn't the brightest crayon in the box, and I was craving intellect. I felt inadequate with Ian because my opinions didn't matter. I was there strictly to please him when he beckoned. We were no longer connecting. When he met me, I had really just got off the bus. Initially, being exposed to the excitement of the NBA was thrilling. Bragging to my friends that I was dating Ian Addison, superstar point guard for the Detroit Pistons, or seeing him on a commercial and know that I was in his bed the night before would pump my adrenaline. I felt privileged to get on a plane and malinger in a big old mansion, lounging around being glamorous. But, that wasn't my plane, it wasn't my pool, and that damn sure wasn't my mansion. I was a visitor!

"Tyler, I'm ready to go. This sun is burning me like a piece of toast."

"That's cool because my head is killing me." Chrissie and I were gathering our shoes and zipping up our cutoff jean shorts when I heard the chiming of my cell. When I finally located the miniature phone, I didn't recognize the number.

"Hello."

"Tyler?"

"Yes, this is she."

"Hi, it's Sasha."

"Hi, Sasha, how are you?" I was surprised to hear her voice.

"Wonderful, your pictures came out fabulous. I can't wait for you to see the final product. But that wasn't what I was calling about. I'm having a small get-together tonight at my penthouse in the Trump Tower and would love for you to come."

"Party at your penthouse in the Trump Tower," I repeated out loud. Chrissie nodded her head yes again and again.

"Sure, I would love to come. Is it okay to bring my friend Chrissie?"

"Of course. I'll see you around nine." Sasha gave me her apartment number and hung up the phone.

"This is so cool. I've never been in the Trump Tower before, no less a penthouse. Your life is so cool, Tyler. Thanks for bringing me along."

"Chrissie, if it wasn't for you, I probably wouldn't even be going." I had a feeling T-Roc would be there, and I wasn't up to seeing him. T-Roc gave me a powerless sense of being that scared me.

I didn't know what to wear. It was burning up outside, so I wanted something sexy but not too revealing. My lime-green satin halter dress by Miguelina would be perfect. I sleeked my hair back in a bun and wore the strappy Emilio Pucci heels Ian purchased for me a couple of weeks earlier. Not to keep Chrissie waiting, I gave myself the once-over and I was the vision of summer perfection.

"Chrissie, why didn't you come upstairs instead of waiting outside?"

"Because I needed to smoke and I know how much you hate the smell of cigarettes."

"Oh, yeah, you did the right thing." Chrissie knew I was damn near allergic to the cancer sticks.

"Oh, my gosh, Tyler, you are unbelievable in that dress. You bitch," Chrissie said, teasing.

"Look at you, Chrissie! You're putting Carrie Bradshaw to shame in that skin-tight powder-blue one-piece short suit." Chrissie loved to wear microminis and microshorts to show off her toned curvy legs. Besides her bottled-blond perfect ringlets, her legs were her next best asset.

For Chrissie, entering Sasha's penthouse in the Trump Tower was like hitting the lottery. I hadn't seen her this excited since she got the deal of a lifetime on a vintage Chanel dress. When Sasha said a small get-together, I figured ten to fifteen people, maybe twenty at the most. But there were about forty people scattered around, and I assumed there were at least ten more lurking around the corner somewhere. Sasha immediately strolled over, giving kisses on both cheeks and a counterfeit hug.

"Tyler, I'm so glad you could make it, and this must be your friend." She approached Chrissie with the same fake kisses and hugs.

"Come have some champagne, and relax. We also have excellent blow and ecstasy available if you like."

"Champagne would be great." Chrissie and I followed Sasha over to a couch in the corner, where the waiter brought us a bottle of Cristal.

"Cheers, ladies," Sasha chirped before going off to mingle with her other guests.

"Her penthouse is amazing," Chrissie said, gazing around. Sasha's place was no doubt beautiful, but it didn't come close to touching T-Roc's grand town house. I scanned the room, but I didn't see him. I was actually disappointed. After thirty minutes of having three glasses of champagne and dissecting every person at the party with Chrissie, I was having a great time.

"Here comes Sasha again," Chrissie complained.

"Tyler, I have a proof of your ad shots in my bedroom. You should go up and see them, and tell me what you think."

"That's okay; I can wait," I said, not feeling all that comfortable about going in Sasha's bedroom.

"No, you have to. I really want to get your opinion."

"Well, if it's that important to you, I'll go. Chrissie, come with me." As Chrissie was standing up to follow me, Sasha grabbed her hand.

"Actually there's this actor that wants to meet her."

"Really?" Chrissie said with eyes beaming.

"Yes, he's extremely cute too," Sasha added.

"You two go ahead. I'll go look at the pictures and let you know what I think." Sasha gave me directions to her bedroom, and once again I put Sasha's behavior on odd. Her aura rubbed me the wrong way. When I finally made it upstairs to her bedroom, the door was slightly ajar, a dim light was on, and the sounds of Lenny Kravitz were playing. I peeked around the door and gawked at the spectacle I faced. After a full sixty seconds of digesting the scene, I stood in the hallway against the wall to catch my breath. There was no way I saw what I just thought I saw. I closed my eyes, reopened them, and scrutinized the spectacle one more time. The picture didn't change; it was still the same. Brianna and Sierra, the stepsisters from the ad campaign, were having a ménage à trois with my Prince Charming, Ian. Brianna was giving him a professional and fingering Sierra at the same time. My, what skills she had. Ian was sucking on Sierra's breasts, and then he flipped her and started fucking her doggy style, while Sierra munched on Brianna's bush. It was all so sick and disgusting.

I wanted to scream, break shit, and fuck all three of them up, but my mouth wouldn't open. My body was numb and my heart was frozen. What was it with men and ménages anyway? One piece of pussy wasn't enough? They had to indulge in two? Ian hadn't even called to tell me he was in town. Instead he rushed over to Sasha's for some fucking and sucking. I closed the door without interrupting the private party. I drifted downstairs, knowing the tears were coming and wanting to leave this place now. I searched the room for Chrissie, and to my disillusionment she was at the table snorting coke with some soap opera actor. It was time for me to go, and when I turned to leave there was T-Roc.

"Tyler, are you okay? You seem distraught."

"I'm fine. Now please excuse me," I said, walking away.

"Tyler, wait," he said, grabbing my arm. "You don't have to pretend with me. It's obvious something is terribly wrong. I want to help you."

T-Roc seemed so concerned, and honestly I wanted someone to confide in and hopefully numb the pain, if only momentarily. "No, I'm not okay. I feel terrible." I put my head down, not wanting T-Roc to see the tears in my eyes. He gently lifted my chin and gazed in my eyes, full of concern.

"Baby, what's wrong?"

"Can we leave here, please?"

"Sure, where do you want to go?"

"Anywhere but here." There was complete silence until we got inside his Bentley, which was waiting outside.

"Tyler, are you going to tell me what's wrong?"

"I don't want to talk about it. Can we go back to your place? I'm not ready to go home."

"Are you sure that's what you want to do?"

"Positive."

That night T-Roc and I made love as if it were our last night on earth. My emotions were disseminated all over the place, which caused me to grasp on to him for dear life. Making love to T-Roc overshadowed the pain Ian had caused me. With every stroke, T-Roc entered my body and Ian left my mind. We fell asleep in each other's arms, and Ian's once warm and secure embrace was now replaced by his cousin's.

"Rise and shine, pretty girl. I know you must be starved." T-Roc had breakfast for me with fresh flowers on a tray.

"Is it some sort of family trait, cooking breakfast for your women friends?"

"Only the special ones." T-Roc smiled. T-Roc was an excellent cook, and I devoured the French toast and home fries and downed it with a Bellini.

"That was delicious!"

"I see! You didn't even come up for air. So are you going to tell me what happened last night?"

"What's there to tell?"

"Why you were so upset at Sasha's party."

"I wasn't upset; I was just ready to go." In the middle of answering T-Roc's question, my cell phone started ringing. It was Ian. I tossed the phone down, not wanting to see his name or hear his voice.

"That's my cousin calling. You're not going to answer?"

"For what? I'm here with you, aren't I?"

"Talk to me, Tyler," T-Roc demanded as he sat at the edge of the bed looking at me. Observing him in his white terry-cloth robe, I saw he was sincere, and that prompted me to open up to him.

"At Sasha's party I walked in on Ian having a ménage à trois with these two model chicks."

"I'm sorry, Tyler."

"Why are you sorry? Ian wasn't using your dick to fuck those two bitches. Call me naive, but I never thought Ian would cheat on me. I thought he was different from my father." The words seemed to just slip from my mouth.

"Your father?" T-Roc asked, clearly surprised by my admission.

"Yes. My father cheated on my mother, but she continued to stay with him because of his money. She claimed she loved him, but how can you love someone and stay with them when you know they're seeing someone else? Now I'm confusing myself, because in the same breath I'm the first to say that all men have secrets. That belief also came from watching my father's behavior when I was growing up. He seemed so perfect on the outside, but soon it became clear that he was just like every other man. I guess I was making myself believe Ian was unlike my father. But I was wrong." Words were coming out of my mouth faster than I could get ahold of my thoughts. Once again I found myself comparing my relationship with Ian with that of my parents. Was I the product of a dysfunctional home?

"I'm sorry, because I know how devastated you must be."

"I'm over the devastated part. Now I'm just empty. Can you hold me? I just want to feel loved." I fell back asleep in T-Roc's arms, wishing I could erase the revolting images of Ian. He completely ruined my fantasy, and I didn't know if I could ever recapture it. As T-Roc held me closely, I thought maybe all hope wasn't lost.

7

Secrets Exposed

When you have a secret, you know it will more than likely come to light. You may cover it with layers of disguises, but eventually any secret worth keeping will be exposed. All you can try to do is prepare for the ramifications once it's unburied.

Dealing with Ian's betrayal was a lot harder to swallow than I thought it would be. I was spending a lot of time with T-Roc, but it still wasn't enough to suppress the pain. While I was sleeping beside T-Roc one night, I woke up crying because I missed Ian so much. "Tyler, what's wrong?" T-Roc asked.

"I'm okay; I just had a nightmare." I didn't want T-Roc to know I was yearning for his cousin.

"Are you sure?"

"Yes, I'll be fine," I said, wanting it to be true, but not sure if it would be. T-Roc got out of bed and went to the bathroom. He came back a minute later with a bottle in one hand and a cup of water in the other.

"Here, Tyler, take one of these." I looked at the small pill in his hand.

"What is this for?"

"It'll relax you and erase any pain that you're feeling."

"It's not harmful, is it?" I asked, needing some reassurance.

"I would never give you something that was harmful. I use them myself when I need to unwind. Just take it. I promise you'll be happy you did." I put the pill in my mouth and washed it down. Within a few minutes I became light-headed, and a warm sensation ran through my body. T-Roc was right: that pill was exactly what I needed.

"Tyler, what would you like to order?"

"Nothing; I'm not hungry. I'll just have a glass of chardonnay."

"Baby, you need to eat something," T-Roc stated in his "I'm your daddy, so listen to me" way.

"Fine, I'll have a salad. Is that good enough?"

"I see you're in one of your moods. Take this. It always makes you feel better." T-Roc handed me one of the tiny white pills I had been taking for a couple of weeks. I called them dolls, like in Jacqueline Susann's *Valley of the Dolls*. I didn't know what was in them or even the name, but they always relaxed me and kept my mind free of bullshit, which meant not thinking about Ian. I hadn't spoken to him since the peep show, and he still didn't know why I wouldn't accept his calls or see him. I went home only once, to get some of my belongings, and I had been staying with T-Roc ever since. I almost broke down a couple of times and called Ian, but then I would take a doll with a glass of champagne and forget all about him. Sometimes I felt addicted, but hey, it was just dolls. It wasn't like it was coke or something. But I was a tad curious.

"Baby, what's in these dolls?"

"All natural herbs and stuff. It just relaxes your muscles so you can feel good." I knew there was more to it, but I preferred hearing the bullshit. Then if things did go bad, I could pretend I was in the dark and unaware that I was willingly taking narcotics.

"Okay, that's cool." I smiled as if I fed into his garbage.

"Don't forget tomorrow you have to meet with the photographer to take a few shots for the promo ads."

"How can I forget? You remind me every other hour."

"Tyler, baby, don't get smart. You know how I detest when you're loose with the lips." T-Roc was exactly like Ian, but more subtle in his controlling ways. Ian would hit me or scream to make me follow his commands; T-Roc would try to bribe me by using logic. If that didn't work, he'd simply hand me a pill. T-Roc excused himself to go to the restroom, and as I began feeling the effect of the pill, my cell rang. It was Ian. I scanned the room and when no T-Roc was in view, I answered.

"You finally answered my call. Baby, why are you mad at me?" Instead of the bellowing I expected from Ian, he was calm and mild-mannered.

"I can't talk about it right now."

"When can you talk about it? Baby, I'm going crazy without you."

"Ian, don't do this. I have so much to say to you."

"Then say it," Ian pleaded.

"Not now."

"Come to Detroit and be with me for a few weeks. What-ever's wrong, I know we can work it out, Tyler."

After leaving the bathroom, T-Roc had stopped to chat with a gentleman, but now he was on his way back to the table.

"Ian, I have to go, but I'll call you tomorrow so we can discuss everything." As I was hanging up, I heard Ian saying he loved me. Could he love me though? Almost all men cheat. The ones who don't probably can't find anyone to cheat with. But a woman is never supposed to know. My ideal man is one who is so discreet and tactful with his indiscretions that they would never get back to me. Because if you don't know, technically it didn't happen. Unfortunately I had caught Ian red-handed, and there was no escaping that. In my heart he was still my Prince Charm-ing, and we belonged together.

"Who were you talking to?" T-Roc asked before even sitting down.

"Just Chrissie telling me about her problems with that soap opera guy."

"How's that relationship panning out anyway?" T-Roc asked, knowing good and well he couldn't give a flying fuck.

"Excellent—if you call fucking and snorting a relationship."

That night after T-Roc got his oral fix and we made love, I lay in the bed mulling over what I should do about Ian. I wasn't ready to let him go, but I definitely couldn't see Ian and T-Roc at the same time. They were cousins, for goodness' sake. This was too much to deliberate. I'd revisit the issue in the morning.

I dreaded getting up in the morning, especially to meet with a photographer. When I scrutinized myself in the mirror, I was a vision of shit. My energy level was nonexistent, and my morale low. Luckily T-Roc had left two dolls to help me through the day. After throwing on some sweats and a T-shirt, I hopped in a cab and headed to the photographer's studio.

"Hi, Dave. What's it looking like today?"

"In and out; Sasha left two outfits for the promo ad, and she wants one with low-cut jeans, no shirt."

"Cool, I can handle that."

"I got something if you need a boost."

"You're a sweetheart, but I'm good." One sure thing in the fashion business: you can always count on having your choice of anything in the candy store.

Thank goodness T-Roc had left me those dolls, because I was completely drained. When I thought my morning couldn't get any worse, Sasha came prancing in in her typical over-the-top attire. Even at eight o'clock in the morning she was in full glamour-girl mode.

"Hi, Tyler. I've missed you. We haven't spoken since my party."

"Yeah, I've been busy."

"So I hear; with T-Roc, no doubt." She grinned. I cracked a half-smile, hoping Sasha would take the hint that I was in no mood to talk. But of course she didn't.

"You must be awfully special for T-Roc to go through so much trouble for you."

"Trouble . . . What kind of trouble?" She had piqued my interest.

"Well, this is between you and me, because T-Roc might get a little pissed if he knew I was telling you this. But personally I think it's flattering that he went through all the trouble." Sasha took her time getting to the point.

"Well, T-Roc asked me to hook up his cousin Ian with

Brianna and Sierra and have you catch him in the act. Can you believe he went through all that trouble so he could have you? You must be amazing in bed." Sasha stood there telling me this psychotic story with a big smile, revealing her perfect porcelain-veneer teeth.

"I knew you were a despicable bitch," I sneered. Sasha did a catwalk stand as if she didn't hear me, so I repeated myself. "You despicable bitch! How dare you make me a part of T-Roc's and your game? That whole "Go upstairs and look at your pictures" was nothing but a ploy to catch my boyfriend fucking the nitwit twins?"

"Tyler, you're taking this way too seriously. T-Roc obviously cares about you a great deal if he would turn on his cousin just to have you. Instead of being upset, you should be honored that someone of T-Roc's status went through the trouble."

"Sasha, there is no sense reasoning with you, because in your pathetic mind you can't even comprehend how foul this is." I put my sweats and T-shirt back on and started to get outta that hellhole, while Sasha stared at me with confusion written on her face.

"Where are you going, Tyler? You have a shoot to do."

"Sasha, I won't be doing any shoots for you ever again."

"You can't just leave. This is the biggest break of your life. You will never get another chance like this."

"Sasha, dear, your *never* and my *never* are two different things. You're right; I hope I never get a break like this again. It comes with too high a price." As I stormed out of the building, I heard Dave calling for me to come back. The poor guy had no idea what was going on. Boiling over inside, I reached in my bag to get my Dasani water and the last doll. T-Roc was playing God with my life, and that was unacceptable.

I arrived at T-Roc's office demanding to see him immediately. When his assistant said he was in a meeting, I just barged in.

"I need to talk to you—now."

"I'm in a meeting, Tyler. Can you wait for a few minutes?"

"No, I can't." With extreme annoyance T-Roc asked the two men and one woman to step out for a moment. After he closed the door, fire was in his eyes, but it was no match for the fire that was brewing inside me.

"You look like shit. Why aren't you at the photo shoot?"

"Oh, I guess you haven't spoken to Sasha."

"Sasha? She actually did call a couple of times, but I told my secretary I would have to call her back. Why, is there a problem with Sasha?" T-Roc was fishing, and I was more than happy to deliver the bait.

"She told me everything. That bitch had the audacity to think it was somehow cute the way you all set me up."

"Tyler, what are you talking about?"

"Don't patronize me. You planned for me to catch Ian in bed with those women. How dare you play God with my life?"

"You don't need Ian; he will never appreciate you. My cousin is just an overgrown kid. You deserve so much more than that, Tyler."

"I deserve what? Someone like you?"

"Yes, I can make you happy. I will provide the success you crave so badly. Ian will never give you that. He'll want you stuck in the house barefoot and pregnant. You have so much more to offer."

"I hate you. I hate you so much. You stomped all over my heart just so you could win and tear Ian and me apart."

"Tyler, you don't love Ian. He is a safe and sure thing for you. There is so much more out there. That's all I wanted to show you. I see so much of myself in you, Tyler, and I want to expose you to the world. Is that so wrong?"

"T-Roc, you don't own me. I'm my own person and make my own decisions. I don't want to be a part of the life you are creating for me."

"So what are you going to do? Go back to Ian? It will never work. He isn't the man for you, Tyler."

"Neither are you."

"You say that now, but I guarantee you'll be back. I'm the only person who will ever understand you and accept you for who you are."

I left T-Roc's office feeling more confused than when I arrived. Although I hated T-Roc, he had an undeniable hold on me. He seemed to know every strength and weakness I had and how to play on it. Because of that, it made it that much harder to free myself emotionally from him. I opted to walk home instead of taking a cab, so I could use the time to reflect. Once I reached my apartment, the first thing I did was take a long hot shower. That had now become a ritual when I needed to wash away my pain. I put on Sade, had a glass of wine, and lay on the couch contemplating what I should do next. Over the music I heard what seemed to be a slight knock at the door. I took my phone off the hook so as not to be disturbed, and hoped it wasn't T-Roc at my door. I peeped through the hole and to my pleasant but shocked surprise it was Ian. As soon as I opened the door, Ian wrapped his arms around my waist and lifted me off the floor.

"What are you doing here?"

"I figured if I kept waiting for you to come to Detroit, it would never happen." As Ian put me down, he zoomed in to kiss me. I turned my face away because I hadn't forgotten why I stayed away in the first place.

"Baby, you still mad at me? What's got you so vexed?" Ian had no idea that I had witnessed his threesome, and after my conversation with T-Roc I almost wanted to forget that it had ever happened. But I couldn't. No matter what role T-Roc played, nobody forced Ian to fuck those two chicks.

"Ian, a few weeks ago I went to a party and saw you dickin' down two bitches," I said point-blank.

"What?" Ian was obviously stunned.

"You heard me. Does Sasha McIntire ring a bell? You were at her penthouse in the Trump Tower, and you were fucking two model chicks named Brianna and Sierra."

"Tyler, I—"

"Don't bother trying to deny it, because I saw it with my own eyes."

"Baby, I'm so sorry. I know you must hate me." Ian shook his head, still trying to digest what I had told him. "Baby, I'll do anything to make it up to you. It was a mistake. I met them hos at T-Roc's place. We were all heading to that chick Sasha's party, and they hit me off with an E pill. That shit had me so open that by the time we got in that homegirl's crib, they were all over me and I couldn't resist. Baby, I had no idea you were going to be there. How do you know those chicks anyway?"

"The ad campaign I did was for Sasha's line; those girls are in the ad with me."

"What? Yo, I had no idea you even knew them."

"Ian, none of that matters. The point is, I can't trust you. If you did it with them, then you're probably doing it with mad other bitches."

"Baby, I swear I'm not. I was so out of it that night. My mind wasn't working clearly. I wasn't myself. Tyler, please don't let some worthless tricks ruin what we have. We belong together;

you know that." Ian was now holding me, and he was wearing the cologne that I loved. I missed how safe I felt in his arms.

"Ian, will you promise never to hurt me again? That pain was too overwhelming; I couldn't go through that all over again." Ian stroked my hair and kissed my forehead in that special "Baby, I love you way" that I craved more than anything.

"Tyler, I promise I will never hurt you that way again. You're my baby; I never want to cause you pain."

"You mean that?" I knew I was going to give my relationship with Ian another chance and decided that I was completely cutting off T-Roc. Going back and forth between them was unhealthy. Part of me wanted to be rid of both of them and start from scratch, but I loved Ian. I truly believed that in my heart.

"I put that on my life. Baby, why don't you come to Detroit and live with me? I know you love me, and I want to be with you all the time. There is nothing in New York for you; your life is with me."

"I don't know, Ian. That's such a big step."

"I tell you what; come for a few weeks and see how you like it. But I guarantee you I will make you so happy, you'll beg me to stay."

"You're that sure of yourself?"

"Positive." Before I could say another word, Ian silenced me with a kiss. He scooped me up, leading us to my bedroom. He slipped off my bathrobe as I wrapped my legs around his back. I rocked back and forth, feeling his arousal through his jeans. After a flurry of loving kisses Ian slid out of his clothes and laid me down on the bed. He lightly sprinkled kisses until my entire body shivered. Then he wrapped my legs around his shoulders, and his tongue entered me. It felt so good that my hands tightly gripped the bedsheets, but I couldn't choke back my moans, yelps, or squeals.

"Baby, I want you inside of me," I said breathlessly.

"Tyler," he said in a serious voice. "Do you love me? Do you want to be with me for the rest of your life?"

"Yes, I do; I love you so much."

"Then let's make a baby. Will you do that for me?"

"Yes, whatever you want. Just please make love to me right now." With that Ian entered me, and I buried my face in his neck to get a faint smell of his cologne. With every thrust I felt our connection coming back to life. Maybe his home was where I belonged.

When I woke up in the morning and Ian's arms were still wrapped around my body, I knew this was where I belonged. Watching him sleep, I examined every tattoo and every defining muscle and saw how beautiful his caramel-colored skin was. I didn't care what T-Roc said. Ian and I were meant to be together.

"Baby, how long you been up?" Ian asked, still half-asleep.

"Not that long."

"What time is it? I have to get back to Detroit today. You're coming with me, right?"

"No doubt; it's ten fifteen."

"I'ma stop at the hotel, pick up my bag, and then come get you. Can you be ready by two?"

"Definitely. Give me a kiss good-bye."

"I'll see you in a few." Ian threw on his clothes and headed out the door. Today was starting off to be a good day. Having Ian back once again made me feel complete. On my way to the kitchen I noticed my phone was still off the hook. No sooner had I put it back on the receiver than it started ringing from a private caller.

"Hello."

"You turned off your cell and had your phone off the hook all night. Are you avoiding me?"

"That's a stupid question, especially since you know the answer to it."

"I understand that you're angry with me, but don't go back to Ian. Take some time for yourself and figure things out."

"It's too late. Ian and I are back together, and I would appreciate it if you stay out of our relationship."

"When did you have time to reconcile with Ian?"

"He flew in from Detroit and came over last night. We talked about everything except you. Which is exactly how I want to keep it. I'm going back to Detroit with him today, and I don't want to speak to you anymore, T-Roc."

"You think you can erase me from your life that easily? Tyler, I control your mind more than you know. You're making a mistake going back to Ian, but like you said, it's your mistake to make. When you need someone to help you pick up the pieces, call me."

There was silence on the phone, and I realized T-Roc had hung up. What did he want from me? I knew he wasn't in love with me, but he was determined to own my mind. Whatever it was, I prayed that he would let it go so Ian and I could be happy together.

"Baby, I should call my doctor and have him stop by. You've been sick for a week straight."

"I'll be fine. I think I have a virus. It's no big deal."

"Tyler, if you're not better in a couple of days, my doctor is coming to see you. I'm serious."

"Ian, your concern is so cute. If I'm not better in a couple of days, we'll call your doctor."

"I'm heading out to get something to eat with TJ; you want me to bring you something back?"

"No, I'm good," I replied. Ian kissed me on the forehead and walked out of the bedroom. I pulled the covers over my face, racking my brain trying to figure out how I was going to get myself out of this mess. I'd been in Detroit for two and a half weeks, sick. First, I assumed it was because my period was about to start. But then I backtracked and realized I was three weeks late. I began rationalizing out loud. "There is no doubt in my mind that I'm pregnant, but I have no idea who the father is. I didn't use protection with T-Roc or Ian. If Ian discovers I'm pregnant, he will assume it's his baby and want me to have it, unaware that it might be his cousin's. I have no choice but to terminate this pregnancy immediately. But before I drive myself crazy, I need to be sure."

I dreaded getting out of the bed, but I had to go buy a home pregnancy test before Ian came back. As I drove to the store, a cloud of depression fell over me. When I was pregnant with Patrick's baby, I knew I didn't want his child. But the circumstances were different this time. If part of Ian was growing inside of me, then I would want to hold on to that. But there was no way I could take the chance that this baby was T-Roc's. Not only would it destroy Ian, but T-Roc would probably end up destroying me. I ran into the store, purchased a pregnancy test, and sped home. When I pulled up, I was relieved not to see Ian's car, but when I took out my keys to open the front door, to my dismay there he stood.

"Oh, my goodness, you scared me. What are you doing here? I didn't see your car out front." My voice was shaky, and I hoped Ian didn't sense my nervousness.

"TJ is running an errand for me, and I let him hold my car. Where are you coming from and what's in the bag?" Ian asked as he reached for it. Before I could yank it away from him, he was already opening it up.

"You think you're pregnant?" Ian asked, his voice mixed with shock and excitement.

"I'm not sure."

"But you must think there's a chance. Maybe that's why you've been so sick. Tyler, this would be incredible."

"Baby, don't get keyed up yet, because it could very well be a false alarm."

"Well, damn, no sense standing down here discussing it; let's go see."

Walking up the stairs to the bathroom seemed to be the longest walk of my life. I took each step like it was my last. By the time I reached the bedroom, Ian had the box open and the test out. At first I considered dipping the stick in some water so the test would come back negative, but Ian messed that up because he wanted to see the process from start to finish. He actually held the cup when I urinated. He kept saying, "I know you're carrying my son; I know that's my son in there."

It was too much to stomach. Ian set his stopwatch, and when the buzzer went off, with a gleeful smile he said, "It's time." When he came out of the bathroom, lifted me up, and wrapped his whole mouth around me to the point I thought I was going to choke, I knew the test was positive.

"Tyler, you've made me the happiest man on earth. I have everything now: a beautiful woman and a beautiful child growing inside you. We have to get married. Baby, I'm serious. Let's go pick out the biggest rock ever."

"Ian, calm down. You're moving way too fast."

"Are you kidding me? I have to call my moms and pops and let them know they're going to be grandparents, and they're getting a new daughter. Tyler, I love you so much; I can't explain how happy you've made me." Ian gave me one last kiss before he picked up his cordless and made calls to share the news with his family and friends. I wanted to pull the emergency brake, but this car was on cruise control and driving itself.

I would have given anything for a doll, but I was carrying a baby inside of me, one that it seemed I would be having. I opted for a glass of juice. I was walking toward the stairs and could hear Ian yelling but couldn't make out what he was saying. Then I heard a loud crash. As I ran closer to the top of the stairs, Ian was running up them, all the color drained from his face. Sweat was trickling down, and his body was trembling.

"Baby, what's wrong? Is everything okay?"

Ian moved up the stairs closer to me, and his eyes were stinging. "I just got off the phone with T-Roc. You were fucking my cousin? Tyler, tell me that bastard is lying! Tell me, damnit!"

"Wait, baby, wait, wait . . . please wait." I was breathing so hard, I couldn't hear anything.

"He said that baby growing inside you could be his. Tyler, please tell me there is no chance that our baby could be T-Roc's . . . Tyler, why aren't you saying what I need to hear?" Ian and I were now face-to-face, and I could clearly see the tear coming from his eye.

"Ian, I can explain." But there would be no explaining. In what seemed like a split second I was free-falling down the stairs. In one quick shot Ian lifted his right arm and gave a blow that knocked me unconscious as I hit the floor.

8

Finding Love

My love life was in shambles, and between Ian and T-Roc I believed I was walking around with a scarlet letter emblazoned across my chest. I convinced myself that I wasn't worthy of love and would never truly experience it. But then again, being the optimistic person I am, I told myself that when one door closes in love, another is sure to open.

"Tyler, it's so good to see you out and about again. I was beginning to worry that you would never come out of your apartment," Chrissie said.

"Yeah, well there was nothing out here I wanted to see. My life is basically empty. Ian hates me and I hate myself." It had been over six months since I'd come out of the house looking halfway decent. After my tragic encounter with Ian, I went into mourning, and I always left the house looking like shit. It was now the year 2000, and half of the new year already seemed to have passed me by.

"How can you care what Ian thinks? He pushed you down the stairs and caused you to lose your baby. You should've brought him up on criminal charges."

"Chrissie, what do you expect? His own cousin told him the baby could be his. Talk about being devastated; I'm surprised he didn't kill me."

"Hello? That was his intention. You just so happened to live. Or maybe he wanted to guarantee that your baby never saw the light of day because he couldn't handle it if it turned out to be T-Roc's. Whatever the reason, he is fucking crazy, and you should be grateful he is out of your life."

"Maybe, but I don't feel that way. I'm lost and I don't know what to do to find my way."

As Chrissie lectured me about getting over Ian while we ate lunch at Da Silvano, an unassuming gentleman walked passed me, made eye contact, and turned his head to smile. Here was another creep undoubtedly trying to get in my pants. I didn't take it seriously. After all, it was New York City, and seeing men flirt with just about everything that had a pulse was the norm. Not thinking too much of the crafty glance, I continued chatting with Chrissie and drinking my Kir Royale.

About ten minutes later the waiter sat the flirtatious guy and his friends right behind me. The one sitting closest to me sparked up some half-assed conversation.

"Hi, sexy. Would you and your girlfriend like a drink?"

"You mean besides the one that is already in my mouth?"

"Excuse me, miss, I was just offering you and your girlfriend a drink."

"No, thank you, we're fine."

"Yeah, you definitely that, so can I buy you a drink or what?" After responding sarcastically to his question, I recognized that he was some up-and-coming would-be rapper. At this point anybody remotely in the music industry was a major turnoff. I was hoping the would-be rapper picked up on my cynicism.

A few minutes later he got up, and I heard someone else say, "That's an interesting tattoo; what does it mean?" I was wearing low-rider jeans, so the Japanese symbol on my lower back was impossible to miss. I turned around and studied the man who made the comment; it was the unassuming gentleman. His eyes were enthralling, and he somehow maneuvered a seat at the table with Chrissie and me.

"So what does the tattoo mean?" the boyishly handsome gentleman asked.

"Freedom."

"Freedom . . . that's interesting. Who are you trying to be free from?"

"Who said I was trying to be free from somebody?"

"Just a thought. So . . . what's your name?"

"Tyler, and this is Chrissie." Chrissie gave a slight wave to show she was annoyed this man was interrupting our lunch. Normally I would be giving the wave too, but something about his subtle cool demeanor was engrossing.

"I'm Brian. I would love to call you, Tyler."

"I'd like that too," I responded. Chrissie was burning a hole through my sweater with her intense glare. I wrote my number on a napkin and handed it to Brian.

I was sitting on my red canvas couch engrossed in a juicy Jackie Collins book when the phone rang.

"Hi, it's Brian. I don't know if you remember, but I met you yesterday at Da Silvano."

"I remember you, silly."

"Oh, I was just checking. I don't know how many guys you know with the name Brian," he laughed. I thought it was cute.

We ended up having a meeting of the minds for hours. He seemed to be everything that I needed in order to put my guard down with a man. Nothing about him was threatening, and that was refreshing. His spirit was unlike that of any other man I had ever met.

The next day Brian and I found ourselves absorbed in another two hours of nonstop chatting. With the conversation never seeming to end, we decided on no more phone talk. We needed up-close-and-personal talk. As I was waiting in front of my apartment building, I kept trying to remember what he looked like because he had on a hat when we first met. I was pleasantly surprised when I opened the car door and saw the cinnamon-complexioned guy with the smooth bald head. He greeted me with a megawatt smile with a dimple on his right cheek. His body frame was small but with strong muscle definition.

Mary J. Blige was playing on the radio, and I was humming along as he drove down Broadway. "Are you a singer?" Brian asked.

"No, why?"

"I'm always looking for talent; I'm a music producer." As the walls seemed to be closing in on me, I realized that throughout the hours of conversation not once did we discuss his profession. I didn't ask and he didn't volunteer the information. The last person I wanted to get involved with was another industry cat. It seemed that when you dated one guy in the music industry, there was a domino effect. Maybe he was new to the industry and wasn't turned out yet. His ride was fly, but niggas can buy that after they sell their first track, which most do.

"So you're a music producer? Who have you worked with?"

"Jay-Z, Jennifer Lopez, Mary J. Blige, Nas," and the list went on and on. He definitely wasn't new to this. There was only one music producer named Brian that I'd heard of, and I was hoping he wasn't him. But I had to ask.

"Are you Brian McCall?"

"Yep, you've heard of me?" he said with a big smile.

"Who hasn't heard of you? You're one of the biggest hip-hop producers in the business. Your beats are classics."

"I'm flattered. Are you in the music business?"

"Hell, no!"

"Why you say it like that?" Brian asked with a frown.

"Actually if I knew you were in the music industry, I would've run in the opposite direction. But then again I should've known. This is New York, you're driving a hundred-thousand-dollar car, and you're young and black. I haven't seen you on the big screen or in any sneaker ads, so you're not an actor or an athlete. What else can you do but be in the music business? You don't really strike me as a pharmaceutical dealer."

"That's a little cynical, wouldn't you say?"

"Call it what you like," I said, fidgeting.

"Does that mean you won't go inside with me for a minute?" I glanced out the window. We were on West Fifty-fourth Street parked in front of the Hit Factory.

"Oh, no thanks, I'll wait in the car for you."

"What's the problem? Who is it you don't want to see?"

"Brian, go handle what you have to do. We'll talk when you get back." He shut the door, a bit put off by my attitude. Between

T-Roc and his flunkies, and Mark and his flunkies, I was bound to run into somebody I knew at the studio. I wanted to avoid an encounter at all costs.

Brian was gone about fifteen minutes, but he came back with the same attitude he left with. He didn't say two words to me until we were sitting down in the American Park restaurant at Battery Park.

"Talk to me, Tyler. Tell me, what ghosts are haunting you?"

"Excuse me?" Brian's question threw my mind in a tailspin.

"For someone so young, you are so intense. What has your mind so damaged?"

"I seem damaged to you?"

"To be quite honest? Hell, yeah—but I want to help you."

"Help me? I'm beyond help."

"Everyone can be helped, Tyler, but you can't be afraid to let people in who want to help."

I spent the rest of the evening divulging all my skeletons to Brian. My disastrous relationships with Ian and T-Roc, my momentary bout as a rapper under the guidance of shady Mark, and even the nightmare I have every night of Trey blowing his brains out. His face truly did haunt me. Eventually I even confessed how my lies destroyed my relationship with Patrick.

Brian sat and listened without interrupting me once. He was so sweet and attentive. With other industry cats I dealt with, it was all about them. Their attention came with strings attached. Brian seemed to genuinely care about the demons I was fighting. He was extremely humble and down to earth, especially for a producer of his status. Not once did he make a move on me. He never so much as tried to kiss me, and unlike Ian, Brian was intellectually stimulating. The combination of his mind and the physical attraction drew me in.

When we pulled up to my apartment, I couldn't hold back. "Brian, will you give me a kiss good night?" I asked, wondering if I sounded as innocent as I felt. Brian leaned toward me, and when his lips and tongue touched mine the chemistry was undeniable. I got butterflies in my stomach and that tingling feeling. It was amazing.

That night my mind was filled with all sorts of thoughts. I kept tossing and turning, thinking maybe he wasn't any good in bed because he wasn't putting the moves on me. I wondered if he was lacking in the area where it counted. I decided to nip my thoughts in the bud. I needed to find out what was going on down there. If he was lacking, there was nothing I could do for him besides be his new best friend.

In my opinion if two people aren't sexually compatible, the relationship is dead before it has even started. Several elements go into making a relationship work, but at the end of the day when they are having problems like every relationship does, then sex is important. If the two don't have enough passion and lust to make love and forget their differences for just a moment, then how are they ever going to get through any real storms? I had to know if Brian and I were compatible sexually, because I was falling for him.

"It's beautiful out here tonight," I said as Brian and I took a nighttime stroll through Central Park. We were laughing and holding hands when I suggested, "Why not play a game of truth-or-dare?"

"Truth-or-dare . . . you're taking it way back to junior high school."

"We can play the adult version."

"Which is?"

"Truth-or-dare and take off your clothes."

"We can skip all that. How 'bout I just dare you to strip down right now?" I glanced around the park and not a soul was in sight. I went behind a tree and reappeared in my midnight-blue bra and panties. Brian scanned me up and down and said, "That's not naked; you basically have on a bikini."

"Really?" with that, I unclipped my bra and slid out of my panties. The whole episode was turning me on.

"That's more like it," Brian said with greed in his eyes. Although I could see how much he wanted me, I respected the way he took his time crossing my path. His hands were touching my skin and gently exploring my body. He obviously had never done any sort of manual labor, because his hands were as soft as a baby's. His touch was sending chills down my spine. His lips melted on my neck, and the nighttime summer breeze on my naked body escalated my arousal. The kisses became more and more passionate, and I wanted to be with him right under the tree. I rubbed down his pants for a spot check, but with his big baggy jeans it was impossible to get a read. I decided to take my chances. This had to happen tonight.

Between kisses and heavy panting I managed to say, "Brian, I want you now; I can't wait."

"Right here under the tree? Tyler, there is nothing but dirt and grass here."

"Well, let's go back to my place." I threw my clothes on, and we headed to his car. Once inside we could barely keep our hands off one another. I was so anxious and overcome with desire that I demanded he pull over.

"You want me to pull over?" Brian asked in disbelief.

"Yes, please," I said in an I-want-you-so-bad tone. Realizing how serious I was, he looked for a quiet place to pull over.

I stripped off my clothes as Brian parked the car. Luckily he was pushing a Range, so there was plenty of room to make it happen. Once he was in the backseat, the fervent kisses back and forth were in full swing. My curiosity was driving me wild. For a minute I thought about LL Cool J's song "Back Seat (of My Jeep)." When I watched the video, I imagined playing a part in one of the scenes, and now the experience was happening to me.

I eagerly undressed Brian, starting with his pants. He stepped in and took off his boxers. I ogled his better half for the first time. Wow, he definitely had nothing to be ashamed of, and he wasn't holding back out of embarrassment. As a matter of fact he was on point; I couldn't have created a more perfect size. I wanted him inside me, and when he entered we became one.

During our ride home Brian and I continued our fervent kisses, and while he ran his fingers through my hair, he grabbed it tightly. He turned my face toward his so we were eye-to-eye, and he asked, "Why are you trying to make me love you?" His mood surrounding the question was eerie yet powerful.

"Because I need you to love me," I said intensely. You know me; I love intense because intensity spells drama and drama spells stimulation—everything I crave in a relationship.

After our night of passion we were inseparable. Even though we loved to talk and laugh at one another, we loved being in the bed even more; our favorite pastime bonded us.

In the beginning of our relationship I don't want to call what we did making love because it was more like obsessive sex. Our lust for one another absorbed our whole minds. We would do it anywhere at anytime. Brian couldn't get enough of my insatiable appetite for sex. It was never enough for me, and I only craved it from him.

"Big Pimpin'" by Jay-Z was blaring from my CD player, and I danced in front of the full-length mirror like I was the star of his video. While pretending to be Jigga, I was getting dressed to go to the movies with Brian. When my phone rang, I didn't bother to look at caller ID because I knew it was him telling me to hurry up. "Brian, I'm almost ready."

"Who's Brian?" a serious voice asked, sounding exactly like Ian. The last time I'd heard his voice was when he came to see me at the Ritz-Carlton in Dearborn. After Ian knocked me unconscious, he had TJ take me to the emergency room. Of course, TJ told the nurses and doctor I'd had an accident, and when I finally woke up I backed his story. Although the nurses took it upon themselves to call the police because of the bruise on my face, I stuck to my story that the lights were off and I hit my head on the stairwell and tripped and fell. The officers didn't seem convinced, but they couldn't prove otherwise. Of course the doctor informed me I had lost the baby, which wasn't a big surprise. I stayed in the hospital for a couple of days, and when I checked out, TJ picked me up.

TJ drove me to the hotel, gave me a room key, and told me Ian would come see me later. When Ian arrived he could barely make eye contact with me. It was like going through my ordeal with Patrick all over again, but this time I didn't kill the baby, Ian did. Out came that same envelope. This time there was no cash but a check.

"Take this," Ian said as he handed me the envelope.

"What is this? I don't want your money, Ian." When I spoke

those words, I meant it. "If this is hush money, you can take it back. I'll never tell the police or tabloids what really happened," I said solemnly. I considered myself responsible for Ian's actions. No way would I bring him further humiliation by letting the world know he caused me to have a miscarriage because I didn't know if he or his cousin was the father.

"No, it isn't hush money. I know you would never do that."

"Then what is it for?"

"Because I can't be with you anymore, Tyler; it would hurt too much. But the baby you were carrying could've been mine, and I was the cause of its death. That will fuck with me for the rest of my life."

"This money isn't going to change that."

"Maybe not, but I'm hoping it will ease my conscience. The rent for your apartment is paid up for the rest of the year. This money will hold you over until you decide what you want to do."

"I don't want it. This is guilt money, and the only one who should feel guilty is me. Ian, I'm so sorry, but you have to believe that I love you and I never wanted to be with T-Roc. After I caught you with those girls, my heart was broken and I felt alone. T-Roc was there to console me, although I eventually found out he set it up to work out that way. If you could only forgive me, I know we can make this work." I walked toward Ian and put my arms out to hold and feel his embrace, but he motioned for me to stop.

"Don't." Ian's voice quavered. "I don't know what will happen in the future, but right now there's no way I can be with you, Tyler. The whole T-Roc situation is fucked up, but it doesn't change the fact that you let my cousin inside what I thought belonged to me. I don't know if I'll ever get over that, but I do ask one thing of you."

"What's that?"

"Under no circumstances do I want you to go back to my cousin. This money should hold you over for a while, and if you do need something, call me. Don't call him. If you ever truly gave a fuck about me, then do what I ask."

"I will do that. I promise I will never have anything to do with T-Roc again." Ian turned around and walked out the door. I opened the envelope, and there was a one-way plane ticket to New York and a check for two hundred and fifty thousand dollars. Once again Ian was using his money to control my life, even if he wasn't going to be in it. For a minute I considered how I could chill with this type of money and not worry financially, but then this was blood money. This check was a substitution for the unborn child Ian took away from me. I ripped the check into tiny pieces and flushed them down the toilet. That was the only way I could free myself from the guilt and pain of my sins. Now here it was six months later and Ian was on the phone, questioning me as if he had never left my life.

"Brian is a friend of mine," I answered, as if it was my duty.

"Your friend, huh?"

"Yeah."

"I was checking up on you because you never cashed the check. Are you maintaining financially, or is your friend handling that for you?"

"I'm okay. I've been working a part-time job and going to school."

"Why didn't you cash the check, Tyler?"

"I didn't want your money, that's all, and honestly I don't want to discuss it any further."

"Well, can we discuss us?" Ian said seriously.

"What about us?"

"Tyler, I was beyond pissed with you a few months ago, but every day when I wake up and before I go to sleep at night, you're all I think about. I want to give us another try. I still love you." Ian's words were bittersweet. I questioned whether Ian ever loved me, but it didn't matter because I now loved someone else. Brian had become so important to me. The first few weeks of us talking for hours and hours, I shared my private thoughts and experiences with him—things I had never shared with anyone. When we made love for the first time, we connected emotionally and physically and it was perfect. We clicked, and Brian was definitely somebody I wanted to share my life with.

"Ian, I yearned to hear those words from you again, but it's too late. The friend I spoke of is more than that. I love him. He understands me and he loves me too."

"Tyler, you couldn't share the same love with him that we have."

"I don't even know if what we shared was love. Maybe we fulfilled a void in each other's lives—your need to control and my need to be controlled."

"No matter what you think, I do love you, and I want you back. If you believe this other guy can make you happy, then I won't try to come between that. But, Tyler, if you ever need me, call me."

I stared at the phone after Ian hung up. He was supposed to be my Prince Charming, but he wasn't after all.

"Yo, Eddie Murphy was so funny back then," I giggled, as Brian and I sat on my couch watching *Raw*.

"Yeah, he was a funny cat. Now he's white-bread all-American. He's definitely not the same Eddie Murphy who came in this game starving and had us crying on *Saturday Night Live*."

"You ain't never lied," I hollered, agreeing with Brian.

"Losing that hunger is what makes you lose your edge. You have to always go at something like it's your first and could be your last."

"Is that how you should proceed in relationships too?"

"Yes, if you believe you've found the one you want to spend the rest of your life with. Just like I think you might be the one, so I'm keeping you under my thumb."

"Oh, that's why we spend so much time together? You want to make sure no one swoops me up."

"Something like that, but to be on the safe side I have an idea. . . . My lease is about to be up and your lease is about to be up; how about we get a crib together?"

"I don't know, Brian."

"What's with all the hesitation? You don't want to live with me?"

"We're having so much fun right now, and having a place of my own keeps the relationship sexy and unpredictable. We have plenty of time to move in with each other." I did love Brian but I wasn't in love, and living together would just complicate things. I was also feeling that whole Destiny's Child "Independent Women" theme.

"I think that's a mistake, but if that's how you want it, then so be it." Brian's statement and delivery were a tad hostile, but I dismissed it and we continued to watch *Raw*.

"I can't believe you managed to meet me for lunch. Every since you started dating Brian, you never have time for me."

"I'm sorry, Chrissie, but you know I love ya, baby." We were having a late lunch at our favorite spot, Da Silvano.

"Whatever . . . I hope you're not here to break news of a baby and horse-and-carriage thing."

"No, not yet. Brian actually suggested we move in together, but I think it's too soon. But I do have to move. My lease is about to expire, and I definitely can't afford the rent."

"Why not ask Brian?"

"Brian is different from the other guys I've dated. I want to show him that I can be independent and stand on my own two feet. If I can do that, then I can earn his respect."

"Oh, brother . . . you've really fallen hard for this guy. I hope he's worth it, Tyler, because you're about to do a lot of struggling."

"Tell me about it. I don't want a roommate, and I can't possibly afford a place in Manhattan, so I think I'm going to have to take it to the boroughs."

"What! You can't be serious."

"I have no choice."

"No. You do have a choice. You could always call Ian."

"I'm not going to do that. I'm committed to Brian. And I was considering moving to Brooklyn. That's where he's from."

"Now you wanna be one of Brooklyn's finest. Where is my friend Tyler? What has happened to her? Excuse me for a minute; I have to go to the ladies' room." As Chrissie walked off, I thought about what she was saying. My lifestyle would change a lot; but I wanted a real relationship, not one that was dictated by money. It was important for Brian to understand that I wanted him for him and not because of who he was or how much money he had. This was my way of doing that.

When Chrissie sat down, I noticed white powder under her nose. "You're not still fucking with that shit?"

"I had stopped—" Chrissie took a deep breath "—but after your confession of this new nightmarish life, I had to medicate myself."

"I'm serious, Chrissie; you need to leave that crap alone."

"It's not that big a deal. I'm a social user. What about you and those pills you used to take?"

"I'm through with all that. Ever since I've been with Brian, I haven't felt any sort of depression. My dolls are a thing of the past," I assured her.

A friend of Ella's knew a couple who lived in the Park Slope area of Brooklyn. They'd had a baby and needed a bigger place, so they were subletting their apartment. Brian went with me to take a look at the place and make sure it was okay. The neighborhood had tree-lined sidewalks, but the flat was a walk-up, and it was smaller than my apartment in the city. Let's just say I wasn't excited about moving in, because it definitely wasn't Sixty-sixth Street and Central Park West. But the price was in my range, and the unit was available. Brian gave his stamp of approval, so it was a go. As Chrissie put it, I began the process of being one of Brooklyn's finest. Some people would have considered it a nice apartment, but I was from Georgia, where I'd always lived in beautiful homes in pretty neighborhoods. I had been struggling in the city, and now here I was in Brooklyn. I definitely wasn't feeling pretty in pink.

After settling me into my new place, Brian had to go to Miami to work with Busta Rhymes for a few weeks. He asked me to come, and though school and work were hectic, I somehow managed to get a few days off. I looked forward to spending time with Brian in a different place and getting some sun. After taking the trip to Miami, though, I had to reevaluate if Brian was really "the one." There are certain traits I believe a man should have, and Brian hadn't developed them yet.

When I arrived in Miami, Brian was at the gate waiting. I had an obviously nasty attitude, so he asked, "What's up? What's wrong?"

"Brian, why did you make me fly coach?"

"Excuse me?" Brian snorted as if he didn't hear me correctly.

"I'm a little—no, a lot—bothered that you had me fly coach instead of first class."

"Come on, let's go." Brian said, ignoring my complaint.

I thought Brian had been in the game long enough that he could afford to put me in a first-class seat. So I was furious that I had had to fly coach. A limousine was waiting for us outside, which added to my fury.

"You have a limousine waiting for us, so you could have put me in first class. Don't half-ass it." I could tell by the way Brian was looking at me he thought I was an obnoxious snob. I wasn't a snob, but when you like something you just like it.

When we arrived on Ocean Drive, my eyes immediately became fixated on the tall, elegant, art deco hotel, the Tides. I was thrilled when I realized we were staying there. When we got to the hotel room and Brian opened the door, I could see the interior was luxurious and spacious. The oceanfront room was decorated in soft tones of beige, white, taupe, and sand. The serenity of the room put me in a romantic mood, and I was no longer agitated with Brian.

We were spending time luxuriating on the beach and dining at the best restaurants, but eventually I became a little annoyed. We weren't doing any shopping! I was sitting in the studio with Brian all night, and I became bored with the whole trip. The only purchase Brian made was some Rollerblades for himself. I thought, Okay, I'm in Miami and you fly me here in coach, and we're not going shopping? This is not looking good.

My biggest pet peeve was a cheap man. Every man I had dated knew that women love gifts. Believing a man should want to pamper his woman with tokens of affection goes back to when I was a little girl, when my real daddy would take Ella and me shopping and would include my friends because he loved to see the smile it would bring to our faces. I had little room for compromise in that belief. But right before it was about to be curtain time, Brian played his trump card.

On the third night in the Tides I can honestly say that I made love for the very first time. Coming back from a late dinner I was feeling exhausted. I took a long hot shower to relax myself and get ready for bed. After drying off and lathering my body with lotion, I felt the bed was calling for me. Brian was already in bed watching a movie. The sky was clear and the moonlight and stars were shining through the windows. It was the type of night when fools fall in love.

The crisp sheets felt so good under my naked warm body. Brian turned off the TV, and the moment I closed my eyes his hands gently spread my legs apart and his warm tongue entered me. Brian was licking me with elegant strokes. My past boyfriends had tried to gratify me this way, but none made me fall into an abyss of pleasure as Brian had.

"Baby, nobody has ever made me feel this way. I don't want you to ever stop." I said, in heavenly bliss. Brian's oral pleasuring gave me a full-flush orgasm. I could feel the powerful gushing of come leave my body. Without so much as a pause, Brian kissed my stomach and tickled his tongue in my belly button. He did it just long enough to give me the right effect. With his hands he caressed my breasts, and I just luxuriated with my eyes still closed, not wanting this to end. As though he was reading my mind, his hardness entered me at the exact moment my body was calling for him. I wrapped my legs around his neck so he could go as deep as possible. His strong arms were pressing down on the bed holding me up as I was clinching his back, and my breasts were pressed against his chest.

I never wanted to let Brian go. I couldn't hold him tight enough. With every stroke, a part of my soul became his, until finally it happened. This explosion of ecstasy overcame my body again. For the first time in my life, I was having my second orgasm in less than an hour. At first I couldn't quite grasp what was happening, because this was a wake-up call. I understood that I had never had an orgasm. All my other sexual experiences, where I just knew I was getting mine, were a mirage.

"Brian, you have sent me to heaven. This is the most unbelievable feeling I've ever had." I realized then that every other sexual experience I'd had was nothing and meant nothing. During the orgasm my eyes had rolled to the back of my head. I had screamed so loud that I startled Brian.

"You meant that?" Brian asked.

"I'm a hundred and fifty percent positive. Out of all our lovemaking sessions this was the first time you ever made me feel this level of pleasure. . . . Baby, I want to marry you," I said laughing. I wasn't actually ready to marry Brian, but his lovemaking skills made him the number one contender.

When I got back from Miami, I called Ella to tell her about Brian.

"Hi, Ella."

"Hi, Tyler. I called you a few times but you weren't home, and you didn't pick up your cell either. Where have you been?"

"I went to Miami."

"Lucky you! Who did you go to Miami with?"

"I didn't want to tell you until I was a little surer the relationship would work, but I met someone. I've been seeing him for a few months now, and I really like him."

"What's his name?"

"Brian McCall. He's a music producer, but he's different from the rest of the industry guys I've dealt with."

"Please tell me that he isn't abusive."

"Not at all; he's as sweet as a lamb. He doesn't even yell. He's incredible, Ella. I can't wait for you to meet him."

"Wow, this must be serious. I'm just relieved that he's not a mental or physical abuser like your previous men. This is great, Tyler, but don't rush it—take your time and get to know him. If it's meant to be, it'll work out."

"Thanks for the advice, Ella. You're the best."

For that brief time I forgot I had flown to Miami in coach or that he hadn't bought me a damn thing. Contemplating a short-lived relationship was out the window. All material gain seemed pointless. All I longed for was that internal calm that enveloped my body.

I hopped on the train, rushing to meet Chrissie in the city. I loathed the commute from Brooklyn to Manhattan, but nothing in life is perfect. I didn't want to be late, because Chrissie said this meeting was extremely important. In Chrissie's last year at NYU she got an internship at a high-profile publicity company. They hired her full-time after she graduated, and she met all sorts of celebrities. Now she'd met a celebrity mother who was launching her own styling company and wanted to bring her on board. Chrissie in turn thought it would be a great opportunity for me, and we were meeting the woman to discuss a potential position for me.

When I reached the office building on Twenty-fifth and Park, I took the elevator straight up to the fourteenth floor. The doors opened directly to office space in a huge loft. The layout was still in the beginning stages, but the color schemes were in place and everything was black, silver, and white.

"I'm so glad you made it," Chrissie beamed. "With your new Brooklyn zip code, I had my doubts you would get here on time." Chrissie was still giving me a hard time about living in Brooklyn, but I was actually cozying up to the quaint, culturally inclined area.

"I'm not coming from the jungle, Chrissie. It's Brooklyn."

"Whatever. Follow me. I want you to meet Cynthia White." That name sounded familiar, but the face and the name weren't clicking.

"Mrs. White, this is Tyler Blake. Tyler, this is the one and only Cynthia White."

Cynthia White was absolutely beautiful. Her caramel complexion and short auburn hair put you in mind of an older Halle Berry. She had great style and carried herself with the highest of class. And although she appeared to be nothing but a complete lady, you could also tell she was a woman not to be taken lightly. She knew how to handle herself and didn't tolerate people trying to get over on her in any way. After taking in her beauty, I quickly realized exactly whose mother she was, and I wanted to wring Chrissie's neck. Cynthia White was T-Roc's mother.

"It's a pleasure to meet you, Mrs. White."

"Why, thank you. You're a very beautiful young woman, and Chrissie tells me you're smart too."

"You're making me blush."

"You have nothing to blush about. When someone pays you a compliment, simply straighten your back, poke out your ample chest, and say, 'I know,'" she teased.

We all burst out in laughter simultaneously. Mrs. White and I talked for two more hours, as though we had known each other for years. We had an instant connection, but I was apprehensive about getting involved in the project because of T-Roc. He would no doubt hit the roof. To say T-Roc was displeased after I cut him off would be an understatement. At this point in his career he definitely got little or no rejection. But something about Cynthia White was positively endearing. I knew we were supposed to be in each other's lives for a reason. Despite the success of her son, she didn't want to ride his coattails; instead she wanted to make her own success. She was smart and savvy enough to do just that, and it made me admire her that much more. I could see where her son got his drive from. I decided to take on the project and assist Mrs. White with her new business venture.

Later that night lying in bed with Brian, I began discussing my new career plans.

"I met with Chrissie today, and she wants me to work with her at a new styling company."

"That sounds dope. You have great style, and Chrissie has that whole *Sex and the City* vibe going. Whose company is it?"

"Cynthia White's."

"I know you didn't just say what I think you said?" Brian snapped.

"Baby, I was taken aback at first too, but working with Mrs. White has nothing to do with T-Roc. I'll probably never even run into him."

"Now you're reaching. You need to worry if she's a crook like her son."

"Please. Mrs. White is definitely nothing like T-Roc."

"Okay," Brian said sarcastically, "but he learned his cutthroat business tactics from somebody. I'm sure the apple doesn't fall too far from the tree. How 'bout this . . . instead of working for Cynthia White, you start your own company."

"What?"

"Yeah, you can do it. I'll fund everything. You said Chrissie was working at some big-time publicity company, and you're going to school for journalism. That's a perfect combination. You all can start your own publicity company."

"Brian, I don't have a clue how to run a business."

"I'll have my business manager oversee everything for you and Chrissie. All you have to do is concentrate on getting clients."

"But I have school, and this all sounds so rushed and crazy."

"Listen, you can still go to school and work part-time while Chrissie is there full-time."

"I don't know, Brian. Would it bother you that much for me to work with Mrs. White?"

"Yes, it would," Brian said sternly.

I knew Brian wasn't offering me this company because he believed in me or even wanted me to have success. To him it was worth investing thousands of dollars just to have power over the situation and not let me work with Mrs. White. That was just one of many telltale signs of the extent Brian would go to to make sure he controlled everything in my life.

I spoke to Chrissie, and she was psyched with the whole idea. We both still had an interest in Mrs. White's company, particularly me with my budding friendship with Mrs. White. I was caught up in the excitement of starting a new company and in my relationship with Brian. Although it seemed like we had been together for years, it had only been a few months. But with all the commotion, I wasn't paying attention to the warning signs in our relationship.

For example, after I'd declined to move in with Brian, we both looked for our own place. Either he was at my crib or I was in the studio with him all night, so it hadn't dawned on me that I had never been to his new place. Although we were together constantly, something wasn't quite right, but I couldn't put my finger on it. Initially I wasn't sure if things were going to last between Brian and me, so I wasn't asking myself questions that should've been addressed a lot earlier. Secretly I wasn't a hundred percent sure I wouldn't go back to Ian. As bizarre as that sounded, a part of me didn't feel Ian and I had had our last dance. But now that my relationship with Brian was becoming more serious, I wanted the answers to the questions floating around in my mind.

Sometimes you get so caught up that you don't focus on evidence that is staring you in the face. But I did what I rationalized as a thorough investigation by dotting my *i*'s and crossing my *t*'s. I spoke to a few of my industry associates about Brian, asking them to find out if he was dating anybody, had any kids, or was on the down low. I know sometimes men get selective amnesia, and forget to give the make-it or break-it information. But Brian's report came back positive. His record was very clean indeed.

With the help of Brian's business manager, Chrissie and I got our new publicity company up and popping in no time. We named it Girl Power PR. For the first few months a lot of money was being spent but no money was coming in. Chrissie was pretty much carrying the company solo, because between school and being with Brian, I barely had time for anything else. Eventually we landed our first client, a female R&B singer who had the number ten song on the Billboard charts—with a bullet.

Just when business was picking up, Brian had to go to upstate New York for a few months to work on tracks for several artist projects, and he wanted me to come along. Of course I wanted to be with him, but I also had school and a new business to help run. But Brian didn't care. In fact, he said, "That company—I pay for it. So that means I pay your salary. You'll get a check regardless. As far as school goes, you can always go back. I need you with me, so get your shit together and let's go."

Because my heart wasn't really into Girl Power PR, it was easy for me to go. And as for school, my first year at NYU was fun only because Chrissie was there. After she graduated, I never really enjoyed it.

Off to upstate New York we went. We stayed in the mountains where the homes looked like cabins, but they weren't. It was a warm and cozy atmosphere. There were tons of artists there, including. Nas, 50 Cent, and some new female group called Divas. The list went on and on. Brian's plan was to complete all their needed tracks within his four-month stay. He had me in his back pocket, so we were around each other 24/7. Playing house made us grow even closer. I would wait on him like we were husband and wife, and during this period I began to love him deeply. Our relationship grew beyond the mind-blowing sex to an elevated level of respect and praise. Brian was a man who had come from almost nothing and had to work for everything he had. When you meet a man like that, you have to admire the grind work he put forth in order to accomplish what he has in life. But some men who go through that kind of struggle become selfish and never learn how to truly take pleasure in life and enjoy their success.

After being in the mountains for several weeks I would go home for a couple of days. I still didn't know where home was for Brian and whether his information was on the up-and-up. So when he was dropping me off at home, I asked, "Brian, where exactly is home for you?" I gazed intently in his eyes, searching to see if his answer was the truth.

Without skipping a beat, he calmly said, "I've been staying with my business manager, Greg. You know he recently purchased a huge house in Jersey, and I'm staying with him until our house is finished."

"Why don't you just get an apartment?"

"That's a waste of money. Greg has plenty of space, and most of the time I'm at your place anyway. And we're upstate for the next few months. What's the point? You're the one who said you weren't ready to live together. I figured we'd test the waters upstate, and by the time we're done there, you'll be ready to make it official." That was the line Brian used on me, and that was the line I ran with and fell for.

A few weeks later it was Valentine's Day, and we were back in New York. I stopped by the office to read some pitch letters Chrissie wanted me to take a look at. Brian was on his way. I figured he would take me to a fancy restaurant and surprise me with a nice little trinket or something. But he showed up with some roses, gave me a kiss on the cheek, and then said, "Baby, I can't stay long. I have to go back to the mountains and finish a track for an artist."

I surveyed him with daggers in my eyes. "Motherfucker, you can't be serious. Because if you are, take your bullshit roses and shove them up your ass."

"Yo, what the fuck is all that about?"

"You must think I'm crazy. It's Valentine's Day, and you have to rush outta here to work on some tracks? What . . . you fucking your track now? That's how you're getting your shit off?"

"You're seriously bugging right now. I swear I have to get this track done for this cat. I'm behind schedule. Don't you think I want to be with you?"

"So why can't I come with you?"

"Tyler, I'm coming back tomorrow. Anyway you told me you have to meet with Chrissie tomorrow to get some shit done."

"Whatever, nigga, your shit is stinking right now. You step in this office with some half-assed roses and some bullshit excuses. I don't know what the fuck is jumping off, but something is wrong. And if it isn't, I can't be bothered with someone as unromantic as you."

I stormed out of the building, and as I walked down the street Brian followed me in his car, pleading his case. There was nothing to discuss. I will let other days slide for someone who is not used to being romantic. But when it comes to Valentine's Day— a day that is stamped on a calendar to be imprinted in every man's head to get on top of his game—and my man comes with some roses and a good-bye speech . . . fuck him!

I went home. I was done with Brian. This shit was for the birds. Not being one to sulk in misery, I picked up the phone and dialed Ian's number, hoping it hadn't changed. I needed to hear a familiar voice and speak to someone who could take my mind off the roller coaster ride I just got off of.

"Hello," Ian answered, and I instantly felt relieved to hear his voice.

"Hi, it's me, Tyler," I said, not sure of the comeback I would get.

"Tyler! I can't believe you called me. I'm actually here in town for a game. I would love to see you."

"Ditto."

"Give me your address; I'll come get you. We can have dinner and talk about what's been going on in our lives."

"Perfect; that's exactly what I need."

An hour later Ian picked me up in a stretch limo, and yeah, he had those same tired red roses (but a lot more of them) that I had tossed back at Brian. But it was ten o'clock at night and he had no idea he was going to see me until the very last minute. Plus Ian had shown me his generous gift-giving side in the past, so that was never an issue. When I stepped in the limo and saw Ian's face, he was as handsome as ever, but there were no butterflies like I felt with Brian.

"Tyler, you look beautiful. Give me a hug; I missed you." When I hugged Ian his smell was still intoxicating, but I yearned for Brian's smell.

"I missed you too, Ian," I lied.

"Baby, what are you doing living in Brooklyn? Your man isn't holding it down for you?" Ian couldn't even wait until we made it to the restaurant before starting in on the slick-ass comments.

"Obviously I don't have a man if I'm here with you, and there is nothing wrong with Brooklyn," I snapped.

"I'm sorry; I just worry about you. Believe it or not, I want you to be happy." I laid my head on Ian's chest, hoping he could somehow fill the empty void Brian left.

While we dined at Asia de Cuba, my mind drifted to Brian and what he was doing. I looked at the waterfall, wondering if throwing a penny in would change Brian into the man I wanted him to be. Ian and I made small talk about what we'd been doing, but my mind was somewhere else. After finishing dinner, I told Ian I was tired and had to get up early in the morning. Using Ian as my crutch wasn't working. When we reached my apartment though, Ian was still optimistic that he had a chance.

"Tyler, I know you have a lot on your mind, but I can help you through it. Get some rest tonight, because tomorrow I have a game and I want you to come," Ian said, confident that I would be there.

"Okay, call me tomorrow." We kissed briefly on the lips before I closed the door.

The silence in the apartment added to my gloom. Being with Ian didn't help me get over Brian. It made me miss him more. At the same time, I knew I needed to let him go because the bottom line was that we were too different. Not giving in to the urge to call Brian, I fell asleep with Brian McKnight's "Anytime" playing in the background.

Early the next day someone was buzzing at my door, and to my delight it was Brian. When he came inside the first thing he saw was the red roses that Ian had brought me. He gave me a quizzical look but didn't question me about them. He simply said, "I love you and I'm sorry. No woman has ever really asked much of me, and I'm finding it difficult to adjust. But I know we belong together, so I'm going to make it right."

"You mean that?"

"With all my heart, Tyler, because I never knew I could love someone as much as I love you." I could feel the tears welling in my eyes. Brian's words touched a core inside that I didn't know existed. My heart filled with warmth that only true love could bring.

"Brian, my heart belongs to you. The love you've expressed to me is the same love I feel for you." Brian and I made love right there on the living room floor.

When we returned upstate, we had an incredible night to make up for our lousy Valentine's Day. While sitting in the car about to go in the house, Brian said, "This is like déjà vu. Have you ever experienced it?"

"No, what is it?"

"It's a feeling of having been in a place or experienced something before. I just had that with you, so I know this is where I'm supposed to be." We had a heart-to-heart about many of my concerns. I explained to Brian that I didn't expect him to give me everything in the world, but that he needed to step his romance game up a few notches. He understood that I wanted him to sweep me off my feet, and not just in the bed. The real romance happens outside the bedroom. He was rough around the edges when it came to that, but for the first time I could see that he was willing to try, and that was a positive sign.

As winter turned into spring, our love affair continued. Our bond seemed stronger, and I loved Brian even more for making such an effort in our relationship. As a surprise, he took me on a fabulous shopping spree up and down Fifth Avenue and didn't even restrict me with a budget. That was a major leap for him.

My heart belonged to Brian. Our relationship was in full

bloom. But once again, a gnawing pain in my stomach told me that something wasn't quite right. The answers always seemed so close but yet so far. One sunny afternoon while walking in Park Slope eating Häagen-Dazs dulce de leche, I felt compelled to speak my mind. "Brian, I feel like you're living a double life," I said candidly.

He looked at me with ice cream dripping from the side of his face, smiled, and said, "You know everything about me." As I took my finger and wiped the ice cream from his chin like we were an old married couple, my sixth sense was telling me otherwise. I couldn't put the pieces together, and since I hated to dwell on anything that I couldn't instantly figure out, I put my thoughts in the back of my mind. But they were all there on reserve, waiting to go in their proper places. Here I was with a man who had made my heart so pink. I knew in many ways we weren't compatible, but he made me love him. I compromised in the belief that maybe there was a chance for us.

9

Shattered Love

I believed I had found true love—not in a perfect package but a very workable one. Brian and I had come so far—we had been together for over a year and I deeply loved him. I knew we could be together forever.

I was sitting in the lounge at the Hit Factory talking to Melanie, a cute young Hispanic woman who was one of Leon's many girlfriends. Leon was Brian's partner and so-called best friend. He was a short light-skinned cat who wore his hair in long braids and swore he was a ladies' man. Out the blue Melanie looked at me seriously and said, "I don't think Brian deserves you," which struck me as odd because I thought she and Brian were close. In fact, she referred to him as her big brother. My antennae instantly went up.

"Why do you say that, Melanie?" I asked.

"People aren't always the way they seem," she replied. With

those words I knew this was the beginning of the end. I asked her point-blank what she meant. What she said next was chilling.

"Do you ever wonder why you've never been to Brian's house?"

Before I could respond, Leon strolled in; he was wearing his oversized Sean John sweatsuit. He glared at me, then at Melanie, then back at me. He immediately sensed the vibe was off and rushed Melanie out of the room. But he was too late. The damage was done. I didn't need for her to tell me anything else. I knew! I knew. I didn't have the details yet, but I knew that the double life that I feared Brian had, was a reality. My mind was spinning. I couldn't believe the lousy sonofabitch had played me like a fool for all this time.

I stormed out of the lounge and went into the studio where Brian was working and spewed out, "You are dead to me. This relationship is over, and I don't ever want to see your lying face again."

He had the audacity to keep a straight face. "What are you huffing about? You need to stop bugging out over bullshit." When I surveyed his face, his eyes were empty and cold. With his right hand he kept stroking his throat as though contemplating his next lie. Then he said, "What the fuck is wrong with you, Tyler, and why are you acting like this?" But he knew exactly what I was talking about.

"You're a sick fuck, and I hope you burn in hell forever for each despicable lie you fed me. If I don't ever see your face again, it will still be too soon."

Brian glared at me as if he felt torture and agonizing pain. Within an instant, he lifted me up by my white Luca Luca leather jacket and slammed me through the door and then up against the wall. My whole body buckled under the pressure.

He was such a little guy, and I couldn't believe he had such strength. Leon ran into the hallway to get Brian off me, but Brian reached around Leon and punched me dead in my face. People started running out of the other studios, wondering what the commotion was about. Brian was ripping plaques off the walls and throwing them on the floor. He screamed, "How the fuck can you treat me like this? I take care of you. You are supposed to be my woman. This is how you repay me?"

I was in shock, upset, and torn all at the same time. Here was the demise of our relationship unfolding at the Hit Factory, with strangers being privy to our dirty laundry. Brian had done a lot of things for me, but put his hands on me wasn't one of them. He had never raised a finger to me. Never! We had had disagreements but he had always remained so calm. I had never seen anything in his character to point toward such a violent temper. But then again, I guess I really didn't know this man at all.

After Brian was finally restrained, I was so overwhelmed that I ran out of the building in tears. Melanie followed me outside to get a taxi and said, "I'll call you tomorrow so we can finish our conversation." I reached in my purse and quickly wrote down my number. Leon was lurking in the back, and I didn't want him to have a clue as to what we were discussing. I went home feeling dazed and confused. I sat on my bed scrutinizing the bruises on the side of my stomach. My eye was swollen, and my leg was also bruised because Brian kicked me while I was on the floor. That's what they do. They kick you while you're down.

Early the next morning the phone rang and jarred me from my sleep. It was Melanie. It was the call that would start to answer so many questions. The soap opera news began rolling out before I could digest it.

"Tyler, I was in Chicago with Leon a few weeks ago, and the

day we were leaving the hotel he asked me to check out. I went to the front desk and they handed me the bill, and I asked for the phone records too, which they were more than happy to provide. I gave Leon the hotel bill and put the phone records in my purse. When I got home I started calling the numbers, trying to find the number to his crib so I could blast his baby mother. One particular Jersey number appeared in the records several times, and when I called, some chick named Beverly answered the phone. I said my boyfriend was in the music industry and this number had shown up several times on my cell phone bill and I wanted to make sure he wasn't calling the next chick on my phone. She tried to ease my paranoia by explaining that she was Brian's girlfriend and the mother of his child. She said my boyfriend was probably calling to speak to him."

My mouth dropped, and I believe for a brief second my heart stopped, if that's possible. The room started spinning and I felt like I was in the twilight zone. I had to sit down because my knees became weak and my stomach was nauseated. I wasn't ready for this. I was still in shock over the fact that Brian had jumped on me, and now Melanie was telling me he had a ready-made family. All this triggered so many mixed emotions. In most of my prior relationships the man was abusive, and because I had serious issues within myself, it made me feel closer to the man when he put his hands on me. My excitement-free relationship with Brian had now taken on a life of its own. I discovered there was a dark and dangerous side of him, and at the same time I got the devastating news that someone I thought was my man really wasn't. He was somebody else's man and they had a child together.

Melanie gave me Beverly's number, and I called her to get the scooby doo. After the second ring a woman's voice said, "Hello."

"Hi, can I speak to Beverly?"

"Who's calling?" the woman asked, sounding apprehensive.

"This is Tyler Blake."

The woman paused. "I'm sorry, you have the wrong number," the woman said abruptly. But I knew I didn't have the wrong number, and I knew it was Beverly on the other end. I said my name again, but this time I asked to speak to Brian and she put him on the phone.

Without hesitation, I told him I knew all about his lies and his other life. Of course, he acted like I didn't know what I was talking about and said we needed to talk. When he hung up, my mind was clogged over the whole situation but I still wanted to hear his side. I tried to absorb all this new information about his other life and replay what I learned over and over. It hadn't dawned on me that my heart was shattered and I was truly crushed.

Brian didn't call me that day or night, because that is what a lot of men do. They play mind games with you. They first try to figure out what you know and believe to be the truth so they can then contradict you with more thought-out lies. They plot and scheme and get all their lies together before they even have a conversation with you. Then they keep you waiting so your anxiety builds up, and by the time you do talk, you don't know what to believe yourself. That's how fucked-up they have your head. I call it the Jedi mind trick, and honey, once they master it, they are not to be fucked with.

Thank goodness I had Girl Power PR, because although I was drained and feeling miserable, it gave me a reason to get out of bed and put on my clothes. I had so many emotions I was trying to sort out. I felt betrayed, used, and lied to, felt that I had wasted over a year of my life. While I was sitting at my desk, the phone rang. It was Brian; he wanted to come over that night to talk. I told him that was fine. When I hung up, I put my head on the desk and hoped that I would open my eyes and find this was all a bad nightmare. But this wasn't a fantasy script I wrote to spice up my life. This was my reality. This was me once again having to accept that the world isn't so pink.

Later on that evening, Brian came over, and the first words out of his mouth were, "Please forgive me for hitting you. I never meant to put my hands on you, Tyler." After looking at my bruises his eyes filled with tears, and in a sorrowful voice he said, "I'm sorry for hurting you this way. I felt overwhelmed when you said you wanted to leave me, and the built-up anxiety from keeping my lies bottled up was weighing heavy on my mind and heart."

(Readers, do you see how men can turn their web of deceit around so that suddenly they are the victim? You can be walking around with a broken arm and a busted lip, but it's all your fault. For all you women who are just realizing this crap for the first time, don't worry about it. You see what kind of drama I had to endure to finally get it.)

I wasn't interested in Brian's words of sorrow.

"Brian, who is Beverly?" I asked harshly.

"She's an ex-girlfriend."

"That you have a baby with? How old is the baby?"

"A few months," he said coyly.

"So you were having sex with her while we were together?"

"In the beginning when you and I were having problems, I started seeing her off and on and she got pregnant. Once she told me she was pregnant, I never slept with her again."

"There was no need. The seed was already planted. Were you ever going to tell me you had a baby, or were you going to keep me in the dark?"

"I knew I had to tell you eventually, but I could never find the right time or the right words. I didn't want to lose you and I still don't. I'm not with her anymore, Tyler, I swear."

"Then why is she living at your house, the house you claimed you didn't have?"

"Beverly doesn't live there. She lives in Brooklyn. I got the place in Jersey when her due date neared. I couldn't live in Greg's house with a baby. She is only staying there temporarily so I can be near my daughter, and so I can help her out." When he said "daughter," I felt a lump in my throat because the child should have been *our* daughter.

"How long is she staying with you, Brian?"

"I'm not sure, but it doesn't matter, because I'm not in a relationship with her. I'm with you and she knows that. Tyler, all I'm asking is that you give me some time. I want to be a father to my daughter, and that means having a cordial relationship with her mother."

"Are you sleeping with her?"

"No, I swear I haven't had sex with her in months. I have no desire to sleep with her. Tyler, I made a mistake, and when I tell you my heart belongs to you, that is the truth."

He told me more half-truths. I had given this man my soul and although I knew I should have left him and never looked back, the other part of me wanted to make him pay. I began the process of collecting on my debt, and at the same time I tried to pull it together mentally in order to handle the cards I had been dealt. It wasn't an ideal situation, but under the circumstances it was my only option. I took Brian back that night. Why, you ask? Because every man I had been with had stomped on my heart and then left me alone. Well, not this time. And since Brian was the one who broke my heart, it was only fair he put it back together.

10

Picking Up the Pieces

I was moving to Jersey. The first thing Brian was going to pay for was my rent. I liked Brooklyn, but I wanted trees, flowers, and grass. And Brian was going to give it to me.

"I can't believe I'm in Brooklyn, but I have to admit I'm somewhat impressed. It's very cute and hip over here. I was expecting derelicts on every block," Chrissie said. I rolled my eyes and continued packing up my belongings.

"Chrissie, would you please make yourself helpful and tape up the boxes? The moving company will be here shortly."

"Well, why don't you have *them* tape up the boxes?"

"Chrissie, I remember when we first met, you were so sweet and down-to-earth. Hanging out with all those celebrities has made you so New York snooty. Take it down a notch. It's not that serious."

"All right, all right. Where's the tape?" Chrissie asked,

annoyed although she knew I was right. Chrissie located the tape on the kitchen counter and continued sizing up my apartment. "I still don't understand why you're not moving back to the city. With the high rent you're paying—I mean Brian will be paying—you can get a beautiful place in the city instead of Jersey."

"Unlike you, I don't want my stomping ground to be my sleeping ground. I'm not up to being bothered with the hustle and bustle of the city. I need peace and quiet. I can't get that in the city."

"I don't agree with your logic, but I understand. I'm just happy you're moving out of this dump. Brooklyn isn't as bad as I thought, but you're so above this place. It's about time Brian put you in the lifestyle you're accustomed to, even if you had to catch him with his pants down to get it. I knew you were making a grave mistake when you stripped away your beliefs in order to prove you were worthy. It never works. Men don't appreciate that sort of sacrifice," Chrissie preached.

"I can't believe this is coming from you, Chrissie. You're the same woman who called me jaded for my views on men and relationships. I remember when you were sleeping with some real estate tycoon and were ecstatic when he bought you a pair of nine-hundred-dollar Jimmy Choo boots. I made the comment, "What, you fucking for boots now? Is that all you're getting out of the deal?" And you blasted me. Now you're telling me that trying to be independent in order to gain the respect of a man is overrated."

"Yeah, that's the long and the short of it. You were right, Tyler. Men don't think any more of you for trying to be superwoman or for pleasing them by giving in to their every need. If anything, you'll end up tired and old-looking from working so hard to please them, and they'll be luxuriating with the chick who was smart enough to put her energy into maintaining herself."

When the door buzzed and I let the moving people in, Chrissie's words were still weighing heavily on my mind. Is that where I went wrong with Brian? I let all the guilt of my past relationships dictate the direction I went in ours, not feeling worthy of the gifts and money men so freely gave me in the past, even though they had done so in order to control me and have me obligated to them. Or maybe I so desperately wanted to belong that I sold myself cheaply for momentary doses of love. Whatever my reasoning, I was more confused than ever.

I stepped onto my balcony with Ella, and we basked at the beautiful view of the city. I was living in a loft apartment located on the Hudson River.

"Tyler, this place is gorgeous. Brian really went all out."

"Yeah, it is pretty great."

"You don't seem as excited as I thought you would be. This place is amazing, nothing like your apartment in Brooklyn."

"I liked Brooklyn."

"So do I, but I love this place. It was so nice of Brian to do this for you. He really must love you, Tyler."

"It's not quite that simple," I said, knowing that Ella needed to hear the truth.

"What happened, Tyler?" she asked, seeing the distressed look on my face.

"Ella, Brian has been lying to me. He got another woman pregnant, and she's living with him. He says it's just temporary, but I don't believe his story. He also turned out not to be the gentle lamb I once described to you. When I confronted him about his deception, he jumped on me."

Ella sat down on the patio furniture taking it all in. She shook her head. "Tyler, when is this going to stop? Brian is a cheat and an abuser, just like almost every other man you've been with. This has to end. Why are you even here living in this place? You should be back in Brooklyn beginning your life without Brian in it."

"I know, but I can't."

"Why can't you?"

"Because as much as I hate him for what he's done to me and as much I'm determined to make him pay for what he's done, I . . . also love him." There the sad truth that has been lurking beneath my anger. I put my head in my hands. "I keep wondering what is wrong with me that men continue to mistreat me and not give me the love that I crave."

"I blame Mother for this. Since you were a little girl, all you've seen is men using physical violence to express their feelings in a relationship. And whether or not you want to admit it, I know you've never gotten over having our real father ripped from our lives. You were always closer to him than me, and it seems all your life you've been trying to fill the void he left. But a man can't do that, Tyler."

"I know, but until I wake up and say enough is enough, being in another crazy relationship is the only thing that brings me some sort of validation that I'm wanted."

"Tyler, you are wanted; you just don't know it yet," Ella said as she hugged me.

After Ella left, I stayed on the balcony and stared out at the Empire State Building. My mind replayed the heartache that brought me here. I was so full of anger. Actually I was beyond angry. I was at the boiling point. I tried to medicate the anger by digging my hands farther and farther into Brian's pocket. While I was spending his money, did it make me feel any better? As a matter of fact, it did.

One night I went to meet Brian at his office (he was now the president at a major label) because we were going out to dinner. It was rather chilly and I decided that I wanted a new coat. A little coat wouldn't hurt his pockets. We were walking down Fifth Avenue, when I saw a beautiful coat in the Fendi window. Of course I dragged Brian in the store. I tried on several other coats, but my heart was set on the one in the window. Not bothering to look at the price tag, I had already made up my mind that I was getting that coat.

"Excuse me," I said to the saleswoman. "Could you please get that coat in the window for me? I don't see it in the store."

"Why, of course." She grinned as if she had dollar signs in her eyes.

I tried on the camel-colored coat and viewed myself in the mirror.

"You look stunning," the saleswoman said. "That is a limited edition. There are only twenty like it in the world."

"I'll take it," I said, not bothering to ask the price. Brian and I walked over to the sales counter, and I lingered on the side waiting for him to pay. He pulled out his newly issued black American Express card and nearly fell to the floor when he realized the price.

"Twenty thousand dollars? Are you crazy? You can put that shit back!" Brian paused and looked at me before he said, "I don't have a twenty-thousand-dollar coat. I don't even have a five-thousand-dollar coat."

His words had no substance because I had already decided that I was leaving with that coat. "Darling, I don't care if you don't have a twenty-thousand-dollar coat. I don't care if you don't have a hundred-dollar coat. Hell, I don't care if you don't have a coat at all because this isn't about you. I want that coat and I deserve that coat," I said in a sweet saturated bitchy tone.

As Brian reluctantly handed his card over to the saleswoman, I put my old coat in the bag, threw on my new money coat, and sashayed out of the store saying, "Mother would be proud of her princess." Some people say money can't buy you happiness, but it can sure make you look damn good while you are disintegrating in misery.

The more money Brian spent on me, the more I asked for and the more resentful he became. Brian felt that if he didn't give me what I wanted and didn't spend his money on me, I would leave him. And you know what? He was right. I would make it clear every day that I really didn't give a fuck how he felt or what he thought. If he concluded, because he had some baby mama and a child, that I was going to be deprived of what I wanted, then fuck him—and them. I became bitchy and said many despicable things about him, his child, his mother, and anybody affiliated with him. But it really wasn't me talking. It was the person inside me, the one who was dying from a broken heart. Overnight I'd become a bitter bitch, and I hadn't even reached my mid-twenties. I had never felt so betrayed, and I wanted Brian to feel the pain that he had caused me. I would say and do things just to bring him grief. I was out for blood, and he was definitely my prey.

No matter what I did, I constantly thought about my situation with Brian, and my anger continued to brew. I became increasingly curious about who this other woman in his life was. I had visualized all sorts of scenarios and wanted my mind at rest. My dear friend Melanie, with her great detective work, was able to obtain Brian's address. I imagined him living in some elaborate house, like the estates in Timberline at Alpine, and playing house with a beautiful woman and an adorable child. If true, it would give me the strength to just walk away. I would have to bow out gracefully because no woman can ever compete with a package like that. I know when something is a losing battle. I can embrace that disappointment and move on.

All women should know that if you ever meet a man who has a beautiful woman and a beautiful child and they are living an ideal life, well, you can never come between that. Even if the man decides to be with you, part of his heart will always be with them. I had to see once and for all if that was what I was up against.

"Melanie, pull over. That's the place right there," I said, pointing to a small condo complex.

"Hmm, this is where big-time music producer Brian McCall lives? I thought he would be living a little better than this," Melanie moaned.

"You know Brian, always saving for a rainy day."

"He must be trying to save for a rainy year by the looks of this place."

"It's not that bad, Melanie."

"For the type of paper he's making, it ain't that good."

Ignoring Melanie's comment, I glanced at my watch, calculating the time I believed Beverly would show up. Brian was at the studio and would be there until late, so I figured she would be home soon because of the baby. Fifteen minutes later we saw a car pull up that resembled Brian's, and a couple of seconds later a woman stepped out. I was on the passenger side so she and I were basically face-to-face. I knew it was Beverly. I politely smiled and said, "I'm sorry. I'm lost; this is the wrong address."

"No problem," the woman said after a long pause. As Melanie made a U-turn, my blood pressure started to rise.

"This is what that nigga fucked up my heart for? A pathetic life in the cut with this chick? Unbelievable! Take me home."

When I got to my apartment I crawled into bed, and all I could say was, Why me?

A few days later Brian and I were off to Los Angeles for the Soul Train Awards. It was freezing in New York, and I knew the LA sun would do me some good. We stayed at my favorite hotel, the L'Ermitage Beverly Hills. The room had a contemporary decor with a delicate infusion of Euro-Asian ambiance. While I was in the spacious walk-in closet getting dressed for the awards, the eye-spy encounter with Brian's baby mother kept flashing in my head. I was rolling my eyes at him, so he finally snarled, "Why you giving me those dirty looks? What's on your mind?" I shrugged my shoulders, avoiding the conversation. But then he had the audacity to say, "If you're wondering if she picks out my clothes, she doesn't."

I wanted to scream, "I don't give a fuck whether she picks out your clothes or picks out your ass! I'm trying to figure out what the fuck is wrong with me, that I'm dealing with a contemptible rat like you!" But I knew that would ruin our evening. I was thinking it so hard though, I wondered if he could read my mind.

I knew I needed to leave Brian, but I wanted to take him down. We were together in the physical form, but there was no respect. In fact, I had zero respect for him. To guarantee that was clear, at any given opportunity I'd embarrass him in front of his friends by being rude and disrespectful. Hell, they weren't my friends. They were the same clowns who stayed in the mountains with me for months and months, hee-heeing and ha-haing. But while they were in my face running off at the mouth, none of them bothered to reveal Brian had a girlfriend and a baby on the way. They were probably too busy hiding their own skeletons. But by this time I didn't give a damn what they thought about me, because it couldn't have been any worse than what I thought about them.

Brian and I were sitting in the third row at the Soul Train Awards, and every time someone came up to him, he introduced me as his girlfriend. "Don't you feel like a hypocrite introducing me as your girlfriend when you already have one sitting at home with your baby?"

"We already discussed this. Beverly isn't my girlfriend. You are," he howled.

"Oh, so she's just your live-in baby mother?"

"Temporarily. I'm working on that. You need to stop worrying about Beverly and concentrate on us. She is irrelevant to our relationship."

"You don't care what people are probably saying behind your back? Oh, he got his baby mother stashed at home and his so-called girlfriend on his arm."

"Hell, no. I don't care. The dirty laundry these motherfuckers got stored in their closets makes mine look sparkling clean."

Brian constantly ridiculed his friends and industry peers for their trifling behavior. He considered himself different and of a higher moral standard, and he would never approve of their indecency. I now had more respect for them than him, because at least they were straight up with the chicks they messed around with. For instance, one of Leon's jump-offs, Courtney, was in LA too, but she knew her position. When Brian and I went to Leon's room to get him, Courtney answered the door in her pajamas. When I asked her if she was coming, Leon said, "Nah, she ain't going. She's staying right here and babysitting this room until I get back. You think I'm taking the chance getting caught out there and letting it get back to my baby mother or one of her friends? Courtney knows what time it is." Courtney kissed Leon as he walked out the door, and told us bye like it was all good.

The next day Brian and I were strolling around the Beverly Center, when all the built-up anger in me boiled over. "I hate you and I hate myself even more for being in this nightmare called a relationship," I bawled, not caring who heard me. These outbursts were becoming frequent, and Brian became so fed up, he flipped out and bitch slapped me right there in the Beverly Center.

There it was once again: the cycle. They hit you once; they hit you twice. They hit you again, again, and again. Violence soon became a normal part of our relationship. I would beat him with my words. He would beat me with his fist. I got back at Brian by making him jealous. The dysfunction continued. And got worse.

I was becoming increasingly aggravated with how slowly things were progressing with Brian. Earlier that day we had gotten into a huge argument because I dared to ask how much longer it was going to take before Beverly was on her own and out of his life. I knew she would never be completely nonexistent, because they shared a child together, but their living under the same roof was taking a greater emotional toll on me than I expected. After our heated confrontation, I stormed out of my apartment and went to see Melanie. When I first left, I refused to answer Brian's calls, but if nothing else, he's persistent.

Pacing back and forth at Melanie's apartment I said, "I'm sick of you and this emotional roller coaster that seems to have no end in sight!" I sat down on her burgundy sofa.

"Save it, Tyler, you're the silly bitch that doesn't want to get off ranting and raving about the same shit over and over again. You think you're fed up? I'm spending more time and money on you than ever before, but instead of being content, you complain like an old nagging wife. Fuck that. You're worse than a wife. If we were married, I wouldn't have to put up with half of your crazy-ass demands. These shenanigans are wearing me down."

"Well, you don't have to be bothered with it any longer. I'm done fucking with you. The next man will be more than happy to pick up where you left off." *Click* was all he heard as he let out a word in response.

Forty-five minutes later we heard a knock. Melanie opened the door, and standing before her was Brian. He shoved her out the way, and with intense rage he lunged at me, grabbed my hair, and said, "We're going the fuck home!" When I resisted, he reached in his dark blue baggy jeans, pulled out a nine-millimeter handgun, put it to my head, and yelled, "I will blast you and then kill myself because I don't give a fuck!" I could barely see his eyes under his Yankees baseball cap. I was panic-stricken.

Melanie was freaking out. She'd forgotten how demented Brian could behave sometimes. As Melanie darted across the room to call the police, she bumped into the coffee table and fell on the floor. Her hands were shaking uncontrollably. Brian peered at her with hate in his eyes and yelled, "You started this, bitch. This is your fucking fault."

After Brian found out it was Melanie who had opened Pandora's box, he loathed her. Now it gave him pleasure to see her helpless on the floor. When Melanie reached for the cordless phone, I begged her not to call the police. She stared at me with confusion. My heart was pounding, but I didn't want Brian to go to jail and I didn't believe he would actually kill me. For a brief second I closed my eyes to gather my thoughts. I spoke to Brian in a soft and easy, almost hypnotic tone. "Baby, I love you; I know that we belong together. Every word I spoke was out of anger and frustration, and I apologize. Please forgive me." The words flowed with such ease that I believed what I said. Brian released my hair and put the gun away.

"Melanie, I know it's asking a lot to excuse Brian's behavior, but please let us handle this on our own." With a look of fear and disgust she reluctantly agreed.

My life was spiraling out of control, and I didn't know how to stop it. Normalcy was desperately needed, but no matter how much drama Brian and I went through or how much pain we caused one another, when we made love we became one. Our chemistry was intoxicating, and whatever Brian's faults, our connection was stronger and more passionate than ever. My heart hungered to go back to the time when I admired him and thought he had the most beautiful soul in the world. Now our relationship was full of misplaced obsession, with no trust or faith. I looked in the mirror, facing my inner monsters. With great stupidity I had believed I could use Brian to get over him, but instead my emotions had fallen into a bottomless pit.

11

Second Chance at Real Love

From the outside it seemed Brian was treating me like a princess. He would send truckloads of flowers to the office, and Chrissie would complain, "Why can't I find a man to show me that kind of love?" It got to the point that she told Brian she was banning him from sending anything else. He had chocolates, balloons, and even all-day gift certificates to plush spas delivered. Or sometimes he'd send an invitation telling me to meet him at a suite in a five-star hotel. When I arrived, rose petals were everywhere, and he'd bathe me and wash my hair in the Jacuzzi while I drank champagne. He stepped his romantic game up to the next level. So the night I surprised Brian by telling him I was pregnant, he promised he would take care of me as his queen for the rest of his life.

"Ella, I wanted to tell you that you're going to be an auntie," I said excitedly while getting a pedicure.

"You're pregnant? If this is what you want, I'm happy for you, Tyler."

"Of course I'm happy. I'll finally have the chance to make things right. I will give this baby all the unconditional love that no man has ever deserved from me. The bond I'll have with this child, no one will ever be able to break."

"Does that mean you guys have worked everything out? Less than a year ago you found out he was living a double life. On top of that, once again you fell into yet another abusive relationship. Have any of those issues been resolved?"

"Things are different between us. Brian promises that soon everything will be completely resolved with Beverly, and the abuse has been nonexistent. He is thrilled about the baby, and he truly wants us to be a family." Not only was I trying to convince Ella that this was true, but I was also trying to convince myself.

"I hope you're right, Tyler, because you deserve to be happy. You've been through so much, and now a baby is growing inside you. I pray that it all works out the way you want it to."

"Thanks, Ella."

"Of course, let's go out to dinner soon and celebrate. I'll call you later this week to find out what day and time are good for you."

"Okay, I'll talk to you soon." I was so glad Ella was being supportive. This was the happiest time of my life, and I wanted to share it with her.

A few weeks later Brian left for a week-long business trip. Because he was a top executive with a ton of responsibilities, I thought nothing of his travel plans. A couple of days after Brian left, I ran into Courtney after work.

"What's up, girl? I haven't seen you since LA," I said, giving Courtney a hug. "What you been up to?"

"Nothing—just working and fucking around with Leon

Crazy-ass. I was going to the diner to get a bite to eat. Come with me so we can play catch-up."

"Sure," I agreed, knowing something was up.

As Courtney ate a turkey burger, she casually said, "You know Brian took Beverly and the baby to Aruba for a family vacation?" She glanced up at me, waiting for my reaction. I was livid, but I wasn't about to let that hating-ass bitch know it.

"Really? He forgot to mention that when he slipped this ice on my hand before he left," I said, coolly placing my engagement ring under her nose and thinking, Eat this, bitch. Courtney sat there with her mouth wide open, annoyed by both my reaction and my ring. I finally said, "Dear, close your mouth before something flies in."

When I left the diner, I was burning up inside, so much so that when I opened my mouth I knew fire was going to come out. Walking to the parking garage to get my car, I was talking to myself out loud. People were staring at me as if I were crazy. I screamed to one passing pedestrian, "This is New York City! Don't act like you've never seen someone talking to themselves!" I got in my car and slammed the door. As I headed toward the George Washington Bridge, my cell phone chimed and Brian's name popped up. Without even a hello I said, "Where are you?"

"You know where I am—LA," Brian said.

"Is that right?" I retorted.

"Tyler, don't start. What the fuck is up now?"

"I heard you took Beverly and the baby on a vacation to Aruba." There was a pause, and I knew it was true.

"That's a damn lie. Who told you that bullshit?"

"Nigga, fuck you! You do you, and I'm gonna do me." After hanging up I immediately dialed Courtney's cell. "How about Mr. Chow's tonight, my treat? I'll pick you up around nine."

When I picked Courtney up, I had on my perfect-fitting Blue Cult jeans and silk lime-green Plein Sud shirt. Although I was four months pregnant, I wasn't showing, and my clothes still fit just right. My plan was to have a ball tonight, and I wanted to dress sexy for the occasion. Brian had been calling me nonstop ever since I hung up on him, and he called three more times while Courtney was in the car. He blocked his number, as if I didn't know it was him. After the fourth unanswered call, Courtney's phone went off. "It's Leon; I need to get that," she said enthusiastically, not putting two and two together. I could hear him giving her the third degree.

"Where you at, Courtney?" Leon demanded to know.

"On my way to dinner," she said, fidgeting with her cell phone.

"With who?"

"Nobody you know—just a girlfriend from work."

"It better not be Tyler, 'cause that's gonna cause a serious problem between us." There was a long break, and then Leon said, "Did you tell Tyler that Brian took Beverly and the baby to Aruba?"

Courtney swallowed hard and replied, "No."

"All right, I'll call you back."

Before Courtney and I could even discuss Leon's call, Brian was blowing up my phone again. Of course I didn't answer, so once again Leon called Courtney. But this time he was on three-way with Brian. I heard Brian bark, "Put Tyler on the phone." Being the Leon pleaser that she is, Courtney handed me the phone. I heard Brian say, "Go home now. I don't know why you think I'm with Beverly and the baby, but I'm not."

I took a deep sigh and squealed, "Go fuck yourself. If you

want to take your baby mother on a trip, then you need to be with her and leave me the hell alone."

"Yo, when I get home, it's so over for you."

"That won't be for a few days, so it gives me plenty of time to enjoy myself," I said. Then I hung up the phone.

Courtney and I dined at Mr. Chow's, and I was enjoying myself. I wasn't thinking about what Brian was doing with his baby mother. I didn't give a damn; it was all about a party for me. Brian continued to blow up my phone, so I turned it off. Then he and Leon started calling Courtney, and of course she got on the phone, entertaining the bullshit. Meanwhile Leon had two kids with his baby mother and about twenty other jump-offs just like Courtney. But in her pathetic little mind, she figured if she acted like a good girl, maybe she would be "the one." Lies, bitch. I asked Courtney to hang up so we could enjoy our dinner, and finally she gave in to my request.

Just then my friend Rob walked in with a couple of guys. He came over to our table and bought us a bottle of Cristal and we started kicking it. Due to my pregnancy I opted not to have a glass of champagne, but instead sipped my juice and watched as Rob and Courtney got tipsy. Rob, who was also in the music business, invited us to go to LA to do a little partying, a little shopping. In my mind I didn't have a boyfriend anymore, and I needed to frolic. Plus Courtney was excited because Rob was the cat she'd told me she had a crush on. Here was her opportunity; Rob was a genuine guy and would treat her right—so she eagerly gave him the digits. Rob and his friends were headed to Missy Elliott's party, so we tagged along. We had a blast. I couldn't help but ask myself why I was going through a whole bunch of bullshit with Brian when whooping it up at the club was so much more fun. I partied until four o'clock in the morning, and by the time my head hit the pillow the sun was rising. That afternoon, I called Courtney. She was acting like everything was cool, not telling me she had talked to Brian again. My phone beeped and it was him.

"Tyler, what do I have to do to prove to you that I'm not with my baby mother? You know if I was going to take anybody out of town, it would be you," Brian pleaded.

"Give me the number of your hotel so I can call to see if you are where you say you are."

"I'm in the car, but I'll be back at the hotel in ten minutes. I'll call you with the number the minute I set foot in my room."

Lounging on the plush white sofa, I held on to the phone, anticipating Brian's call. It was a beautiful afternoon and the sun beamed through the huge bay windows. I rubbed my stomach, fantasizing about the baby growing inside me when a knock at the door brought me back to reality. Thinking maybe it was the concierge delivering a package, I opened the door. To my despair, standing before me was Brian with the look of death in his eyes.

Before I could utter a word, one left hook landed me on the thick off-white carpet, pleading for Brian's mercy. But there would be no mercy. He turned around, slammed the door, and proceeded to stomp with his Timberland boots over my entire body, staying clear of my stomach. "You were out all night fucking around with Rob, you fucking whore. . . . I set you up! You want to act like a whore, I'm gonna treat you like a whore!" he said, grabbing my hair and dragging me into the bedroom. I could feel the carpet burns on my legs. "Suck my dick like the whore you are," Brian growled when we reached the bedroom. Then he pushed down my head, forcing me to perform oral sex.

As the tears streamed down my face, Brian continued with

his tirade: "You deserve to die, you trifling bitch. I'ma show you how whores get fucked." He grabbed my arms, threw me down on the bed, and had rage-fueled rough sex with me. Tears were rolling down my face, and I turned my head to the side, praying for the moment this depraved act would be over. Brian was breathing hard, and his adrenaline was pumping as if the repugnant episode was turning him on. After pounding my body, he stood up, took all of my clothes and shoes out of the closet and drawers, and threw them on the floor. He ranted and raved for the next fifteen minutes, finally bellowing, "Have this shit cleaned up by the time I get back." Then he left.

Feeling ashamed, I sat on the bed and cried for hours until falling into a deep sleep. Later that night Brian's warm body against mine woke me up. He whispered in my ear, "Tyler, please wake up."

"I'm up," I said quietly.

"Baby, I should've never gone off on you like that, but when Courtney said you were with Rob all night, I lost it. You're sacred to me. I put you on a pedestal, and the thought of anyone touching you drives me crazy."

"But Brian, I wasn't with Rob like that. We're old friends, nothing else."

"Well, Courtney said you were going to LA to hang out with him."

"Courtney was saying an awful lot. Did she mention that she gave Rob her number because she wants to date him?"

"Nah, she didn't mention that."

"I figured as much. She was so busy trying to score brownie points with Leon that she sold me out. . . . But Brian, that doesn't change what you did to me today or your going to Aruba with Beverly."

"Tyler, I swear I wasn't in Aruba with Beverly. How the fuck am I going to be in Aruba with her yesterday and be back here today with you?" I asked myself the same thing, but still I believed he had been in Aruba. Thinking about what I might do knowing he was with Beverly drove him so crazy that he cut his trip short and came home. It was just as easy for him to catch a flight from LA as from Aruba.

Whatever problems Brian had, I couldn't escape the realization that I was sick for staying in the relationship. I needed to put the welfare of my unborn baby ahead of this sickness I shared with Brian. But before I could make a final decision, there were some questions I needed answered.

Sitting on the barstool tapping my finger on the glass table, I picked up the cordless to place a much needed phone call. "Hi. Is this Beverly?" I asked solemnly.

"Who's calling?" she responded with underlined attitude.

"This is Tyler Blake."

"What do you want?"

"Listen, I'm not trying to cause you problems, but I need to ask you a few questions. I'm at a crossroad in my relationship with Brian, and I hoped you could clarify a few of my concerns."

"Crossroad?" She paused and smacked her lips. "What do you mean, a crossroad?"

"A turning point. I was told Brian took you and the baby on a vacation to Aruba. He has adamantly denied it and says your relationship is solely based on your daughter, that there isn't any sort of romantic dalliances jumping off. Is he telling the truth, or is he making you the same sort of promises he's making me?"

"I can't speak for Brian because he is his own man, but I will tell you this. I'm the mother of his child, so no matter what you think you have with him, it doesn't compare to our bond. You know he has a child with me, so you need to just let him go."

"For your information, Brian didn't tell me about you or his daughter; I found out from a mutual friend. After being caught in his lie, he took responsibility and said he only wanted to be there for his daughter. I'm trying to find out if his lies are continuing or if he is being honest with me about his relationship with you."

"I'm not about to ease your mind, because now you do know about me and the baby. If you were any type of woman, you would let Brian go so he can be with his family. But you're probably nothing but a whore anyway."

Do people ever grow tired of throwing the word *whore* around? It's so juvenile and pathetic. It's as if you can't extend your vocabulary and think of anything better to say, so you just use the *whore* word.

After hanging the phone up with Beverly, I was more torn than ever. Brian had her so programmed that she wouldn't reveal any of his dirt. But she still managed to leave me feeling guilty because of their daughter. But I too was carrying Brian's child, and our son or daughter deserved a stable life. I was so confused and couldn't comprehend any of it. What you don't understand is what you fear the most, and I was tired of being afraid of the unknown.

As Brian strolled through the front door, my legs became weak and I sat down. When he walked down the hall toward me, I admired his perfect cinnamon complexion and beautiful smile, and I visualized the gorgeous baby he would give me.

"Hi, baby," Brian said as he kissed me on my forehead. He

walked back toward the kitchen and went in the refrigerator and pulled out a Heineken.

"Brian, we need to talk."

"If it's about your conversation with Beverly, I'm not mad. I understand you have some concerns and questions. Did you get the answers that you need?" I was so surprised by Brian's laid-back attitude that I almost lost my train of thought. But I quickly regrouped and continued.

"Actually I did." Brian's eyebrows raised, and he ogled me quizzically. He'd assumed that Beverly hadn't told me a damn thing, when what she didn't say spoke volumes.

"Really, what was that?"

"Brian, we can't be together anymore. I want you to be a part of our baby's life, but our relationship is over." I let out a long sigh, feeling relieved the words had finally come out.

"Tyler, if you're concerned about my relationship with Beverly, it's almost taken care of. I'm going to let her have the condo, and you and I are going to get a house together. I was trying to be diplomatic with her because you know how women can get sometimes. I was afraid she'd wild out and threaten to keep my daughter away from me and take me to the cleaners for a whole bunch of child support. But we've worked past that, and she's accepting the fact that we're not getting back together."

"I don't believe you, because the Beverly I spoke to hasn't accepted anything. But for argument's sake, let's just say you're telling the truth. It's too late. The damage has already been done. I should've left you when I first found out about Beverly and the baby, but I couldn't let go. I was determined to make you suffer and feel the same pain that you caused me. You ripped my heart out, Brian, and I wanted to rip out yours. But it didn't work. All I accomplished was further destroying myself."

"Tyler, just stop; stop this nonsense. You know we belong together, and no matter what you say, you'll never leave me."

"I believed that to be true at one time, but it isn't the case anymore. When I look in the mirror, I don't like the person staring back at me. I continue to go from one abusive relationship to another, and it has to stop. This relationship is so twisted that you actually recorded my phone conversations so you could know my every thought. You're sick, and so am I. Somewhere in my life I stopped loving me, and now I have to find that love again, because without it I'll never be happy." Brian moved near me and stroked my face, as he knelt his head down to place a kiss on my lips. I turned my cheek.

"Baby, I love you," Brian whispered.

"Sometimes love isn't enough," I said, pushing him out of the way.

"Are you sure this is what you want, Tyler?"

"Yes, this is what I need to do for me and our baby. Our child doesn't deserve to grow up in a household full of dysfunction. We owe it more than that." Brian stood there shaking his head, speechless. "I do want you to be part of the baby's life and mine, but as a friend."

"That's funny. You honestly believe that with all we've been through we can somehow be just friends? I don't think so . . . and I'll tell you what else. I'm not going to make it easy for you to walk out of my life. That baby you're carrying is mine. I own it, just like I own you. By the time you give birth, you'll be begging me to take you back because you'll have nothing."

"What are you talking about? Are you saying you're not going to give me any financial support during my pregnancy?"

"You're fucking right. You think I'm going to pay you to leave me?" Brian grabbed my hand and snatched off the engagement ring he had given me less than six months earlier.

"This isn't about you. This is about the child I'm carrying. How am I supposed to support myself?"

"You should've thought about that before you stepped on your soapbox." Brian turned his back on me and walked away. I sat down to digest the conversation. Would Brian really leave me pregnant with no sort of financial assistance? I couldn't fathom that reality.

The phone rang early in the morning. To my dismay I had fallen asleep on the couch. The microwave clock said it was only eight thirty, and for a moment I wished I had taken the phone off the hook. When I answered it, Chrissie was hysterical. "Tyler, what the fuck happened? I came in the office this morning, and the locks were changed. All my stuff was packed up in boxes and stacked outside the door. When I called the building manager to find out what the fuck was going on, he said Mr. McCall told him the company was under new management and to change the locks."

"What!" I said, stunned.

"You fucking heard me! When I called Brian, he said my services were no longer needed and any further questions should be directed to you. So what the hell happened?" By this point I had lain back on the floor spread-eagle style, looking at the ceiling and believing I was caught in a nightmare.

"Chrissie, I'm so sorry."

"I don't want your damn apology. I want to know what the fuck is going on. I put my heart and soul into this business, and Brian in a blink of an eye can just pull the rug out from under me? This is outrageous!"

"It's a long story, but Brian and I broke up. The decision was mine and I knew he wasn't happy with it, but never did I think he would go this far."

"This man is turning my life upside down over some girlfriend-slash-boyfriend drama? You have to be kidding me. He's not going to get away with this. I will sue that psychotic motherfucker."

"Chrissie, wait," I said, but she had already hung up. Brian sent his message loud and clear. If possible he would take everything from me and leave me with nothing. Immediately my mind kicked into survival mode. I called my bank to check the balance in my savings account. I had ten thousand dollars, which would barely cover two months' rent. I looked down at my ringless finger and went to my jewelry box to see what items I could sell. I had a couple of tennis bracelets, diamond studs, a Chopard watch, and the diamond necklace Ian bought me. The items would bring me a nice piece of change, but my bills were large, and on top of that I had medical expenses due to the baby. My head was spinning and I needed to calm down. Without a second thought, I called Mother.

"Mommy," I shrilled, sounding five years old when Mother picked up.

"Tyler, what's wrong and why are you calling so early?" Mother was never an early bird, but this couldn't wait.

"Mother, I told Brian that I don't want to be with him anymore but I want us to remain friends for the sake of the baby. All has gone downhill since then. He shut down Chrissie's and my business, and he has threatened to cut me off financially."

"Pull it together, Tyler, and stop all that crying. What did you expect for Brian to do, roll out the red carpet? You need to swallow your pride and tell him you want him back," Mother stated firmly.

"But, Mother, he's abusive, and I don't know what his relationship is with his baby mother. There are just too many issues, and they are making my life miserable."

"Get over it. Brian is an excellent provider and you're carrying his child. His baby mother is irrelevant as long as he continues to give you everything you want and need. It's time for you to get your priorities in order."

"But, Mother, I want someone to really love me."

"Stop living in a fantasy world, Tyler. Brian does love you, the best way he knows how. I'm not saying he is perfect, but he treats you good and will always take excellent care of you and the baby. What more do you want?"

"Self-respect, honesty, and a little loyalty would be nice," I said sarcastically. Mother was so caught up in the financial security Brian could provide, that she ignored my cries of abuse. In her mind she assumed it was mental abuse, and Mother believed that was just part of the torture you endured in being with a man. No, I had never told her that it was mental *and* physical abuse, but part of me wondered if it would've made a difference.

"I gave you my advice. Take him back, enjoy your pregnancy, and relax. You're making this way too complicated."

"Mother, I don't want Brian back. Our relationship isn't healthy. I need you to help me, Mother. Would you please send me some money?"

"No." Mother said point-blank. "I'm not going to fund your stupidity. You have a man right there who can give you anything that you want. Call him."

"Don't you hear me? I hate myself when I'm with him. I'm begging you to please help me."

"Sorry, Tyler, you're on your own. I hope you will come to your senses and reconcile with Brian, because I will not be sending you any money. And don't even think about calling your father because he is in the south of France with his new wife."

"Mother, don't do this to me. You never take my feelings into consideration. All my life you've done what you wanted and ignored what was going on inside of me. You've never even apologized for taking my real father away from me. But what makes it worse is that he never came back for me. If my own father didn't want me, I could never believe that any other man would. That's why I allowed myself to be mistreated for so long, because I never felt worthy of love. I still don't. But I have a baby growing inside me, and I refuse for this child to have the same miserable existence that I had."

"Stop being so dramatic; your hormones are in overdrive due to the pregnancy. You have no idea what you're talking about. But this too shall pass, and it will all work out. You and Brian will be back together in no time. After the baby is born, I'll come visit you. Now, dear, I really want to get a couple more hours of sleep. I'll speak to you later." Once again Mother wrote off my cry for help, leaving me to turn to a man who constantly hurt me.

I called Brian and pleaded with him one last time to do the right thing and help me financially. He simply said, "You should never bite the hand that feeds you," and hung up.

I sat back for a minute trying to determine exactly when my life went to shambles. Here I was six months pregnant, contemplating my financial resources in order to get through my horrendous circumstances. I scrolled through the yellow pages, calling all jewelry stores that bought merchandise and seeing who offered the best prices. I narrowed my search down to three, gathered my goods, got dressed, and headed out.

• • •

"Ms. Blake, Mr. Dunn will see you now," the pretty receptionist said, escorting me through the glass doors. When Brian refused to budge financially, Chrissie said it was time to get an attorney. She referred me to some top dogs in Woodbridge, New Jersey, and luckily I got a decent amount of money for the jewelry I sold, so I could afford them.

I'd felt quite intimidated when I first entered the building. Forget about having an entire floor; the law firm owned the whole damn building. There were glass and marble everywhere, and wraparound staircases. The place was just plush, plush, and plusher. They were way out of my league, and it would take every cent I had to retain them.

"Good morning, Tyler, it's nice to finally meet you," the distinguished older gentleman said, smiling.

"It's nice to meet you too, Mr. Dunn."

"Stop with the formalities; call me Richard." We shook hands, and I sat down on an antique leather chair.

"Okay, Richard," I said meekly.

"Let's get right down to it. I went over the notes from our conversations and the one with Mr. McCall's attorney."

"He has an attorney already?"

"Yes. As a courtesy to you I mailed a letter to Mr. McCall to see if he was willing to sit down and come up with an amicable solution, and his response was a phone call from his attorney, Ted Armstrong."

"What did he say? Are they willing to try to work things out without a court battle?"

"Unfortunately, no. It's actually going to be a longer and more complicated procedure than first anticipated."

"What do you mean?" I asked, confused.

"Not only does Brian want a paternity test, but he is also seeking custody of the child."

"What? There has to be a mistake."

"I'm afraid not. It could well be a legal ploy, but Mr. McCall is his own man. He doesn't have to do anything that he doesn't want to. From what you told me and from my conversation with his attorney, your ex is trying to make this as difficult as possible. I'm sure he's betting that you can't survive a long drawn-out battle, and that you'll throw the towel in. From what you've said, your finances are extremely tight, but we can try to schedule an emergency hearing to get you temporary support. I'm not sure how successful it will be since you and McCall aren't married, but he has been your sole means of support, so it's worth a shot."

"Can he actually try to get custody of my child?"

"New Jersey law states that he can, but in all likelihood, he will not prevail. But a custody battle is costly and time consuming."

"So where do we go from here?"

"As I said, I will file an emergency hearing to try to get you temporary support, but I don't know how successful that will be. It is important, however, for you to stay at your current residence and maintain your expenses."

"Why?" I asked, wondering if he was trying to make me go broke.

"Because your expenses will be an indicator of just how much child support you're entitled to. When you fill out your Case Information Statement, the higher your monthly cost of living, the more you can ask for in support."

"But, Richard, I'm living on a hope and a prayer right now. The last bit of money I have is going toward your retainer."

"I understand, Tyler, but see what you can do. Your baby will be here in a couple of months, and after the paternity test, the case will pick up in pace."

"Push, Tyler, push . . . I can see the head. Come on now, push a little harder," the doctor instructed.

"I can't; it hurts too bad," I screamed breathlessly, falling back down on the hospital bed.

"You can't stop; you're almost there. I'm going to count to three, and I want you to take a deep breath and push harder than you ever have before." I glanced down at my swollen hands and sweat-drenched body, feeling that I had nothing left in me to push with. I had been in labor for twenty-eight hours, and now the baby's head finally wanted to appear. I was tempted to tell the doctor that I'd done my part and the baby was going to have to do the rest. Realizing that wasn't an option, I closed my eyes, called on the angels above, and mustered all my strength for one last and final push before hearing the cries of joy. The last words I heard before passing out were, "Tyler, it's a boy."

When I woke and the nurse brought my little angel to me, I gazed into his dark eyes and decided he was the most beautiful baby I had ever seen. He was perfect. I nicknamed him Poncho because he resembled a little Indian. With his dark reddish complexion and jet-black straight hair, I was in awe and I couldn't believe he was mine. I held my angel and he naturally latched on to my breast, and in an instant our bond was cemented. As I smelled, touched, and held my son, all I could think of was Brian, that he made this possible. On February 12, 2003, I received the greatest blessing in the world, and because of that Brian would forever hold a special place in my heart.

12

The Battle Begins

Don't ask me why, but for some reason people like to fuck with me. They get the impression that I'm weak and soft. They don't understand that I follow Teddy Roosevelt's advice, "Speak softly and carry a big stick." The point is, don't ever let them see you coming. I like it when people make the usual assumptions because that means they always underestimate me.

"Tyler, he is gorgeous." Chrissie grinned as she held my three-month-old baby. It was her first time seeing him because, as always, Chrissie had landed on her feet. She gave up her fight with Brian and was now heading the publicity department at MTV and traveling constantly.

"Who would have thought that something so beautiful could cause so much pain? Honestly I didn't think I was going to make it. But then I concluded that if I didn't pull through, Brian would raise him, so I found the strength," I halfway joked.

"But wasn't he worth it?" Chrissie asked in baby talk.

"Yes, and then some."

"You still haven't told me his name."

"Christian Andrew Blake."

"That's beautiful, Tyler. You're so blessed to have such a beautiful baby."

"I am blessed, especially since everything else is going downhill. After not paying my rent for four months, I finally got an eviction notice."

"I'm surprised they let you get away with it for that long."

"I know, but the building manager felt sorry for me. When I finally revealed why my life was spiraling out of control, she said she would hold off on the eviction process for as long as possible. I figure it will take another two months for them to put me out, and by that time hopefully the judge will have ordered temporary support."

"You still haven't received any support from Brian? What the hell is the holdup?"

"Brian's attorney keeps having the case postponed, using a million and one excuses. In the court of law, one thing money can surely buy you is time. Brian is still probably trying to figure out how I've been able to survive for so long. He didn't count on the fact that I'm a child of God, and with faith God will deliver me from any dark path."

"Praise the Lord to that, Tyler! Honestly I don't think I could've been so brave. Your strength is amazing. I know I've told you in the past that I admire you, but it was always for superficial reasons. But now I admire you for being the strongest person I know. You had this baby against all odds, and now look at you. This is the happiest I've ever seen you."

"I am happy. During the last few months I had a lot of time to do some serious soul-searching. For so long I was yearning for love from every man I was with. Finally it dawned on me that everything I need to be happy is inside me. The greatest love one possesses is self-love. I have that now. It took a lot of bullshit to get here, but now that I've found it, I'll never let it go."

"Oh, Tyler, I love you," Chrissie cried as she gave me a long tight hug.

"I love you, too."

"Tyler, did you receive the documents that I mailed over?" Richard asked as I tried to eat, read, and talk to him before Christian woke up from his nap.

"Yes, I'm still stunned and haven't quite digested all those lies."

"Well, Mr. McCall is definitely playing hardball."

"Could you please call him Brian?" I said, interrupting. "Calling him Mr. McCall makes him sound like a respectable human being, which obviously isn't the case."

"I apologize, Tyler, but calling him by his last name is my way of keeping it impersonal. I'll be more than happy to call him Brian if you wish."

"I understand; please continue with what you were saying."

"With the allegations he is making, he's definitely hitting below the belt. I must ask you though, Tyler, did you have a coke addiction?"

"Hell, no! I briefly dabbled with pills, but that was way before I even met Brian, and I surely wasn't addicted to them."

"What about the allegations that you broke up because he found out you were a stripper and a call girl? He says that's why he is demanding a paternity test."

"More lies. Why would I need to be a stripper or a call girl when he was taking care of me? I didn't need the money."

"He says it was to support your costly coke habit."

"That is a bunch of crap!"

"Have you seen Brian at all?"

"As a matter of fact, he has been over here just about every day since Christian was born."

"Really? What has the conversation been like?"

"I don't really talk to him. I let him spend time with his son, and then he leaves."

"Interesting . . . He is demanding a paternity test, but yet he is coming over to see a son he says he doesn't know is his."

"Don't you get it? Brian knows Christian is his son. He is trying to drive me crazy. Aren't you wondering why Christian is six months old and Brian still hasn't taken the paternity test?"

"Tyler, I never doubted that Christian is Brian's son. I assumed Brian would play the I'm-not-sure-he's-my-son card, at least until we got to court. By visiting Christian on a regular basis, his actions show that he believes he's the father. That's not going to sit well with the judge, especially since Brian isn't giving you a dime."

Two weeks later, Brian finally took the paternity test, and to no one's surprise he was the father. It still didn't motivate him to write a check, but he insisted on seeing his son. None of my friends understood why I was allowing Brian to visit with Christian when he refused to provide any financial help. I tried to explain that when you keep a man away from his child to punish him, it doesn't only hurt the man; it hurts the child, too. Also, if you keep a man away from his child long enough, he will get over it. Especially if he has another child that he is able to be with whenever he wants. The first couple of years are the most important, because that is when men and their children bond. I didn't want my antipathy toward Brian to interfere with the bond I hoped he would share with his son.

After talking to Richard, I was weary and needed some fresh air. I was on my way out the door to take Christian for a walk when the phone rang.

"Girl, turn your radio on to 107.5," Ella shrieked.

"I can't; I'm one foot out the door with Christian. Why, what's up?"

"Wendy Williams is talking about Brian on her show."

"What? What is she saying?"

"She is blasting him. She's talking about how he threw his first baby mother, Beverly, out of the house with no car and no money, and sent her packing back to Brooklyn. Now she's talking about the court battle he has going on with you. She says Brian needs to check himself because when you do dirt, dirt comes back to you."

"Are you serious?"

"Serious as a heart attack. That's what his trifling ass gets. Brian needs to get over his God complex. He thinks because he has money and a little fame he can walk all over people. Obviously nobody has taught him about karma."

"I can't believe Wendy blew him up. But that's why women love her, because she's all about female empowerment."

"You got that right," Ella said. "Well, I have to get back to work. I just wanted to let you know that Brian's secret is out of the bag. Everyone knows what a jackass he is."

Brian was on his way over to see Christian, and I hoped we could resolve our problems and put this nightmare behind us.

When I opened the door the first words out of his mouth were, "You ready to end this useless battle?" Surprised by his attitude, I had a glimmer of hope that things would be easier to resolve than I had thought. Maybe he didn't like the fact that the Queen of Radio had put him on blast.

"Always have been," I said coolly.

"No, you wanted to be Miss Free and Independent. But I've brought you to your knees, so I'm sure you're ready to end this."

"Excuse me?" I said, shocked by his cocky and over-the-top attitude.

"Tyler, listen. I always knew the baby was mine, but I needed concrete proof. You never can be one hundred percent sure these days. But now that I have my proof, it's time to move forward and end the bullshit. You read the documents, and you know I've got you in a fucked-up predicament. Why don't you stop with all this I-wanna-be-a-single-mother bullshit and come back to me? I still love you, never stopped."

"Brian, you never loved me, and if you did, you have a bizarre way of showing it. And whatever predicament you think you have me in is a figment of your imagination. I've never done coke, and I definitely wasn't a stripper or a call girl. No judge is going to believe your lies. By the time we do go to court, the judge will be so turned off by your theatrics that you'll be begging me to settle."

"I see you're still the same naive bitch I met three years ago. Do you not know who I am? I already have my witness list prepared. They will all testify about your out-of-control drug habit and how you sold your body to maintain it. Baby, you're in the big leagues, and money can pay for any lie you need. A broke bitch like you just needs to count your blessings that your baby daddy got long paper. So you can either enjoy the benefits of having some of my paper, or you can watch me win custody of my son and give you nothing."

"Do you think a judge will give custody to a man who has put a gun to my head and who beat me throughout our relationship? I don't think so."

"So what if I did those things?" Brian said arrogantly. "You'll never be able to prove it. And if you think you can get Melanie or one of those other dizzy-ass broads to testify on your behalf, dead it. Leon has those dumb bitches so wrapped, they don't move without his permission. Enjoy these last few weeks with our son, because soon he'll be calling the next chick Mama and you'll be a distant memory."

(Ladies, it is true what they say: God bless the child who's got his own. You really need to have your own. I don't care how much money your husband or baby daddy or boyfriend has. It doesn't make a damn difference. You need money to fight money. It's as simple as that. If you don't have money, you can't fight to get any money. You know that saying, Innocent until proven broke? Because there is such a thin line between love and hate, if a man still has feelings for you and he still cares, he will do anything to make you miserable because he is miserable. With Brian, I was dealing with a psycho who was chipped. There is nothing worse than that. If I had my own paper, I could tell him to go fuck himself and think nothing of it.)

I tossed and turned the whole night, replaying the revolting threats Brian made against me. I was staring into the eyes of evil when I listened to his bold-faced intimidation tactics. It blew my mind that this was the same man I had believed I was in love with. Now he was plotting to take away my son, a baby he didn't pay a single expense for. All he had tried to do for the last several months was bring me down, emotionally and physically. He was cold and calculating, not giving a damn about what was best for our son. The Brian I thought I knew was dead, and a monster had emerged. As I watched Christian sleep, I found comfort in how peaceful and pure he was. He gave me strength to fight, to realize that although Brian seemed to be winning the battles, the most important thing was for me to win the war.

13

My Fate

As I said before, we all must fight battles and face obstacles in life that we sometimes feel we can't endure. But as the saying goes, "If it doesn't kill you, it will make you stronger." I believe that statement is true to life because when you are going through a war with someone, it's the battles that eat away at you little by little. You start off tall and sturdy, but if you are not made of a strong and durable substance, then piece by piece you will crumble and eventually break down. In most cases people want to give up because the likelihood of defeat is too great and the fear overrides their motivation to succeed. But when someone is kicking you hard, you have to reach deep down inside and uncover the strength we are all born with. I knew with every bullet Brian fired at me, that that was one less shot I had to dodge. If I kept bobbing and weaving, eventually he would run out of ammunition. That fact is what kept me pushing forward every time I wanted to give in.

When I was walking out the door, my phone rang. It was Ella. "Hi, Tyler, I know you're probably in a rush, but I wanted to wish you good luck today."

"Thanks so much for calling, Ella. I needed that."

"Of course, I'm your big sister. I'm always rooting for you. Just remember that everything happens for a reason, and you will get through this stronger than ever."

"You really think so, Ella?" I said, not feeling as confident as I hoped.

"Positive. Tyler, you've grown so much, and your heart is in the right place. Keep your head held up high and know that I'm praying for you."

"Ella, thank you, and I love you."

"I love you too."

When I arrived in court I saw, as promised, Brian had brought along his well-prepared witness list, which included the ever-so-down-ass chick Courtney, the ever-so-loyal partner Leon, some wannabe lead singer of his girl group Divas, and some two-bit players who consisted of industry groupies, label flunkies, and well-paid assistants. I was hoping that if it came down to it, the truth would speak for itself and the judge wouldn't fall for the circus show that Brian and his attorney wanted to put on. I was ready for the next chapter of my life. My greatest concern was getting custody of Christian.

While Richard was going over all the paperwork that Ted Armstrong had submitted, it was revealed that Brian had hired a private investigator to be all in my personal business. What he conjured up was more lies that Brian fed him. He claimed that in checking my phone records, he discovered I was fucking a player from the Washington Wizards for money. The thought flashed in my mind that if I was, I wouldn't be in such dire straits financially.

"Although these are all lies, how damaging is this stuff?" I asked Richard.

"Tyler, it's not good. Brian has used all his financial resources to paint you as the harlot from hell. In all my many years of practice I've never seen a man go through so much trouble to depict a woman in such a foul manner. You would think you were seeking half of his past and future earnings, instead of what your son is entitled to, which is child support."

"Richard, take this," I said sternly, handing him an envelope.

"What's this?"

"Take a moment and open it before you go in the judge's chambers."

"Tyler, I really don't have time. The judge will be calling for us any minute."

"Make time. It's worth it."

Richard asked the court clerk for a few extra minutes, and he excused himself to another room. I was hoping things wouldn't come to this, but Brian was playing for keeps. He was determined to ruin my life and that of my son by removing me from Christian's life. His lies were relentless and his behavior erratic. He left me no choice but to pull out all the stops and protect what was mine. Brian stood across from me in his seven-thousand-dollar Valentino suit, speaking to his overpaid, crooked attorney and making haughty smirks. He believed he had the case all sewn up. That overconfident sonofabitch deserved to rot in hell.

"Why are you just giving me this now?" my attorney asked, seeming somewhat irritated.

"Richard, you startled me." I was so fixated on observing

Brian and his obnoxious attorney, that I hadn't seen Richard walking toward me.

"I'm sorry but, Tyler, why would you sit on this type of information?"

"It was going to be my last resort. Do you really think I want to air all my dirty laundry in a courtroom in front of a bunch of strangers? But Brian is leaving me no choice. I have to protect my son because his father is a borderline sociopath."

"You've been recording your conversations with Brian ever since you were four months pregnant, and you have printed out documentation from e-mails and two-way messages he sent you. You have every promise he made and broke, and every threat he is playing out. Some of this stuff is criminal. If a judge hears a word of this, Brian will be lucky to get supervised visitations. How in the world did you know back then that you would need this sort of ammunition?"

"I suppose I was lied to and deceived one too many times. I was hoping that Brian would have a change of heart and do the right thing on his own, but he has shown me he has no conscience. I don't believe any woman truly wants to bring down the father of her child, but when your back is pushed against the wall, you have no choice."

"Well, excuse me, Tyler, I have some negotiating to do," Richard said, shaking my hand and heading toward Ted Armstrong. Brian still wore the same smirk that I wanted to smack off just a few minutes earlier. Now I actually pitied him.

When I was a little girl, my father once said, "Beware of the fork in the road; sometimes the hunter gets captured by the game." Brian was caught, and he didn't even know it yet. But in a few minutes, he would be well aware of his fate.

After fifteen minutes both attorneys appeared, and the

grievous look on Ted Armstrong's face said it all. From the short distance I saw the once condescending look on Brian's face turn to pure devastation. His normal glowing cinnamon complexion was now hollow and gray.

"Congratulations, Tyler. You have outsmarted us all. I gave Ted Armstrong until Friday morning to present a credible offer, or we will be more than happy to go before the judge," Richard said, delighted by his victory.

"Thank you, Mr. Dunn."

"Tyler, you should be ecstatic. You've won! I guarantee you'll be more than pleased with the settlement deal I will get for you. By the way, what's with this Mr. Dunn? Call me Richard."

"I haven't won anything. My son isn't a prize. He's actually the one who will suffer and get the short end of the stick. He will grow up with two parents who will forever be at odds. No one wins in a situation like this, except the attorneys. And by the way, I won't be calling you Richard. Mr. Dunn keeps it impersonal. Have a good day."

As I walked out of the courthouse furious at how attorneys care only about the bottom line, Brian grabbed my arm and said modestly, "I underestimated you. I can honestly say I never saw it coming. Is it true what they say? When a man is sleeping, a woman is thinking?"

"I don't know, Brian. I haven't given it much thought."

"Tyler, is it too late to say sorry?"

I chuckled for a second before saying, "Brian, the only reason you're sorry is because you didn't get what you wanted. You were willing to destroy the mother of your son because of an overinflated ego. But no matter what you have done this past year, I'm not mad at you. What started off as your curse ended up being my salvation. I finally love me, not because of admiration from a man but because of the admiration I have for myself. I'm truly every woman." I walked down the stairs not even bothering to read the expression on Brian's face. His ideas were meaningless and held no importance to my newfound freedom. As the cold breeze hit my face, the self-love inside warmed me up. This journey had truly made me discover how to embrace all of my Dirty Little Secrets.

14

Freedom

"Cheers," Chrissie said as we toasted what they insisted was a victory. Cynthia White, T-Roc's mother, and Ella were also in attendance at our celebratory dinner at Spice Market, a hot restaurant in Manhattan's meatpacking district.

"I have something to say to the woman of the hour," Mrs. White said, banging the spoon on her champagne glass. "You know you've always been special to me, Tyler, and it broke my heart to see that man put you through hell. But with sheer determination you came out on top. I'm so proud of you. God has blessed you with a beautiful baby, and I know whatever dreams you want to fulfill, no one will keep them out of your reach."

"Thank you. That means the world to me," I cooed as I gave Mrs. White a hug.

"My turn, my turn." Ella yelped. Then standing up, she said, "You are my baby sister, and I always felt that I had to protect you.

But in the last year you've grown up overnight into a woman I truly admire and respect. I know the decisions you've made weren't easy, and the average woman would've broken down and folded. But not you, Tyler. You fought for what you wanted and believed in, and that makes you a winner. I love you, little sis, and I hope to grow up to be just like you. . . . Oh, before I forget, Mother sends her best and wishes she could be here, but she's out sealing the deal for husband number three." We all burst out laughing.

"Wait, I have something to say," Chrissie said humbly. "Growing up in Temecula, California, if someone had told me my best friend was going to be a black woman from Atlanta, Georgia, I'd have laughed in their face. But not only are you my best friend, Tyler, you're my sister. We've both gone through so much since—as you like to put it—'just got off the bus,' but it has all been worth it because we have a bond that will last for the rest of our lives. We're family."

"Yes, we are." I hugged Chrissie and said, "You all are my family. Not only are we bonded by love, we're bonded as women. Each of you has been a part of my support system, and if I didn't have your strength, I couldn't have gotten through this. Every woman needs support and understanding from other women, because as a team we are so much more powerful than if we stand alone. The three of you are my team. I hope that other women are blessed enough to have the same all-star lineup that I have."

"To that, we need another bottle of champagne. *Waiter!*" Chrissie screamed.

Months had passed and I was finally at peace with my life. Driving down River Road with the sunroof back and blasting track fourteen of Jay-Z's classic *Black Album* on an unseasonably warm day, I felt alive. This was the first time in so long that I had no man to answer to about what Tyler wanted. I had the power to decide what I wanted to do and who, if anybody, I wanted to be with. I like to think of myself as an optimistic person, but my disastrous encounters with men had tarnished my views on relationships. I no longer trusted the ideals of loyalty and commitment. I'd seen too much and been through too much to think otherwise. But the pink in me hadn't given up all hope. I was waiting for that special man to walk up to me with a sign on his head reading, God Sent Me to You. But until then I decided to focus on my career, and felt it was time to now pursue my dreams and aspirations. The blueprint to my path was a little shaky, but I wanted to pursue my dream of becoming an actress—not just an actress but a movie star. I wasn't eighteen years old anymore and just getting off the bus, but I felt that I had talent. And if you put your mind to anything and focus, no goal is out of reach.

I enrolled in an acting workshop to get my creative juices flowing. I had a fabulous teacher, who immediately took to me. She told me that I had incredible natural talent and should continue to nurture it. Between giving all my love to Christian and studying monologues and the history of Hollywood, I barely had time to realize that I hadn't been intimate with a man in over a year. It was very empowering though, because I knew if I wanted to, I could have a different man in my bed every night. But I chose not to. Mother used to tell me that when you sleep with a man, whatever is inside of him goes into you, and whatever is inside of you goes into him. In the past I had given my body to men who weren't worthy. Now I decided that I was holding on to all my positive energy. Any man I slept with would have to be able to have positive energy to give me, because like they say, "Fair exchange isn't robbery."

One day at my acting workshop William Donovan, a famous movie star turned director, was our special guest. He wanted to give the class pointers about how a movie came together. I was immediately drawn to the tall and unbelievably handsome middle-aged man. He looked even better in person than on the movie screen. Although he was married, I had always dreamed of sharing a passionate kiss with the gorgeous star. He had the perfect deep-brown complexion, and even though he was in his late forties his body was solid. His eyes were dark and beautiful. You could stare into them and see an abundance of wisdom. I hung on to his every word because I knew he was the man who would change my life. William Donovan would take me to the next chapter of my life and help me become a star. I sensed it through my whole body.

"I would like for two of the students to perform a monologue in front of the class. When you're finished, I will critique your performance," Donovan said, as if he knew whoever performed would do poorly.

The teacher pointed to me and a student named Michael. Instantly I started getting butterflies in my stomach. I didn't want to fall on my face in front of the man I knew was going to be my mentor. We did a scene from Frank D. Gilroy's play *The Only Game in Town*. I stepped up to the front of the class, and I killed it. Michael did very well too, but something about my performance encompassed raw emotion that ignited the room. There was dead silence as everyone paused and stared at Donovan for his reaction. When he stood and applauded, the teacher and the entire class joined in.

"That was excellent. I must say I'm shocked but pleasantly surprised. My only advice to both of you is to continue with the path that you're on. I see great things ahead," Donovan said.

When the class ended and I was on my way out, Donovan stopped me and formally introduced himself. "Hello, my name is William, and your performance was superb. You have a bright future as an actress."

Hoping that I wasn't blushing too hard, I managed to say, "Thank you, Mr. Donovan. That is an honor coming from you."

"No need to be formal; call me William," he said as he gently touched my shoulder. "Are you in a rush? Because there's a lounge across the street, and I would love to talk to you about your goals for the future."

"I'd like that too," I said sincerely. We stayed in the lounge and talked for hours. William was the most intelligent man I had ever met, and I wanted him in my life. After that evening, I knew this was the beginning of a long and prosperous relationship.

A few days later William called and asked if I could meet him at his office in the city. Of course I agreed and decided to put on my pink Diane von Furstenberg wrap dress. I was definitely feeling pink, and I could sense that something amazing was about to happen for me. It was a beautiful day outside as I made my way through Jersey toward Manhattan. When I reached the Lincoln Tunnel and there was no traffic, a smile crossed my face. It was definitely a good day.

Soon I stood outside the tall building in Midtown, gaping through the glass doors and wondering with delight about the possible news coming my way. I could no longer keep my destiny waiting, and I took the elevator to the top floor. Sitting in the reception area waiting for William, I was a little antsy. A million and one thoughts were flashing through my mind, driving me crazy. William finally emerged from his office wearing a pair of jeans that fit his bowlegs perfectly, and he gave me a warm hug.

"You look beautiful, Tyler," William said as he gently spun me around, admiring my Marilyn Monroe–inspired wrap dress.

"Thank you," I said.

"Come with me to my office. I want to introduce you to someone named Albert Moore." I wondered who Albert Moore was, and why William wanted me to meet him. With a beaming smile spread across his face, William lovingly grabbed my hand and put up his arms as though introducing the new homecoming queen. "Albert, this is Angel," he said. Who the hell was Angel, and what did she have to do with me? I thought. I could tell the short pudgy white man was giving me the once-over. He started at my silver Manolo's, and worked his way up my pink dress to my glossy pink lips. When a small smirk appeared on his face, I instantly felt he liked what he saw. Albert Moore finally spoke for the first time, and I realized my mouth was wide open. I was dying to know who he was and why William felt he was so important.

"It seems you have found your Angel—and a potential superstar," Moore said with a wide smile.

I couldn't contain my enthusiasm and blurted out, "Superstar? Me?" William smiled and gave me a proud look, like a father seeing his daughter graduate from an Ivy League college.

"Tyler, this is Albert Moore, the head of Icon Pictures. He just gave the stamp of approval that I needed for my project." Then William explained that the character Angel had the lead role in the upcoming movie he was directing, and he wanted me to play her. One tear began to roll slowly down my cheek. William wiped the tear away and said, "My beautiful Tyler, don't cry. You're in good hands, and I will make all your dreams come true." He didn't understand yet, but that was why the tear fell— because in my heart I knew he would do just that. I prayed to the sky and changed my stars. I finally changed the cards that had been dealt me. This was a new beginning.

After a few weeks of preparation I was on my way to Hollywood. Of course, Brian tried to make a big hoopla about me taking Christian, but with the top attorney that William had gotten me, the judge came up with a temporary visitation schedule for Christian. Brian would have to come to LA to see him. Of course, that was just the beginning. I was positive that Brian would try to fight me tooth and nail to have Christian back in New Jersey. I couldn't let that worry me, because too many extraordinary things were happening in my life. I was on my way to Hollywood to become a major movie star, and there was no looking back.

Logan Olivier

National bestselling author JOY DEJA KING, also known as the Literary Sweetheart, has written young, hip, and sexy novels that introduce readers to street life in all its complexity and the glamorous yet toxic entertainment industry. With over fifty novels under her belt, she was the #1 ESSENCE Bestselling Author seven months straight for her title *Queen Bitch* from her hugely popular Bitch series, and in 2019 winning the African American Literary Award for Best Street/Urban Fiction for *Assassins . . . : Episode 1 (Be Careful With Me)*, Joy has solidified herself as a mainstay in the urban street fiction genre. Joy made her literary debut with the release of her first novel, *Dirty Little Secrets* (under St. Martin's Press), and followed it up with the sequel, *Hooker to Housewife*. Learn more about Joy @ joydejaking.com.